WENDY LOU JONES

I was born and raised in West Sussex and moved to Birmingham to study Medicine at University, where I was lucky enough to meet my husband. We now live in a little village in Herefordshire with our two grubby boys. I discovered a love of writing not long after my youngest son started school. And if you were to ask me what it was that made me make the switch, I'd tell you quite simply, that it started with a dream.

You can follow me on Twitter @WendyLouWriter.

The Songbird & the Soldier

WENDY LOU JONES

Harper*Impulse* an imprint of
HarperCollins*Publishers* Ltd
77–85 Fulham Palace Road
Hammersmith, London W6 8JB

www.harpercollins.co.uk

A Paperback Original 2014

First published in Great Britain in ebook format by Harper*Impulse* 2013

A catalogue record for this book is
available from the British Library

ISBN: 978-0-00-755975-6

Automatically produced by Atomik ePublisher from Easypress

This book is dedicated to my dad, who sadly did not live long enough to see my name in print, but who gave me the courage to try. And to my long-suffering husband, who stood by my side every step of the way while I did.

Chapter 1

Sergeant Andrew Garrington was in control: his house was in order, his shirts were crisp and his career was on track, so the fact that he had caught on to his men's misplaced notion of finding him some new witless woman to pander to didn't bother him unduly. He played with his beer mat as he listened to the men chat. His attention was caught by a rowdy set entering through the front of the bar and disappearing out of the back.

Corporal Dean Fletcher scanned the room for female life and Spike spotted him. "Uh-oh, Romeo's on high alert."

Dean looked back and grinned.

"Well, found anything?"

"No."

"Aren't we meant to be finding a bird for the Prof?" Miller asked.

Andy twitched an eyebrow. "Oh no you don't."

"Come on, Prof. You've been single for far too long now. You need to get yourself a woman," Spike said.

"I seem to be managing quite well by myself, thanks."

"But you need a good woman."

"Oh, a *good* woman, well why didn't you say so? No."

"Andy, think about it. You need someone to keep you sane while we're out there. Remember last time? It's no good if you've got no one to drag you back up again when shit's going down,"

1

said Miller shaking his head.

Claire had walked out before his last tour in Afghanistan. Andy remembered. It had been hard, but he had got through it on his own. He was a stronger man now than he had been then, a better soldier. He had learned in that time that women and relationships were generally disappointing. They were too needy to fit into his lifestyle.

"One day you'll meet a girl who really gets under your skin and it'll completely poleaxe you. You might even find yourself getting…" Miller held up his hands to make parenthesis in the air, "emotionally involved."

The guys laughed. Dean's laugh was the loudest. "The Prof? You've got to be kidding. I've seen more emotion in a potato."

"Whereas you seem to fall head over heels in love with each and every one of them," Andy replied.

"Absolutely."

"For about five minutes."

"Seems long enough to me!"

Spike patted Dean on the back and Andy left the table, rolling his eyes. He approached the bar. Leaning forward, he raised his hand to get the bargirl's attention. She looked across at him while pulling a pint. She smiled and then raised her eyebrows in question.

"Hi, sorry," he called, "um… which way to the… er-?"

"Down the corridor and on your right," she called back, trying to make herself heard over the general hubbub of a busy Saturday night. Briefly she watched him walk away and then returned her attention to the matter in hand.

Andy made his way through the crowd and out into the relative peace of the corridor. Along the walls, small shaded lights lit up old photos of the pub as it had been in years gone by. Wooden panelling hung heavily on either side of him and the dusty stone floor beneath his feet echoed as he walked. Near the end of the corridor he could hear the muted sound of voices chanting. The noise grew louder and louder as he neared the back room and then a cheer went up and he could hear people clapping. Two girls came bustling out of the room, passed him and went off to the right, sending a wave of light and sound crashing around him. They disappeared into the toilets and the door to the back room swung slowly closed again.

As the bright light began to fade, Andy could hear a beautiful voice begin to sing a soft, haunting melody. It was unlike anything he'd heard in a pub before. The song wreathed itself around him, made him stop in his tracks for a moment and listen. He checked for anyone who might notice and then caught the edge of the door with his hand and peered inside.

The room was alive with colour. Banners and balloons hung all around the walls. As he watched, Andy noticed that everything inside the room was now still. Only the girl singing on the far side of the room moved. She was swaying slowly in time with the music, the microphone in one hand and the other reaching out with the grace of an angel. Andy was captivated.

Her hair was brown and waved gently downwards below her shoulders, restrained only by one satin flower tucked in behind her ear. She was wearing patterned blue jeans and a sea-green top that looped up and around her neck leaving the pale skin of her shoulders quite bare. She was neither fat nor thin; in fact her body seemed to flow effortlessly from one supple curve into another. He leaned against the doorframe and watched and listened as she sang. He couldn't say what the song was about, or who had originally sung it, but one line swam repeatedly through his head: 'Until you're resting here with me.' His pulse quickened. She was beautiful. And then in a moment of wondrous clarity, he realised that it was her. It had to be. The girl he had kept close to his heart for the past six years. The girl who had kept him going whenever anything went bad in his life. It was Sam.

Andy felt his heart race as the years fell away. His mouth went dry and his brain refused to think clearly. It had to be her. Of course she wasn't exactly the same, but it was still her, wasn't it? The two girls emerged from the toilets and pushed past, back into the room, their loud chatter and giggles jarring him.

Andy seized the moment and reached out to them. He caught one of them by the shoulder. "Excuse me. Who is that girl?" he asked, pointing to the singer.

The two girls gave each other a look and giggled some more, but quieter now. "The girl who's singing?"

"Yes." He nodded.

"That's Sam: Samantha Litton. Do you know her?"

Andy shook his head slowly and the girls walked away giggling together. As he watched, heads began to turn and look round at him as they realised someone was there who wasn't meant to be there. He started to feel self-conscious, but then Sam finished and everyone clapped and turned back again. Sam re-joined her group and smiled bashfully at the things people were saying to her, until somebody whispered in her ear and pointed him out. She turned and looked directly at him.

Sam felt herself blush.

"Well go on then," Kate said. "He's gorgeous."

Sam looked across at Chloe. "It's your birthday, Chlo'. He's probably here to see you."

"I don't recognise him," Chloe said.

Kate rolled her eyes. "Oh you're bloody hopeless, you are. Look, if you don't get your butt over there and at least talk to the guy in the next thirty seconds I'm going to leap over there and nab him for myself," she said, hitching up the side of her cerise strapless top.

Sam was relieved. "Okay."

"No it's not okay, 'cause it's you he's drooling over, not me. Now get yourself over there and snog his face off!" She poked Sam hard in the ribs.

Sam jumped and turned to stare daggers at her friend, but Kate was just as determined. Sam hesitated and looked down at the glass of wine in her hand.

"Just talk to him, Sam. He won't bite."

Sam took a deep breath and stood up. A rousing chorus of whoops went up from her group of friends as she slowly made her way around the tables and across the room in the direction of the handsome stranger.

Andy stood up tall in the doorway and tried very hard to breathe. His mind was racing, searching for what he was going to say. He looked down at the floor and shifted his weight. He fidgeted with his clothing and then looked up again. She was almost at the door.

"Hello," she said. "Are you here for the party?"

Andy felt a firm slap on his back.

"So this is where you've got to. We thought you'd gone AWOL." Dean had come looking for him. The next singer took the microphone and Dean moved round to Andy's side. "Shit, what is that wailing?" Dean noticed the girl standing in front of them. "Oh, excuse me. Hello, gorgeous."

Sam smiled politely and turned back to Andy. "Are you one of Chloe's friends?" she asked.

"Absolutely," Dean continued, "whoever she is."

Andy's head was spinning. Somewhere along the line he had lost the ability to connect with women on anything more than a superficial level and mostly that was the way he liked it. But this was different, this actually mattered. The angel, who had come to mean so much to him in the years since they'd last met, was standing before him again, only now, he was a shadow of the boy he had once been.

Dean's eyes were all over her, drinking her in and it twisted a knife in Andy's side just to see it.

"No," Andy managed, "I was just listening-"

"You deserted your mates to listen to this?" Dean said, obviously appalled.

Andy stiffened in irritation. He looked at Sam, desperately

hoping she would understand what he was thinking. She had to know that he was not like Dean, a brash lad who acted so loudly and unrefined. He studied her, trying to work out how to speak to her without frightening her off, or looking a complete fool in front of one of the guys. Her beautiful brown eyes melted him. They had a shy curiosity that made her look so utterly vulnerable. Her skin was flawless, her expressions were enchanting and her lips were… were… tantalising.

Sam's brow twitched and she turned to walk away.

"Don't go," Dean suddenly called out. "You can't just leave us here."

Sam turned round and raised an eyebrow.

What was Dean playing at? Andy didn't understand. Hadn't he already annoyed the girl enough, ruining his chance of being with her again? He needed to speak up, fight for what should be his. He couldn't let her slip away. He looked across and saw the friends she was sitting with. Maybe she'd changed. Maybe she wasn't the same girl he remembered from back then, back when he was first starting out.

"We could get back to the bar to find the others have already gone and we'd be left on our own," Dean said.

"You're big boys," Sam replied. "I'm sure you'll cope."

"I can beg," Dean dropped down on one knee, "loudly." Others in the room began to look around.

Sam walked back over, embarrassed. "Get up, you daft fool."

Dean stood up. He turned to Andy. "Did she just call me a fool?"

Andy wasn't sure what was going on, but at least the girl was still with them. He nodded. "I think so."

"And us about to risk life and limb to defend our country. All we ask is a little respect."

Sam looked uneasy. She glanced from one to the other. "Are you soldiers?"

"Corporal Dean Fletcher at your service, Ma'am." Andy watched as Dean turned on his most charming smile.

A light went on behind Sam's eyes. "Dean Fletcher? I didn't recognise you." She looked back at her group and then back to the lads. "We went to school together. You're Kate's next door neighbour, aren't you? Your parents, I mean."

"Katy? Yeah, you know her?" Now it was Dean who seemed a little unsure.

"Of course. She's my best friend. I'm sorry. You just look so different… in a good way."

Dean beamed and Andy's heart raged. He had lost her. One moment of recognition and he had simply faded into the shadows.

"Well you should be sorry, especially for treating a guy as coldly as that."

"I didn't mean to."

"Well, I'll forgive you, perhaps… for a kiss." He held out a cheek.

Smooth. Very smooth, Andy thought, resenting every syllable Dean spoke. He realised he had been out-classed. He, on the other hand, was rusty. But she wouldn't actually fall for it, would she?

Sam hesitated for a moment. "I don't think so. I know about you lot. A girl in every port, isn't it?"

Dean clutched his chest. "I'm hurt." He turned to Andy. "She's vicious, this one."

A blonde girl approached Sam from behind. "Hello, Dean. Are you harassing my friend? And that's sailors, Sam, not… well… actually-"

"-Katy. A pleasure, as always." An uncomfortable tension prickled between the pair of them.

"Come on," Kate said, urging Sam back to her friends.

"A date then?" Dean called. "Dinner? A drink, just a drink?" Sam stopped and turned back toward Dean. "Give me your number. Come on, you know you're tempted. Come on… for me?"

Sam sighed and, smiling, she walked back up to him. Dean whipped out a pen and rummaged for a piece of paper. Sam took the pen and wrote her number down on his hand.

"I'll call you," he said.

"No you won't" Sam told him.

"I will. You'll see." Sam walked away with her friend, deep in conversation. "Goodbye, Gorgeous," he called and then slapped Andy on the back and walked back into the corridor. "Come on, Prof, the guys are waiting."

Sam retook her seat to a round of applause.

"Well?" Chloe said. "What was he like?"

"Gorgeous," Kate said, "But Doofus here was too busy being chatted-up by Dean Fletcher, my pillock of a next door neighbour."

Sam blushed. "But he's lovely."

"He's an arsehole, Sam. You've just never seen past his twinkling blue eyes, that's all."

"I didn't recognise him. He's… fitter. And taller, and he's got a bit of a tan." Sam sighed.

Kate stuck two fingers down her throat. "Yes, well maybe he has got better looking with time, but it's still… him."

Andy followed Dean back up the corridor and the door to the back room shut behind him. They took some stick from the rest of the lads about how long they'd been. Dean took out a piece of paper from his jacket pocket and scribbled down the number next to the word 'brunette', and then he licked the back of his hand and rubbed hard to erase all sign of the phone number Sam had written there. The lads sighed in groans of understanding and he popped it away back in his pocket and grinned. The last of their pints were emptied and they filed outside in happy union, in search of the next drink of the night.

Outside it was dark. Plumes of mist sprang from their mouths as they walked down the back road to the King's Head. In the streets not far away, Andy could hear people laughing and calling, their voices punctuated only by the echo of their footsteps from the quiet, cobbled lane.

Andy thought about how casually Dean had treated Sam. As

soon as he had her number he seemed to lose all interest. He quickened his step to walk alongside him. "So are you going to ring that girl?" he asked, trying to sound as indifferent as possible.

"Yeah, I might."

"But I thought you were seeing Sophia?"

"Soph? Right, yeah… and Jules."

"Jules?"

"Yeah. Nice girl. Met her a few weeks ago at Hacker's bird's do." He opened the pub door and gesticulated. "Great tits."

Andy shook his head. "I don't know how you keep up with them all," he said.

"It's a gift. You've either got it, or you haven't." Dean looked around and beamed. He searched among his friends for the one he was looking for. "Right, Smithy, it's your round, I believe. Get 'em in, boy." He turned around to look for a place to sit. "Shit." He tried to hide his face.

A girl walked across, dressed up to the nines and not looking at all pleased. "Soph. I didn't know you were going to be out tonight?"

The group around them quietened, waiting to see how Dean was going to handle the situation.

The girl raised her eyebrows. "Well you wouldn't, would you?"

"Ah, you know how it is. We haven't had much time off recently, have we lads?"

A general murmur of agreement went round.

"You could have rung. You didn't even answer any of my texts. I was beginning to think you'd gone out already."

"And miss seeing you again? Never." He pulled her toward him and kissed her full on the lips. The girl struggled for a moment, pushing him away with the palms of her hands and then all was forgiven. The odd cheer went up, but mostly it was a resigned sigh.

He'd done it again, thought Andy and his mind went back to Sam. What a stark contrast there was between her and the girl currently being won over by Dean. That delicate songbird had been far more sensual, naturally beautiful, without all the glitz and war paint that this girl was wearing. He cursed his timing and lack of faith. She *had* seemed just the same as the last time they'd met, but what could he do about that now? If only she had seen him a few minutes earlier, or Dean had found them a few minutes later and given them the chance to actually speak before Romeo had got his claws into her, then maybe he could have been the one with her phone number in his pocket right now. Some guys just didn't appreciate what they had. But that's how it was with Dean. No matter how badly he treated them, he was always lucky with women. Still, all was not lost. He would find a way. He had to. Andy knew how she could be traced and Dean had her phone number. All he had to do now was be patient. He had no doubt Dean would mess it up soon enough and then he would make his move. But what if he didn't? What if Dean actually realised how wonderful she was? And did he have the time to wait? But first things first. Sam hadn't recognised him.

Andy thought about Sam more and more over the following weeks. She possessed him, invading his mind and tormenting him every time he was alone. Dean never spoke of her in the mess with the lads, although his other women came up again and again, so Andy made the decision to break cover and to do some recce for himself.

"Did you ever call that brunette from the pub?" he asked, when they happened to meet whilst walking into barracks early one morning.

"Which one was that?"

"You know, the one who was singing. When we hit the pubs the other week. Sam, was it?"

"Oh, Sam. Yeah."

"And?"

"What?"

"What's she like?"

Dean turned a curious expression on him. "Okay. Why do

you wanna know?"

"No reason. She just didn't seem your type, that's all."

Dean let out a big breath. "Yeah? You may be right. She's a schoolteacher. Not a vision I've ever fantasised about myself, a bit of an ice maiden actually. But I'll give it a bit longer before I knock it on the head. Why, do you want her?" They showed their passes and walked in through the gate. "You two would go well together, thinking about it. You're both as dull as each other." Andy went to cuff Dean around the head, but he ducked and punched him back in the ribs, chuckled and jogged off to find the rest of the lads.

It was her. It had to be. He remembered Sam had told him she was just about to go off to train as a teacher. It had been the summer after her A-levels, when he had just finished university. He remembered how he must have looked different then: not as much meat on his bones and longer hair. They were both on holiday with their friends in Tenerife and he had spotted her one day in a café not far from their apartment. She had been sneaking bits of food into her napkin. Andy had wondered what she was doing, until he saw her later outside their complex, feeding a frail-looking dog. That's when he met her. He watched her tenderly gaining the poor dog's trust and feeding it the scraps from her plate, then a sudden sound had made it skit away and he emerged from where he had been watching and started talking to her. They spent the rest of the night together, first chatting around the pool, and then later in the evening they met up again at the party put on by the owners of the complex. They had talked until dawn, when they had, he thought, reluctantly parted, with the most amazing kiss he had ever experienced. They arranged to meet up later that day to spend the last of their time together before his flight left that evening. And that was the last he had seen of her.

When she didn't turn up, he searched all over, but with no luck. While checking out of the hotel, he was given a scrap of paper with a note written on it explaining that she had had to dash off to hospital with her friend and wishing him a safe journey. Nothing since had come close to that night.

Andy tried to get more from Dean on a couple of occasions, but only succeeded in reigniting Dean's attention to his love life. "We've got to get you a woman of your own, Prof," he said one day. "Leave it with me," he winked and, giving the other lads a grin, slipped out to make a phone call.

A couple of days later he revealed that he had planned a blind (on Andy's part) double date.

Andy sighed. "Not a chance."

"Oh go on Sarge," the lads called out.

"Absolutely not. No way. Like I'd let you set me up on a blind date, especially with you there to laugh at me."

Dean held up his hands. "Okay. I'll tell Sam it's off then, shall I?"

Andy looked at Dean. "It's one of Sam's friends?"

"Yeah."

"So it'll be you, me, Sam and…"

"Her friend, yeah."

Andy rapidly weighed up the opportunity of seeing Sam again and spending time with her, despite Dean's presence, against the likelihood of being stuck making small talk with the ugly friend. He decided it was worth it. "Okay, I'll do it."

The day of the double date arrived, several weeks later in the end. It was the lads' last night of freedom before heading off on pre-deployment training. Dean and Andy arrived at the bowling alley and looked around. There was no sign of the girls. They approached the bar and got a round in. A few minutes later the girls turned up. Dean kissed Sam. "Sam, this is Andy."

Sam's smile was warm and kind. They shook hands. "We meet again," she said.

Andy smiled and his heart lurched. Had she remembered?

"And this is Kate," Sam told him, turning to her friend and

introducing them. No, she hadn't.

Andy peeled his eyes away from Sam and looked at Kate. She was nice enough. He recognised her from the day he had seen Sam several weeks before. A pretty girl, wearing a little too much make-up in his opinion, but she seemed okay. "Hi, Kate," he said, leaning forward to kiss her on the cheek. What was he doing here? He had no interest in Kate at all. But of course, he knew the real reason. It was her. Sam. As painful as he knew it would be, to get to see Sam again was worth it. Miller had been right. She had got under his skin and to be able to be near her was worth any price.

The game was close and the banter was lively throughout, but half an hour after the game had ended, Kate got a call from her mum and had to rush off. Andy stood up and offered to walk her home, but Kate said she would get a taxi as it was quicker and that she'd be just fine on her own. Sam wanted to go with her too, but again Kate would have none of it and Sam said she'd ring her when she got home.

Andy soon began to feel like a gooseberry. He knew he should really make his excuses and leave Dean and Sam together, but he couldn't. He had no more will to tear himself away than a moth had from the flame.

Dean's mobile buzzed and his eyes flitted down to the screen. "Sorry, gorgeous, I'd better take this. It's my gran." He slipped out of his seat and wandered away to the front of the building to take the call.

Sam turned back to Andy. They were alone. Andy leant in across the table, holding her gaze for as long as he could bear. "So, how long have you been singing, Sam?" he asked. A delicate blush spread across her face and Andy was in heaven.

"A few years, I guess. I was bullied into it at college by some friends and I caught the bug I suppose. Silly really, but it's a bit of fun. And they're a nice lot down at the Crown, very forgiving."

"I doubt that. I think you just happen to be very good."

Sam looked briefly down at her lap. "So what's *your* hidden talent then?" she asked.

Andy chuckled. "Talent? Not sure I have one of those. I don't seem to have enough time to dedicate myself to acquiring one."

"A hobby then? What about stamp collecting?"

Andy raised an eyebrow.

"Skiing?"

Andy thought. "No, that's my golden brother's domain."

His tone made Sam stop. "You don't get on?"

"No, it's not that. He's all right, we're just chalk and cheese that's all. And for my parents' part, cheese is just preferable to chalk." Andy laughed, quite taken aback at how quickly he had unravelled. "I like to walk, Sam. I like mountains, the countryside and trees. Is that too dull?"

"Not at all. It sounds lovely." She smiled.

Andy knew he didn't have long. Somehow he had to get through to Sam without giving away too much. If he had only managed to actually speak when they had first met, he wouldn't be in this mess right now. He leaned back in his seat, trying to give the impression of easy confidence. "Do you ever travel, Sam? Abroad I mean."

"Not much. Why, do you?"

Andy smiled.

"Of course you do." Sam rolled her eyes. "But what about for fun?"

"Now and again." He was watching her closely. "I've been to Greece," he said. "Switzerland was impressive and, er… Tenerife."

"Oh, I've been there. I went with some friends a few years back." She smiled and Andy hoped she might be remembering.

"All girls together?" he asked.

"Something like that."

"Did you ever discover a café on the west side of the island, Café Aurelio, I think it was called?"

Sam hesitated, her face suddenly becoming unreadable. Andy's heart hammered inside his chest as he waited for her to reply. Sam took a deep breath. She opened her mouth to speak, but just as she did, Dean plonked himself back down by her side, making her jolt with surprise.

"Dean! Is everything all right? Is she okay?" Sam asked and Andy's eye's fell briefly closed in defeat.

"Who?" Dean asked.

"Your gran."

Dean tucked his phone back into his pocket. "Oh, yeah. Yeah, she's fine." He looked from Sam to Andy and back again. "So, what'd I miss?"

Sam glanced across at Andy, her expression searching, but his time had slipped away and the moment was gone.

The rest of the evening was torture and ecstasy in equal measure, talking and laughing with this girl who was now with someone else. She was perfect- intelligent, funny and seductive all in one. He loved the way she tilted her head when she was unsure, exposing just a little more of her delicate neck, and the way she bit her bottom lip when she was trying to tease was sweetness itself. Life just wasn't fair. Dean got any girl he wanted with his film star looks and gift of the gab. They fell for it every time. Why did it have to be her?

His eyes fixed on Dean's hand moving slowly up and down Sam's side. His shoulders tensed. Dean leant in closer, his lips whispered into Sam's ear. It was agony. Why had he not been more of a man and fought for her at the outset, instead of letting Dean snatch her away from him right under his nose? It was Dean who was allowed to touch her sensuous body, Dean who could whisper softly into her ear and the thought of what was going to happen the moment Andy left them that evening was almost too much to bear. But watching helplessly from the sideline was better than not being near her at all.

By ten o'clock, Dean gave up with subtle signals and when Sam excused herself and popped to the ladies' for a minute he made his feelings plain. "Okay, Prof, on your bike. I'm never going to get any action here with you hanging around."

Sam returned and Andy smiled at her warmly and reluctantly stood up to take his leave. "Anyway, it's been great, Sam, but I'd better get back: early start in the morning." He picked up his dark blue puffer jacket and slid out of his seat.

"Oh? You sure you won't stay?" Dean asked, sliding round the table closer to Sam.

Andy looked at Dean and then back to Sam. "I probably won't see you again until we're back now," he said. "Take care, Sam."

Sam stood up and kissed Andy on the cheek. "No, you take care, all right? I want both of you back here in one piece, you hear me? Both of you, or I'll definitely have something to say about it," she added.

"Cor. Are you going to keep me after school and thrash me, Miss?" said Dean, grinning like the Cheshire Cat.

Andy smiled, his brain barely functioning now. "I'll, um…" he gestured toward the door, "be off."

Sam straightened. "I'm serious."

Andy could see that she was. He looked into her eyes. "I know. I'll take care of him. I promise." He smiled and then left her with Dean, walking out into the harsh winter night.

He must try and forget about her now. The next nine months he was to be a soldier and nothing more. The army was his home and the men were his brothers, even Dean. In the grand scheme of things Dean was still his brother: an annoying younger brother, but someone he would gladly lay down his own life to protect- but God, how he sometimes just wanted to smash his head against a brick wall. He put on his gloves, zipped up his jacket and walked away from Sam and towards war. Back inside, Sam was left wondering about the familiarity of that kiss.

Chapter 2

Sam was round at Kate's house, slouching in the big pink beanbag underneath the window. Christina Aguilera sang quietly in the background and Kate traced the pattern of the duvet cover on her bed with her finger. "I still can't believe you're going out with creep-features," Kate said.

"He's nice. He makes me laugh and you've got to admit he is very good looking."

"Oh he is better looking now, I suppose, but… really? Dean?"

Sam smiled, remembering his tall handsome features, his blue eyes gazing down at her, making her feel like a million dollars.

"He's a twat, Sam. A womaniser."

"He is not."

"You're really into him, aren't you?"

Sam sighed and hugged the soft white pony she found lying nearby, to her chest.

"You've always been soft on him, even back in school days when he was ugly."

"He was not ugly."

"Yes he was. I remember." She took a long look at Sam. "I give up. You've been a lost cause ever since he used to put his arm around you at break times. You know he was only doing that so that you would give him your Kit Kat. He was really after Big-Tits

17

Bunstead," she said, slumping back down on the bed.

Sam lobbed the pony at her. Kate was obviously teasing. She didn't believe for a minute that Dean had really used her like that. He was the one who had stood up for her when Tom Finley had teased her about her braces. He even said he would have taken her out only his parents had put their foot down and insisted he stay at home and work. "Just because he was a hard worker and not cool and trendy like all the boys you got off with," she said.

Kate spluttered out a hail of laughter and lobbed the pony back. "Cheeky mare!"

"Listen, you never did tell me what the matter was with your mum the other night? Is she all right?"

Kate propped herself up on one elbow again. "At the double date?"

"Yes."

She sat up. "You really didn't notice anything out of the ordinary with that guy then?"

"No. He seemed really nice. Sort of… reassuring: like you've known him for ages, but you haven't. You know what I mean? Why?"

"'Cause he was gawping at you the whole night. I told you back at Chlo's party that he was into you and you, like a plonker, went and gave your number to old smarm-breath. Why Dean thought he would be interested in me I have no idea."

"But your mum?"

"Oh she was fine. I'd just had enough of blending in with the wallpaper. You know 'shrinking violet' was always more your style than mine. I'm not going spend my evening hanging around babysitting some poor love-struck squaddie."

Sam looked thoughtful for a moment. "Dean said he'd been married a few years back, but it had ended, and well… in his words… he wanted to get him…'back in the saddle'."

"And you thought of me? Cheers, I'm touched."

"It wasn't like that. Dean said he was a nice guy, a few years older than us and it was one of those rare moments in time when you didn't actually have a boyfriend."

Kate gasped again, picked up a pillow and threw it at Sam. "As opposed to my timid little church mouse, who usually runs away if a boy even looks at her?"

"I do not!"

"You do too."

"I'm going out with Dean, aren't I?"

Kate threw her hands in the air. "Miracles!" and Sam chucked the pillow back.

For weeks Sam heard nothing. There was no reply to her texts and no phone calls came. She wasn't sure if this was normal or if something was wrong. All she could do was sit and wait.

Up in Norfolk the men were being put through the training for battle in Afghanistan. There were long exercises in simulated conditions, as close to the scenarios they would probably be facing as they could be in a cold wet February in England. Those on their first tour were eager to get going, to face the war they had all been trained for.

Dean approached his second tour with a mixture of exhilaration and dread. He knew what it was like to feel the scorch of heat on his back. He had picked up fallen comrades and lived through the nightmares that stalked his sleep. For him and those like him, the war was a more subdued affair. It was more than a vocation. It was a deep-rooted brotherhood that bound them all together and made them want to stand side by side and protect each other. That was what carried them when Hell raged.

Andy was learning to control his thoughts about Sam, visiting them only when he was at leisure to do so. Dean hadn't mentioned her once since their arrival and Andy hoped that no stronger feelings could be created between them while he was gone. So he trained and he learned and prepared himself for what was to come.

As the first glimpses of spring took hold on the quiet, peaceful fields of England, the men of 9 Rifles were busy in a muddy ditch preparing for war. Their time in pre-deployment training was almost at an end, and the calm of inevitability descended upon them.

"How's it going with you and 'lover boy' then?" Kate asked several weeks later.

"Fine… I think," Sam replied.

"Fine? That doesn't sound very good. I was hoping for something more like 'fab', or 'great', or 'smoking!'"

"I don't know. I haven't heard from him in weeks. Don't get me wrong, he's great- I just sometimes feel a little in the dark… inadequate, even."

"Inadequate?"

"You know. He's so… perfect."

"He is good looking, I'll give you that, but…"

Sam gestured to her own body. "But look at me."

"What? Hell you're no fatso yourself. You do all that cycling to and fro, all over the place. You're in better shape than I'll ever be and I've never had a guy complain about the state of my body. You're fine, Sam. Your taste in men sucks, almost as much as your taste in music, if I'm honest. But you're smart, way smarter than me. Look at you. You went to university for Christ's sake and have a real job, not like me. I'm still bumming around and living with my mum."

Sam cleared her throat and held up her hands.

"I know, but you'll be out of here soon. I'll still be living at home when I'm 40."

Sam smiled.

"Of course I'm not saying it wouldn't hurt you to brighten yourself up a bit now and again. Keep them on their toes." Kate stood up. "You've got to be like, 'Hey boy, this is what you'll be missing out on if you don't treat me right.'" She nodded at Sam, who burst out laughing.

"I wish I had your confidence," Sam said.

Kate sat down again. "Just think of men as mischievous puppies. They need plenty of ground rules, a slap if they misbehave and loads of affection and treats if they do things right. Remember that and you'll have hordes of them eating out the palm of your hand."

"But I don't want hordes of them. I just want one good one: a nice, kind, decent man, who's easy on the eye and reliable. I want a little house with a bit of garden and two or three kids."

Kate's mouth gaped open. "I so do not want any of that. I'll tell you what. I'll trawl through all the guys out there and if I find a boring one who fits the bill I'll pass him over to you, okay? I want to live a little before I die. I want to travel, see the world. I want to get pissed in seventeen different countries and get thrown out of at least two."

"Good grief," said Sam. "How are you going to manage all that? Sleep your way around Europe?"

Kate feigned shock. "No. I'm going to win the lottery," she said.

"But you don't even play the lottery."

"Then I'll find myself a rich man," Kate concluded.

"Hussy!"

"Mouse!" Kate shot back.

The two girls grinned and giggled. "I can't imagine you married with kids," Kate said. "You've still got a rag doll."

"Says the girl with the Zac Efron bedding," Sam replied.

"Tea's ready, girls," Sam's mum called up the stairs and Kate looked at her watch and got to her feet.

The two girls peered round the door of the dining room.

"Kate, love, there's plenty enough for you as well, if you want to stay," Mrs Litton said. Kate looked at Sam, who nodded eagerly. Mrs Litton smiled. "Give your mum a ring and make sure it's okay." Kate stepped out of the room.

"I left your cheque on the dresser this morning, Mum. Did you get it?" Sam asked, passing the salt and pepper from the sideboard to her mother by the table.

"Yes thanks, love. And do you want me to pick up a paper in the morning again? See if there's anything new?"

"Haven't we got rid of her yet?" her dad asked, walking in with the large dish from the oven and winking at his wife.

"No. I'll probably still be here when you're sixty, Dad. Sorry,"

A groan escaped her dad's mouth but he smiled. Kate walked back in. "Knowing my luck Kate'll still be with us too," he said.

Mrs Litton bashed him and he smiled mischievously. "Don't you take any notice of him, love. Did your mum say it was all right?"

"Yes."

"Good. Take a seat and ignore the grumpy one over there. He loves having you here, both of you. Don't you? Now who wants some shepherd's pie?"

Sam's dog, Humphrey, trotted in.

"Oh no you don't," Mrs Litton said. "Sam, put him in the living room while we eat, love. You know I won't have him near the food."

Sam walked Humphrey out to the living room, where his basket lay in the corner beside one of the armchairs. It was small and smart with a tartan blanket folded up neatly inside to make it soft. Up in her bedroom Sam had a squidgy old soft bed for him, but one of the conditions of her being allowed a dog in the house was that her mum's living room would still look 'presentable'. Sam told him to get in and lie down and then stroked his head affectionately. "You only had your tea an hour ago, Humph. You can't possibly be hungry again yet. Good boy." She walked away without a backward glance. She was hopeless at resisting the sad eyes he turned on her whenever he wanted something and had learned it was better simply not to look.

"So, Kate, what exciting things have you been up to recently?" Mr Litton asked over dinner.

"Oh you know… um…"

"Still no luck on the job front then?"

"No. I've got a bit of casual work next week. I'm helping out in a warehouse for a couple of weeks while they get a big order through, but that's all. But, I did hear through the grapevine that Sally who works at the leisure centre is pregnant, so fingers crossed, there might be some work coming up there soon!"

"Well at least that's something. And what about you, Sam? Has Jimmy managed to drive the music teacher to drink yet?"

Sam smiled. "Close, I think. No. Nothing exciting really."

"Apart from pining after Dean," Kate added, and Sam kicked her under the table. "Ow!"

"What's this?" Sam's dad put down his knife and fork. "Sam? You didn't tell me you had a boyfriend?" He looked at his wife for her reaction, but she looked just as surprised as him.

Sam cringed. She had been trying to keep the whole thing under wraps. The last time her mum and dad had got involved it had complicated matters, so she had wanted to keep this one to herself. And Kate knew that!

"Is it anyone we know?" her mum asked.

"No. I don't think so."

"His name is Dean Fletcher. His parents live next door to me," Kate offered, and promptly received another sharp blow to her ankle for her troubles. "Ow!"

"Dean?" Mrs Litton said.

"He's a soldier."

"A soldier?" Mr Litton seemed a little more wary.

"I'm going to kill you," Sam said under her breath, and Kate grinned.

"That's not your usual type," her dad said.

"It's no big deal," Sam said trying to calm the excitement down. "We haven't been going out long."

"Two months," Kate mouthed.

"And are we going to meet this young man?" her dad asked.

"Not for a while," Sam said. "He's off to Afghanistan in a few weeks."

"Oh." The mood changed.

"What's he like, Kate?" Mrs Litton asked.

In an instant Sam was put aside and Kate was asked to describe Dean to her parents. Afghanistan, Sam thought. Yes, that was something of a conversation-stopper. Only a few more days and he would be back from training and getting ready to go out. Sam looked up.

"Well, at least if he's on the other side of the world I won't have to worry how he's treating you, will I?" her dad said.

"Dad!"

"I'm sorry, but that Rick fellow was bad news, Sam. He treated you exceedingly badly and you refused to see it. I guess you were just too young and too besotted."

Sam rolled her eyes. "Now look what you've started."

"Sorry," Kate whispered back, unconvincingly. "We're just trying to look after you, love," said her mum.

Sam's dad changed the subject and the meal continued. At the end Mr Litton thanked Kate for staying to tea and told her she was welcome to come again anytime. Sam declared that she was not.

Kate left soon after. Sam waved her off and then took Humphrey upstairs again. She sat down on her bed and thought back to the last time she had seen Dean.

It had only been a quick visit. Dean had turned up at her school five minutes after the bell and surprised her while she was clearing up the classroom at the end of the school day. Sam had felt awkward when Dean started to make a move on her while people were still in the building. Dean had been very persuasive, obviously turned on by the whole schoolmistress thing. Had she been a different person, Sam might have had a great time. Nobody surprised them, no one even came in after he had gone, but it was all too stressful for Sam and eventually Dean gave up trying and left.

Sam finished tidying the classroom and battled with the guilty feeling that she was probably a disappointment as far as girlfriends were concerned. Oh well, she thought at last, there was nothing she could do about it now. Hopefully she could make amends when he got back from training in a couple of weeks.

Sam got up from her bed and walked over to where her big flower press lay on a pile of large books on the floor. Soon, she thought. Soon she would find a house of her own and then she would have a place for everything. She picked up the flower press and lugged it over to the bed. She sat down and patted the space beside her. Humphrey needed no second bidding. He jumped up and made himself comfortable. Sam hugged him to her and then played with his ears. "If only all men were as easy to love as you, Humph," she said.

Sam carefully opened up the press and counted out the flowers she had saved there. Thirty-two. Good, that gave her one each for every child in her class and a few left over for mishaps, and knowing little Jimmy Richards there were bound to be mishaps. She had seen her flowers turned into crowns, fairies, the sun and endless footballs, but it was those with the imagination to see beyond the obvious that always excited her. She closed the press again and placed it onto her desk with her school diary and the verse she had written out about flowers to go on the classroom wall. She sat back down. "Do you want to go for a walk, Humph?" Humphrey was on his feet in a flash, his stubby little tail wagging eagerly. "Come on then, let's get out of here."

Dean called Sam once after he got back from training and Sam asked for his address out in Afghanistan, but despite him giving it to her, he was still too busy to catch up. The time passed when he was due to leave and Sam had heard nothing. She wrote, not too emotionally, as she was still a little unsure about whether he would actually get the letter and who else would see it on the way. There was no reply.

Nearly three weeks passed and still she heard nothing. In place of eager anticipation, she greeted the fall of the mail each day on the mat with the resigned habit of just checking.

On Wednesday, Sam had had a particularly wearing day in school. Jimmy Richards had been caught stealing another child's tooth to try and extort extra money out of the tooth fairy. Bethany-May had managed to make her whole group of friends hysterical in front of a school inspector over a class pet hamster who had somehow been let out of his cage, (by whom she had yet to determine) and to cap it all off, Peter Davies chose that very same day to bring up his entire lunch all over Lucy Eccles' lovely long hair.

Sam walked into the house and dropped her bike helmet and bag to the floor. Her mum walked out of the kitchen to greet her. "Oh. As bad as that, was it?"

"Worse."

Sam's mum ushered her inside and sat her down with a cup of tea while she heard all about Sam's miserable day. She tried very hard not to laugh, but by the end of the tale even Sam could see the funny side of things and she felt a whole lot better. "It's all right for you," she said. "You only had one child to deal with, I've got 28 and Jimmy's got to count for at least two."

Mrs Litton laughed. "I'm sorry, dear, but you just couldn't write the stuff you come home with," she said, composing herself again.

"Something smells nice," Sam said.

"Baked ham," her mum told her.

Sam sniffed at her hands. "Ugh! I stink of sick."

Mrs Litton smiled and told Sam to go for a nice warm shower and wash her hair as there was plenty of time before tea.

The following day, all was well with the world again. Mary Appleby had a nice shiny fifty pence piece from the tooth fairy, all the pets stayed safely contained and no one was sick over anyone else. Sam cycled home feeling much better about the world. Her job was great, she had a lovely family and the weather was finally starting to feel like spring.

Sam got in and hung up her things. She found her mum sat at the dining room table with the local paper spread out in front of her.

"Anything interesting?" Sam asked.

"There might be actually, yes."

Sam walked around the table and looked over her mother's shoulder. Mrs Litton pointed to a terraced house, on the other side of town, with a tiny front garden and next to a street light. Sam looked at the price and then read on.

"What do you think?" her mum asked.

"Well, yes. It looks okay, doesn't it?"

"Shall we have a drive past and nose about this weekend?"

"Yeah, why not." She grinned excitedly. Have you got anything sorted out for tea?" she asked.

"Not yet. Your dad rang a short while ago. He's popping round to Uncle Gerald's after work, to help him with his car, so it's just the two of us tonight."

"Great. Let's get a Chinese. My treat."

"What a good idea, but I'll pay. You can pay when we go to your house for tea."

Sam laughed. "I won't be able to afford a Chinese once I've got my own place."

"So, we'll eat beans on toast. But tonight, I'm paying."

Half way across the world, Andy was settling into life in theatre. It was a basic way of life, with few of the luxuries of modern living that most people take for granted. Boredom was commonplace and the food, by necessity, was uninspiring.

The vast expanse of sky had been the first thing to hit him when he stepped off the plane in Kandahar. It had been the middle of the night but the sky was clear and it was hung with a myriad of stars. The atmosphere had changed perceptibly en route, with the excitement of the beginning of the flight subduing by mid-flight and then replaced with a more contained sense of tension by the end.

The empty stretchers on the plane had been a chilling reminder of where they were heading. When they transferred onto the Hercules for the short stretch to Helmand, donning helmets and body armour for a blacked-out approach, the adrenaline had definitely begun to flow.

Camp Bastion, in northern Helmand, was the closest to civilisation they had, with its facilities and air-con pods, but it carried with it its own shadows. The hospital for all the casualties was based there too. But for now, home was a forward operations base to the south near Lashkar Gar.

This was a compound that had been deserted by fleeing locals during some fierce fighting a couple of years before. Andy looked around him at his fellow soldiers. They were all back safe. Relief was expressed in the whoops and cries of the men in his team as they dispersed to their various corners and took off their kits.

Andy checked in with the guys who had been on guard that day, to see if there had been any more contact while they were away. There hadn't. He looked about him. Piles of water bottles were stacked up under a tarp in one corner and Andy wished he could dive in and bathe in every single one. He was filthy. Dust had got in everything. Mud caked around the bottom of his legs from crossing the drainage ditches and tacking in and out of the fields. It baked hard in the sun as he walked and added to the considerable weight he carried around with him. He took off his helmet and started to remove his body armour. Tomorrow was their turn to man the base while the other team ventured out, so he could wash his clothes in the morning and they would dry out in the heat of the day. He checked his rifle and made sure it was clean and then went in search of food.

The following day they took a delivery of mail, one of the highlights of the week for most of them, but Andy didn't lose too much sleep looking forward to it. A letter from his mum every couple of weeks and the odd parcel was the most he could expect. However, if one of the lads happened to have a birthday while they were there, you never knew what treat might wing its way over to them.

He decided to take personal responsibility for distributing the mail that day. He wandered through the compound calling out the names and delivering the post to each in turn. Some men got loads. Andy assumed they must have a harem back home constantly writing to them, while others got only one or two. Where they were, they received deliveries of mail about once a week. In larger bases there was internet communication, but he knew from experience that those in other more remote posts had it worse. He shoved his letter from his mother into his pocket and carried on calling out the names.

In a shady, mud-floored room in the corner of the compound Dean answered his call. Andy walked in and handed over a bundle of letters. Dean thanked him and started rifling through his post to see who his letters were from. Spike looked over at the number of letters Dean had received and rolled his eyes. Andy handed Spike his letter from home and he lay back and began to read.

"How's Sam doing?" Andy asked, turning back to Dean momentarily before studying hard the name on the next letter in his hand.

Dean looked up. "Shit, check this out, guys." He held out a picture of a girl Andy did not recognise. She was a blonde girl wearing a bikini and posing provocatively. Dean snatched the photo back. "Hey, don't wear her out! Spike." He held the photo up for Spike to see.

"Got any of those going spare?" Spike asked.

"I'll swap you for your sister."

"On your bike."

"Your sister is my bike."

"Piss off!" Spike launched a dirty sock across the room and the lads laughed. "Cocky little shit!" he mumbled.

Dean grinned and threw the sock back. He looked back to Andy, still standing in the room. "What?"

"Are you and Sam no longer an item?"

Dean rifled through his things and pulled out a handful of old letters. "Oh, I've got one in here from her too somewhere…" He flicked through, flipped a letter over and read the back. "Yeah, here you go. This one's from her."

Andy's guts twisted. He wanted to tear him limb from limb for treating Sam so thoughtlessly, but he knew he couldn't say a thing. "Who else have you heard from?" Andy asked.

"Oh you know, Mum and Dad, Jules, two from Soph, a couple of mates. How about you?"

"Parents."

"Never mind, Prof."

Andy stiffened and looked back at the letters in his hand. He turned and called out the next name in the stack.

A little while later Andy found a shady spot up against a wall and pulled out the letter from his mum. His older brother, Simon, had got engaged to a girl called Helen from some rich family in London and they were going there to meet them in a couple of weeks' time. - Andy remembered the day he had told his parents *he* was getting married. For once he had done something right and everyone seemed happy… for a while. – But back to the present: Simon's business was thriving and he had just bought a new Audi to drive around town. His dad was apparently fine and the garden was looking lovely. Great. He put the letter back in his pocket and felt Sam's letter lying there.

After lunch it was his turn to go on watch. He manned the lookout post with his binoculars trained on the tree line. His men were in position, covering all sides of the compound.

Privacy wasn't a word synonymous with army life and the letter languished in his pocket for a few days. Eventually it was rescued from being ruined by being washed and hidden away in Andy's box of personal things. Finally, Andy decided he had to take a chance and write to Sam. But what was he to say? How could he write a letter without hurting her feelings? It took him a few days of racking his brains before he came up with an idea.

Chapter 3

April arrived and with it, at last, a letter from Afghanistan. Sam got home from work and her mother greeted her, smiling from ear to ear. She pulled out a blue envelope from behind her back and Sam's eyes lit up. "He wrote!"

Mrs Litton handed her the letter. "Go on. Go up and read it. I'll have a cup of tea ready for when you get downstairs again."

Sam hung her coat and helmet on the rack behind the door and skipped off upstairs, excited to finally be hearing news back from Dean. Humphrey followed her up the stairs, barking eagerly. He panted and wagged his tail at her feet as she sat on her bed carefully opening the folded envelope. He barked loudly and got the attention he desired. "Come up, Humph," she said and patted the bed. Humphrey hopped up on to the bed beside her and rested his head on her lap. "It's Dean," she told him. "Let's see what he has to say after all this time."

Sam started to read and then checked the name at the bottom of the letter. She was confused. She checked a second time and then began to read again from the beginning. When she had finished she was at a loss as to what to make of it. She stared at the wall for a few minutes, trying to work through her thoughts. Eventually, she got up and took the letter downstairs. Humphrey seemed happier to stay where he was.

Sam found her mum in the living room, with the biscuit barrel open and a hot cup of tea waiting on the little table beside the settee. Sam walked over to her mother and handed her the letter. "What do you make of this?" she asked and took a seat by the cup of tea.

Mrs Litton's brow furrowed in concern. She put down her cup of tea, reached for her glasses and started to read.

Dear Sam,

I know you will have been expecting a letter from Dean. Please do not concern yourself, he is quite well, but he has been moved with a small team of men to a rather remote checkpoint and therefore will unfortunately be unable to send or receive post for the duration of his time here. I know this must be hard for you and I wondered if you would care to write to me instead. I can keep you informed about how things are for us out here and maybe you would feel more connected in that way.

I will, of course, understand if you would rather not, but on my part, I would be honoured if you would write to me. It is always good to hear from home and how things are going back there. And to hear the song of a nightingale would be a cool relief in the blistering heat of an Afghan day.

Yours faithfully,

Andy Garrington

Mrs Litton looked down at the address on the back of the envelope. "Sergeant?" she said. She lay the letter down in her lap and looked at Sam. She took a deep breath and said nothing.

"I know," Sam said. She had no idea what to think, or even how to feel. On the one hand she felt abandoned, foisted off onto the next available soldier as if one was just as good as the next. On the other hand, did that mean that Dean was in far more danger? He couldn't write to her at all? Sam racked her brain for an explanation. Keeping in touch had never been Dean's forte, it was true, but…

It occurred to her then that she may have just been dumped. Was this how soldiers did it? Passed you on to the next guy? How was she meant to feel about that? She liked Dean: he was charming and handsome and he made her laugh- but he was very unpredictable and definitely not reliable. But she did like him, a lot. If she'd known some of the other wives and girlfriends at the barracks, or The Patch, as they called it, she might be able to get some answers, but Dean never took her there, not once. Army life was still a foreign language to her. At least she could be pretty sure whatever he was doing, he wasn't cheating on her.

"Do you know this Andy Garrington?" her mum asked.

"Sort of. I met him a couple of times with Dean."

"What sort of chap is he? Is he nice?"

"Mum!"

"Not like that. I mean kind, considerate, that sort of thing, or was he, you know, laddish?"

"No, he seemed nice, quite quiet. Do you think he's dumping me?"

"Who, Andy?"

"No, Dean."

"I don't think you could say that, not without something more… direct. But it's strange, I'll give you that. What are you going to do?"

Sam walked over and took back the letter. She shook her head. "I don't know. It feels wrong to write to someone else, like I'm being unfaithful or something."

"Yes, I can see that, but maybe it doesn't have to be like that. This chap… Andy might not have anyone else to write to. You two could be like pen pals."

"But what would I say to him?"

"I don't know. Anything. Talk to him about your day, what the weather is doing, just pretend he's another girl. It probably doesn't matter. Sometimes it's the receiving of a letter, when somebody's taken the time to write to you, that's the special bit, not what they've actually written."

"Mm, maybe." Sam could see the sense in this, but it still felt very odd.

"Sleep on it. You don't have to decide right now."

Sam thanked her mum and went back upstairs, grabbing a couple of chocolate chip cookies from the biscuit barrel on the way. She still had plenty to do before school the next day.

That night Sam lay in bed thinking about the letter. If Dean had been sent to a remote outpost, why hadn't he sent word before he left, or called? She tossed and turned on this matter for an hour or more and in the early hours of the morning found herself at her desk. It was cold in the night. The heating had long since gone off and Sam wrapped her fluffy dressing gown around her and hugged her knees up to her chest. She had a pile of forces' blueys in her desk drawer just waiting for an excuse to be used. She picked one out and began to write.

Dear Andy,

I am not sure how to respond to your request, but thank you for thinking of me and taking the time to write. It seems strange to be writing to someone I barely know. I don't even know what to say. What could I tell you that you might be interested in? I'm afraid that us writing would never really work, but keep safe and thank you again.

Sam.

The next day she posted it and then worried that she had done the wrong thing. She had assumed it was all over but just under a week later Sam received a second envelope.

Dear Sam,

Thank you so much for writing back. I know you feel uneasy about this and I can understand that. I am glad, though, that you did. We know little about each other, it is true, but are we not all strangers when first we meet? As for what to say? Say anything. Just to hear a kind voice and to know that somebody is thinking about you matters so much out here. Tell me about your day. Tell me about things you like doing and things you don't. Tell me about yourself and soon we will no longer be strangers. Shall I go first?

My name is Andy Garrington. I am 28 and a sergeant in B Company, 9 Rifles. I am not married and have no kids. I was born in Surrey, where my parents still live. I studied English at Bristol University, before joining the lower ranks of the army at 22, much to my father's disappointment – he would have had me in officer training – but there we had to disagree.

Likes? – Fish and chips/ rock-climbing/ marmite/ kayaking/ loyalty and the colour red.

Dislikes? – Horoscopes/ dishonesty/ Facebook/ moaners/ gherkins and Sellotape.

So there you have it. Now you know everything there is to know about me. I doubt you have any bizarre idiosyncrasies that could compete with mine. You're probably far more together and self-assured.

Yours,

Andy

Sam felt a quiver of excitement ripple through her, like a school-girl with a new boyfriend, a new boyfriend she couldn't tell anyone about. She reminded herself that he was not actually her boyfriend, merely a pen pal that she was writing to while she waited to hear where she stood with Dean. She pulled out a fresh bluey from her drawer and poised over it for a minute, deciding what to say, and then she put pen to paper.

Dear Andy,

Thank you for your letter. It certainly made me smile. So you think I have no little foibles of my own, do you? Well, you're in for a surprise. After this you may well decide to go and join Dean at his remote check post just to escape. I hope you're sitting comfortably, because this may take some time!

You know my name – Samantha Litton – but the secret I have been burdened with all my life is a hideous middle name (Gayle!!!) Tell a soul and I will have you shot! This must never be referred to again. It's an old family name and I hate it. I am 24 years old, 25 next week and as you probably know, a teacher. I teach six to seven year olds at a local school, which has its moments, I can tell you. You may do battle with the Taliban on a daily basis, but until you have faced-down a class full of riotous six year olds you know nothing of torture! (I'm joking. I can't imagine what you are going through over there. If it is something you feel able to talk about I would like to try and understand if I can.)

Anyway. I'm currently back living with Mum and Dad, but am searching for a place of my own. One looked promising the other day, but when we went round to look at it, it was falling to bits. Oh well. Soon, maybe.

So, as for idiosyncrasies? Well it may be difficult to beat Sellotape - ??? You're going to have to explain that one.

Likes? - Music - particularly Dido and Stevie Nicks (blame my Mum), singing in the shower, Humphrey (my wonderful little Westie), Marmite, of course, fresh linen and summer days.

Dislikes? – Drunk people (they scare me) and bagpipes – surely that has to count as bizarre?

Over here the days are getting warmer and the gardens and parks are looking lovely.

Are you still there, or have you run away? If I don't hear back again I'll know the verdict.

All the best,

Sam.

PS Do you have a middle name that can be spoken of?

Sam folded up the big blue page stuffed with writing and hurried off to the post box at the end of the road to send it.

On Sam's birthday the girls met up at Kate's house to go ice-skating. They packed into Chloe's red Polo and drove off to the edge of town. Inside it was chilly. They strapped themselves into the uncomfortable boots and tottered over to the gate. At first they were all a bit unsteady. It had been a while since they had stepped out onto the ice. Sam and Kate held onto the edge on their first time round, but a few circuits in, they were finding their balance, some more than others, and they began to glide around with not too many bumps and scrapes.

After forty minutes they came sailing off for a drink at the side. They clomped across the rubber mats to the café at the end of the rink and sat down. Sam was enjoying herself immensely and had a big smile on her face.

"You seem unnaturally happy tonight," Chloe said. "Have you won the lottery, or something?"

Sam shook her head. "No. I'm just having fun. It *is* my birthday."

Kate looked at Sam. "No. She's right. There's something else. You're not normally this chirpy."

"Are you saying I'm normally a miserable cow? Thanks very much, guys."

Kate licked her lips and looked at Sam. "It's a guy, isn't it?"

Sam didn't say a word.

"You haven't finally heard from Dean, have you?"

Sam shook her head. "No."

The girls waited to see if Sam would spill. They watched her face in silence.

Sam felt the weight of expectation on her. She was desperate to tell them all about Andy, but what would they think? Surely she was being a complete bitch? Or was she doing the right thing? She hesitated on the brink of speaking for many moments and then she cracked. She pulled a pained face. "There is somebody."

"Go girl! I never thought you had it in you." Kate said, loudly.

"What about Dean?" Chloe asked.

"Oh bugger Dean," Kate shot in, "he's been crap anyway. Tell me everything." Her eyes shone with excitement.

Sam took a deep breath and told them about the letter. Both girls agreed it was odd, but after a quick recap through Dean's lack of boyfriend-like communication even before he left, they quickly lost interest in the moral dilemma and wanted to know about Sam's new man.

When Sam told them the name of the other guy Kate sat back in her chair. She nodded in understanding. "Yep," she said.

"What do you mean, 'yep'?" Sam asked.

"Oh you have to have seen that coming? Not the disappearance of Dean, I mean, but Andy."

Sam and Chloe looked puzzled.

Kate sighed and leaned forward on the table.

"Why did I say I walked out of the date we had a few months back?"

Sam wracked her brains. "It was something to do with your mum, wasn't it? No, wait, you thought he liked me more than you, didn't you? But-"

Kate was shaking her head impatiently. "He couldn't take his eyes off you. I told you. Andy, that is. I might as well have turned up butt-naked with 'shag me witless' tattooed across my arse. He wouldn't have noticed."

Sam was stunned. Her mouth fell open. "Do you think I should stop writing to him?"

"Hell no! He's a hot guy who's actually paying some attention to you, instead of leading you a merry dance. Don't you dare stop writing to him."

"But what about Dean? He is still my boyfriend, technically. And what if he *is* stuck out somewhere where he can't write to me?"

"He may not be able to get online, but I seriously doubt he can't do anything."

"What's he like then, this new chap?" Chloe asked.

Sam's heart fluttered and her eyes lit up. "I don't know. But I get this feeling about him that I can't explain. He's nice." She smiled despite herself.

"Nice is good. It makes a change for you."

Sam gave Chloe an offended look. "Yeah, all right. I know. I'm rubbish when it comes to men."

The girls nodded. "But this one is nice?" Chloe asked, "and hot?"

Kate nodded. "Oh yeah."

"So? What else?"

Sam told them most of what she knew about Andy from the two letters she had received and the girls did their best to allay the guilt she was harbouring about the way she was feeling about him.

"My mum said that in other wars, girls wrote to soldiers on the front line as a sort of morale thing" Sam said.

Kate grinned. "You don't want to ask your fella to get me a hunky soldier to write to, do you, Sam?"

"And me," said Chloe. "Ooh, you could be the forces matchmaker."

"Tell you what Chlo', let's go back to my place and take some fab pictures of us and then Sam can send them out to her fella and get us a couple of gorgeous guys to write to." She turned to Sam. "We don't have to actually physically write to them, do we?"

"No. I think you can do it online. I looked into it when Dean first went out there."

"What do you think, Chlo? Are you up for it?"

"Absolutely! Right, I think that's enough exercise for me for one week."

The girls clambered their way down to the boot kiosk and released their aching feet. With their faces rosy from exercise and their eyes bright with excitement, the girls laughed and joked as they walked back to the car and, picking up a burger on the way, they hurried home to get the ball rolling.

Sam sat on Kate's bed while the other two got ready. She wondered how their plan was going to work. "You know he may not know any single guys for you to write to," she warned them.

"Course he will," Kate said. "Who wouldn't want a bit of this?" She pulled a sexy pose. Sam rolled her eyes. "Just tell him to get me one with big muscles, all right? And preferably, this time, someone who's not madly in love with *you*."

"He is not!" Sam protested.

"Yeah? Well, we'll see. Muscles, remember."

"I'm not guaranteeing anything," Sam said, amused at the silly way her two friends were acting that night. "Smile." Sam took some shots. "You're both barking mad. You're loons."

A couple of days later the welcome blue post dropped onto the mat again after Sam had arrived home from a stressful day at school. Parents' evening was coming up and there was a lot of paperwork to see to before she was ready. She had spent half the afternoon trying to get the classroom in order, but what with Jimmy's gluing calamity and Rochelle, the new girl in class, in a state over wetting herself on her first day in school it was a bit of an uphill struggle. It was almost five o'clock before she got home. As soon as she took off her bike helmet she saw it there. It was lying on the dresser, just inside the kitchen door. Sam smiled. She hurried inside and grabbed the letter, calling out a greeting to her mum as she swept in and out again and off up to her room. She ignored the whimpering of Humphrey at the bottom of the stairs, wanting to be carried up, and raced up the stairs to open the letter. It was long.

Dear Sam,

Happy Birthday!

I hope you have a wonderful day. It was so good to hear from you. Life here is pretty basic. I seem to spend half my time out and about getting covered in mud and dirt and the other half trying to wash it off again. Why is there never a Hotpoint around when you need one? I tell you, you wouldn't want to sing in our showers – you wouldn't reach the end of the first chorus and the water would have run out. Although I have no objection to you trying if you should feel so inclined.

What do we do out here? Well much of our task these days is diplomacy. We still have to patrol contentious areas like schools and clinics and keep roads clear for safe access, but more and more there is a limit on what we can actually do and more emphasis on assisting the local forces. Which I guess is how it will have to be if we are ever going to get out of here, but it's a little frustrating for the men. There has been far less contact with the Taliban than the last time I was out here, which has its pros and cons. At least in a face-to-face fight you know who your enemy is.

Try not to worry; we don't have it too bad out here. We have a laugh when we can. Anyway, enough seriousness. Back to those peculiar foibles of yours!!! I'm shocked. I thought you were a normal girl!?!

I promise never ever to mention the middle name (although I fail to see why it's so bad?) and in compensation for this spectacular show of faith I will also admit to one thing the guys must never, EVER find out about me: I am a big fan of bird watching. There, I've said it, I'm a twitcher, but if you speak a word of this to anyone else, I will have to shoot you!

So, bagpipes, huh? We'll get back to that one later.

Sam turned over the page.

Okay… the Sellotape… I was badly traumatised as a child by a mother who wrapped every exciting present I ever had with rolls and rolls of Sellotape, leaving not a single edge to help me in my quest to get to the prize beneath. I'm still having counselling about that one. As for middle names? No. Not one that can be mentioned.

Write soon, with photos.

Andy

Sam picked up the photos that had dropped out of the letter. She looked at them. The first one was of Andy with the lads standing in T-shirts and combats, posing in front of a mud wall and the other was of Andy by himself. Sam gazed at the photo. Yes, that's what he looked like. He was gorgeous. Why hadn't she noticed before? He was lean, his arms were well muscled, his hair was dark, almost black and his eyes were…she couldn't tell what colour, and he had a kind smile. She gently stroked the picture and bit her bottom lip. He reminded her a little of someone, but she couldn't think who.

Sam placed the photo at the back of her desk, facing her and looked at the other. She flipped it over. 'The lads,' it said. Underneath, in small writing, Andy had written the names of all the soldiers in the picture. 'Spike, Miller, Harding, Lofty, Zippo, Baker, Evans and Me. And the one in the background unaware he was being photographed is Lt Durbin'. Sam looked closely and noticed the tiny figure at the back that looked like he was picking his nose. She laughed and placed the second picture alongside the first.

She wrote straight back.

Dear Andy,

I was so sad to hear about your tragic childhood. I hope the therapy is doing some good. Sorry to disappoint on the 'normal' front, but at least we will always have Marmite! As for our feathered friends? Your secret is safe with me.

I am enclosing photos of two of my best friends. Kate is the blonde one. She is also 24. She's bubbly and always popular with the boys. Chloe is the one with dark hair. She's 21 and the more reserved of the two, although the photos may suggest otherwise. The point is they are currently without boyfriends and were wondering if there were any nice single guys out there who would like to write to them. Oh yes, and Kate requested someone with big muscles. I'm sorry, you can't take her anywhere. Do you think you could help?

Surely any middle name you could come up with couldn't be worse than mine? I'm intrigued. What are we talking about here? Bartholomew? Alfred? Lesley?

Thank you for your photos. They are up on my desk, looking at me as I write.

What are the children like out there? Are they very different from over here?

What do you miss when you are away?

Write soon,

Love, Sam

Sam looked at the ending: Love Sam. Should she have put that? Was that too much? He might just see it as friendly. She drummed her fingers on the desk. Her stomach tightened and she folded up the letter and walked it down to the post box already anxious about the reply.

Chapter 4

Andy was out on patrol. They had been given the task of maintaining a presence at the local bazaar. He walked along the street, alert and vigilant. The enemy, he knew, could be anywhere and anyone. The sun shone down without mercy. Despite this, he felt like this was a good day. The local people seemed relaxed and happy. Children smiled and waved as traders went about their business. Days were not always like this. Some days Andy had been out patrolling the same ground and muted faces had stared back, afraid. Children looked on in silence and people hid away. These were the days when anything could happen. In Afghanistan, people who looked scared always had good reason.

A small group of boys kicking something that looked like a dried up old fruit started to walk along beside him. Andy smiled at them. The patrol stopped and Andy shook their hands, still very much aware of what was going on around him. He got the order to move off again and signalled to his team. One of the boys kicked the makeshift ball out into his path by mistake, and Andy deftly back-heeled it to them as he passed, winking as he did. It was the little things like this that made his day.

Back safe in the compound when the patrol was over and everyone was at ease, Andy was handed his mail. His face struggled hard not to give away his delight, as he removed himself to a shady corner and carefully opened his letter.

He read, too quickly. He should not be so rushed. He read again, word by beautiful word. She had written some more about herself and Andy needed to know. He needed to know everything about her. He remembered little from before. They hadn't spent much time talking about the past, only the present, their holiday and what they were going to do in the future. He looked at the photos. You stupid girl, he thought fondly to himself. I didn't want pictures of your mates, I wanted them of you.

He rummaged around in his things for the means to reply.

Dear Sam,

When I asked for pictures, I meant pictures of you! Don't worry, I have a couple of chaps in mind for your friends and if I'm wrong, it won't be long before I find some willing volunteers. But I won't let them see the photos until they agree, or I could have half the platoon wanting to write to them, and a lot of them are married!

You asked about children out here. We frequently come across groups of children and mostly they are very friendly. They smile at us and shake our hands, but the more unsure ones just watch us with big round eyes. I've learned a few words from our translator that help to break the ice, but we see little in the way of bad behaviour. Maybe you should try carrying a rifle around at school and see if your kids' behaviour improves!?!

I like the sound of Humphrey. How long have you had him? Is he yours, or your family's? Do you think he would like me?

He paused, unsure of how to go on. Should he let on a little of how he felt, or would that just scare her off? Maybe if he was light-hearted about it?

Back to your list of likes and dislikes – Do you have any idea how many letters I receive every week? Maybe you think I have hordes of mail. A good-looking chap like me, of course I do. Actually, no. Apart from my mother's ramblings once every couple of weeks, telling me just how wonderful my brother is, there is only you. Shocked? I know, it's unbelievable! Then you must be able to see how dangerous it is to write the words 'shower' and 'fresh linen' so close together in a letter to a soldier on a six month tour… Beautiful woman, shower, bed… Bagpipes, bagpipes, bagpipes! Okay. I'm all right again now.

Tell me about the kids you teach and about the parks in bloom.

Send me a picture, please.

Your lonely soldier,

Andy

PS Middle name? – Not even close!

Was that too much? Andy almost screwed it up and started again. But he stopped. Faint heart never won fair maid, he thought, and sealed it up and wrote her address carefully on the front.

He wrote the name, age and address of both the girls on the back of their photos and shoved them in his pocket then folded up Sam's letter, placing it neatly away with the others he had hiding in his things. Deed done.

Sam read Andy's next letter and blushed. She had never intended to be provocative. It had been an honest mistake. Well, not a mistake, but she had never even thought how her words might make him feel. 'Beautiful woman' he had said. Her? He was picturing her. Sam's stomach clenched. What was this she was feeling? She looked at the photo smiling at her from the back of her desk. But there was Dean. So how should she reply?

Dear Andy,

I'm not sure where the school stands on teachers carrying arms in class, but I shall certainly look into it.

Humphrey is mine. I've had him about 18 months and he's adorable. But would he like you? Probably not. He's not very good at sharing my attention, but don't be afraid, he's not the kind of dog to savage a man. He might lick you to death, but apart from the odd yap, he's completely harmless.

I bike through a beautiful park on the way to school and back every day. The grass is very green at the moment because we have had quite a bit of rain. The borders are full of colour and the pond is dappled with quacking ducks. A weeping willow hangs lazily on one side and I have to duck down under its branches on my way through. I know I shouldn't be riding through the park, but there's no one around at that time of the morning, so don't tell, okay?

What do you get up to in your time off? Do you get time off? I'm sorry; I'm a bit of an idiot when it comes to knowing anything about the army.

It got up to 22 degrees over here today. How hot is it with you?

I've got parents' evenings coming up this week - ugh! - So long days and lots of work for me. I need my pillow.

Three days later a small terraced house came up for sale on the edge of town. It was an old place, but it had been well kept and updated over the years. It had one good-sized bedroom, a little room and a bathroom upstairs and a living room, cloakroom and kitchen downstairs. Sam took her mum and dad along to see it, hoping for their approval and she wasn't disappointed. Sam had been left a large amount of money by her grandmother a few years before and had been saving as much as she could ever since to afford a place of her own. So when the next letter arrived, she had plenty of news to tell.

will not do. Unless it is in the style of a hot Mills and Boon novel, of course? Ahhh! Bagpipes! No, I couldn't take it!!! Nuns. Nuns. Okay.

I take it this is a pushbike you ride every day? You're not a Hell's Angel, are you? The park sounds wonderful. What I wouldn't give to walk barefoot around the soft green grass in that park right now.

Yes. In answer to your question, we do get down time. Some guys play cards, some listen to music. There is time to write letters and re-read old ones. The mundane things that back home would take a matter of minutes take a lot longer out here, as everything has to be done by hand, so that fills up a bit of time too. Guys like Spike tend to keep fit - tell your friend Kate to expect a letter very soon – and others like Karl – Chloe's guy – just top up their tans. My hidden talent, it seems, lies in poker. I'm getting pretty good, even if I do say so myself.

The weather out here is hot, with intermittent bouts of scorching sun to break-up the monotony. It got up to a balmy forty three today! I'll send you some over if you like.

Write soon, WITH PHOTOS!

Yours,

Andy x

PS Still no!

Sam had reached a watershed. To go on now would be to admit there was more to this relationship than just friendship. Friendly banter had gone and flirtation was now definitely on the table. Was this really what she wanted?

For the first time, Sam decided not to write back straight away. She understood this would mean the reply would also be delayed because of this, but it was important to be sure of what to say. She pushed the letter to the back of her desk and looked hard at the handsome soldier who smiled back at her from there. She rang Kate and arranged to go out the following night and then went downstairs to see her mum.

After a while, her mum said, "You're not your usual self tonight, love. Is anything wrong?"

Sam shook her head.

"Only you're usually full of the joys of spring after you've had a letter."

Sam thought about this. "Just a tiring day, I guess."

"But the house is still going ahead all right, isn't it? No problems there?"

"Oh yes, fine."

"Right then. Lasagne and chips okay?"

The following evening, Sam met Kate at a pub in town and confided her dilemma. Kate had few reservations about what Sam should do. "Okay, so let me get this straight. You're worried that you might be two-timing a guy who may or may not be bothered about writing to you and was basically a bit crap when he was around anyway, with a dark brooding horny Adonis who thinks you're the best thing since sliced bread? And you are hesitating because…?"

"You're probably right, I know. But what if Dean really is in the back of beyond? What sort of a woman would that make me?"

Kate took a big swig of her drink. "You're thinking way too much about this. Just go with it. What's the worst that could happen? It's not exactly life or death. I say screw Dean and go with Andy."

"Put so eloquently, now I see perfectly what I need to do." Sam sagged. "Oh, why are men so complicated?"

"They're not. They're very simple. It's basic science, Sam. Effort equals results. Andy is the one making all the effort. He should be the one getting the result."

"You *were* awake in Science class. I'm impressed."

Kate thumped her playfully.

"Still," said Sam, "it would be nice to know, one way or the other."

When Sam did eventually write back she felt it was important to maintain a holding position of friendliness. Not dismissive enough so as to put him off, but nor should she give him any reason to hope. She crafted her letter very carefully, giving herself more time to think, but still keeping the lines of communication open between them.

Dear Andy,

Great news: I have found a house. I put an offer in on a little terraced house a week or so ago and it has been accepted. It is all systems go at the moment, so keep your fingers crossed that it all goes well. I'm hoping I can move in over half term week. Mum and Dad will probably hold a party to celebrate finally getting rid of me – not really! I think Mum will secretly be sad to see me go. Who will she cluck over when I'm gone? Dad? I'm not sure he's ready for that.

So, my own place? Wow. All it will have in it is a beanbag, a dog and a laptop, but it will be all mine. I think I may have to do a lot of shopping over the next few weeks, don't you?

Now, Rumplestiltskin, about that middle name. Is it Timothy? Sheldon? Sturgis? Ooo, I know, Rupert? I'm not giving up on this, you know.

Write when you can,

PS Kate has heard from Spike and she's grinning from ear to ear. Thank you.

She checked through the letter again to make sure nothing could be construed as suggestive. No, it was fine, not too cool and she had stuck to safe topics. She called Humphrey over and tickled him under the chin. His stubby little tail wagged happily. "Walk, Humph?" she asked. She carried him down the stairs and walked out up the road, stopping briefly at the post box along the way.

On Sunday night, Kate rang. Apparently she had walked in on her mother having a chat with Mrs Fletcher, her next-door neighbour and she had asked if there was any news from Dean. His mother had said he was fine and seemed to be in good spirits.

"But how could she know?" Sam asked.

"I know. So I asked her, just for interest, how often she gets to hear from him and you'll never guess what? He only writes every week. And I'm afraid she also mentioned meeting his girlfriend in town the other day."

Sam was silent. How could he? He hadn't even had the decency to break up with her. She was hurt. No, she was angry.

"Look, Sam, I'm sorry, but I always said he was no good. At least now you know you can forget about him and get nice and friendly with Andy. Guilt free."

Sam heaved a big sigh. "What is it with men and me, Kate?"

"Oh, you're just one in a long line of girls that have been taken in by that one, I'm sure of it. Cheer up, you're free."

Sam swapped ears and paused. "Hang on a minute. But that also means that Andy lied to me about Dean."

This time it was Kate's turn to come unstuck. "I guess."

"Oh bloody men! Bugger them all, that's what I say." Humphrey whimpered in his bed. "Not you, Humph. You're lovely," she called across her room and patted her lap and Humphrey happily obliged.

"Give me five minutes. I'm coming over," said Kate.

Kate arrived soon after and gave Sam a big hug. "Come on, let's put some music on and stick pins in a Plasticine man."

"I haven't got any Plasticine," Sam said.

"Call yourself a teacher? You've got to have some Plasticine somewhere?"

"Yes. At school."

"Oh well, we'll improvise." Kate searched around Sam's room for inspiration and started looking through her music collection. Various sounds of dismay and disbelief were uttered as she sifted through the stack of CDs. "At last. This'll have to do. At least it's recent and not miserable to listen to," she said and she popped on some Pussycat Dolls. Kate jumped up and started singing along with the tunes. "Come on. Up you get!" she said and dragged Sam reluctantly to her feet.

The following day Sam wrote again.

Dear Andy,

I know Dean could be writing to me if he wanted to. I also know he has another girlfriend. Why you lied to me I do not know.

Sam

So few words on such a large piece of paper; but Sam found she couldn't bring herself to say any more.

The days lumbered past, filled with housing and its demands, leaving the affairs of the heart in second place. Then one day, not long after Sam had got in from school, the phone rang. Her mum answered it on the landline in the living room. She called Sam urgently to the phone. Sam ran in and cautiously took the phone. A man's voice answered from a long way away.

"Is that Sam?"

"Yes?" she said.

"Good. Sam, it's Andy."

"Andy? Good God!"

"Now listen carefully, because I haven't got long. I've sent you a letter explaining everything, but I couldn't let you sit around thinking the worst of me. I only did what I did to protect you. You have to believe me. I care about you too much to ever hurt you. You mean more to me than you can ever know."

Mrs Litton was concentrating hard on her daughter's face, searching for any clues as to what was going on. Sam's lips spread wide into a happy grin and her hand jumped up to her lips. Mrs Litton breathed a huge sigh of relief.

"Sam?"

"Yes,"

"Do you trust me?"

"…Yes." Sam's heart filled with joy.

"Good." Andy sounded relieved. "Look, I've got to go, but read my letter, okay? Promise me."

"I promise."

"Bye, Sam."

"Bye." The phone went dead and she put down the receiver.

"Well?" her mum asked.

Sam's smile spread across her face. "It was Andy. Everything's all right."

"Are you happy again now?" her mum asked folding Sam in her arms and Sam nodded and hugged her tightly.

That evening Sam was desperate to write to Andy again and make up for the lost time, but it seemed silly to write before she had read his next letter. Instead she thought of all the things she would say to him now. He had rung her. From across the world, in the middle of a war zone, he had thought her opinion of him so important that he had rung her. She tried to wipe the smile from her face, but it was no use, she was too happy.

Finally, the letter arrived. Sam ran up the stairs two at a time, leaving poor Humphrey trailing in her wake, to the privacy of her bedroom, where without the usual reverence she ripped the envelope open and began to read.

Chapter 5

Dearest Sam,

You are obviously angry at me and I am very sorry that I have upset you, but you must believe me when I say I was only ever thinking of you.

From the moment I set eyes on you, singing so beautifully in the back room of the Crown and Anchor that day, I have wanted to be part of your life. Unfortunately for me, that day you were won over by Dean and I had to respect that, even though you can have no idea how much I have wished it had been me you had seen that day and not him. But you slipped through my fingers, and I fell into the shadows, and there I thought I might have stayed, had it not been for the foolish nature of your friend and mine. Then I was given a second chance.

I hadn't wanted you to find out, but on that day, Dean offered your letter to anyone who would take it. I refused, knowing it was him you cared for and not me, but when he refused to take the letter back, I slipped it into my pocket and there it stayed until I got up the courage to write to you.

Even then I had no idea if you would ever care to write back. And for a while I thought you might not. But you did, and I cannot explain how much your friendship has come to mean to me. More than friendship, I hope.

Out here you come to appreciate how fragile life can be and how you have to take your chances where you can. Please, Sam, if I have any chance with you, tell me now. I look forward to your letters every day and the thought of one day holding you in my arms is what keeps me sane in the darker times out here.

So there you have it. Now you know why I felt I had to lie to you. But I cannot apologise for caring about you the way I do. And please, forgive me.

All my love,

Andy

Sam's hands were trembling. He had poured his heart out to her and what a wonderful heart it was. She could barely believe that this amazing man was so besotted with her. Dean's hold over her was gone and she was Andy's now. Sam quickly pulled out a bluey to open her heart in return.

Dear Andy,

What can I say to make it up to you? Thank you. Thank you for thinking of me. Thank you for caring about me and thank you for never giving up on me. Thank you too for calling me the other day to put my mind at ease. I was feeling so low, and then to hear your voice… It feels like a huge weight has been lifted from me and I am smiling from ear to ear.

More good news: fingers crossed, I move into my new house on June the 6th. (I'll write the new address at the bottom of the page.)

I still can't believe you've liked me all this time. I'm so sorry for what I've put you through. Why have I fought so hard not to feel anything for you for all these weeks? I thought I was the one in danger of being unfaithful to Dean! What a relief to be able to smile at your picture without feeling guilty at last.

Write soon. Sooner if you can.

Your Sam

PS picture enclosed – be kind!

The days that followed could not pass quickly enough for Sam. She was hopeful and happy. In school she was lenient and fun. Her nesting for her new place was coming on swiftly, with each new purchase silently assessed for Andy's approval. But the days wandered past: nine and ten, eleven days and then twelve. Sam started to watch every news bulletin she could for the words she never wanted to hear. It crossed her mind that the whole thing could have been a cruel joke on her. Maybe he was out there right now, laughing with the lads at her expense? Surely he would not be that cruel, would he? But then hadn't Dean done much the same thing?

The day of the move came and Sam walked into her new house with nervous anticipation and there on the mat lay a blue envelope. Sam quickly scooped it up and folded it away in her jeans pocket. She longed to be free to read the words Andy had written, but this was neither the time, nor the place. Her parents were helping her move in and there was a lot to be done before the end of the day.

As the hours passed, opening the letter began to take on almost ceremonial importance, so much so that by the end of the day, when her parents had said their goodbyes and driven off in the box van they'd hired for the day, Sam found herself barely able to move. Instead, she made sure everything that needed to be done, was done. She even got herself ready for bed before she finally felt able to open the letter she had waited so long for. She took a deep breath.

Dear Sam,

So much to say. I am overjoyed and filled with relief that you find you harbour feelings for me too. I promise you I will not let you down. Thank you for the lovely photo you sent me, although I needed none. I can still remember every detail of your face, the way you laugh and how you kissed my cheek the last time we said goodbye.

Sorry you will have had to wait a bit for this letter, but for a while half of us were laid up with a vomiting bug. There was an outbreak in the compound and as soon as we were well enough to venture out, we were dispatched on a four day operation into previously held Taliban country, to assist in flushing out insurgents that were starting to encroach on one of our positions again. No one was injured, but we were all pretty exhausted after that. We have a couple of days down time now to rest up before we're sent out again. After that, though, I am off on R&R. I have to spend a bit of time with my folks first, but after that... I was hoping to be able to see you. What do you think? Could I maybe stay for a couple of days, or is that a bit presumptuous of me? I don't need a proper bed. Trust me, soldiers can kip anywhere. You should see how little we can sleep on if we have to: bed rolls and mud floors, camp beds or a mat, each other when push comes to shove,

*whatever's going. So a clear strip of carpet, or a settee would
be fine. I should be there on about the 17th?*

*If you write back straight away it should get to me before I
check out. If not, I'll take my chances and prepare myself in
case you show me the pavement. (Please don't!)*

*Has Chloe had a letter from her hunky soldier yet? I think
Spike is on R&R shortly after me, so give Kate the heads up.*

*Your picture is up on the wall by my things. I am looking at
it right now. Can you feel it? Look at my photo guilt free and
write back soon.*

Your Andy x

*PS you could send me an e-bluey instead, to make sure I get
your answer before I leave here. Or both!*

Sam read the letter through again. It was real. He did still like
her. The poor guy had been ill and working hard. He was nothing
like Dean. She had been foolish enough to follow her childhood
fantasy and had been quickly caught up in the abundant charms
of Dean. But his attentions hadn't lasted long and now she had
the chance to get it right. Andy had come to mean more to her
in the short time since they had been writing to each other than
Dean had ever been. And now he was about to walk up to her
front door and be there in the flesh.

She looked over at the picture of Andy, in pride of place, beside
her bed in her new bedroom. Andy was coming here to see her,
to her tired old house, badly in need of an injection of colour and
life. Sam looked at the calendar – eleven days. She shifted nervously. How she hoped it would go well between them. It could
so easily be awkward. He may be a rubbish kisser, she thought.

No. She could be a rubbish kisser? Yikes, that was a far worse thought. What if she was a disappointment to him? How awful would that be? It was the scariest first date ever.

Sam decided to think logically. He liked her. He had seen her and met her and spent a little time with her and he still wanted to see her again. And she liked him. She may not have given much thought to the guy before they were deployed, but she was increasingly aware that she was falling at considerable speed for the man in the picture, whose words had melted her heart and whose distant voice had turned her body to jelly.

Now it was her turn to plan a military manoeuvre. She had to be looking her best. She checked again. He was due a week on Friday. What if she found him on her doorstep when she arrived home from school all sweaty and helmet headed? No. It would be the end of half term. Oh why couldn't he come earlier, then she could spend half term with him? No matter, she thought, at least that gave her a few clear days to prepare.

Sam walked into the room that would one day be her office; until then it was a box room that was certainly living up to its name. She cleared the desk and opened up her laptop. Damn, she remembered she had no internet access for a few more days. School would be all right to send an e-bluey, she thought, and so she wrote a note that she would never need, to remind her to send a message in the morning. And then she wrote a letter too, for good measure, ending it with:

I hope you won't be disappointed when you get to know me better. Please like me.

I am looking at you right now. Can you feel it?

Come home soon.

Sam

Returning from a patrol, Andy found a group of his men back from a secondment after a joint operation. The lads reunited with friendly banter and talk of their various encounters.

Spike saw Dean first. "Romeo, how's it hanging?"

"Ready as ever."

"You don't know anywhere round here I could get a burger and fries, do you?"

"Sorry, mate, but we did get some fresh supplies in today, so who knows? Is Evans with you?"

"Yeah. He's over there with Miller and the Prof."

"I'm glad to see you kept my space warm for me," Dean said, having found his old spot still free.

"It's right where you left it," said Spike.

They walked into the building inside the compound and Spike laid down his kit underneath several very suggestive pictures of a blonde woman. Dean sat down opposite and picked his photos off the little ledge in the wall where they had been balancing.

Spike lifted an eyebrow. "What's up, Romeo? Trouble in paradise?"

"Bloody women," Dean said. "Had the two of them nicely simmering, waiting for my R&R and they go and fucking meet up, don't they?! Turns out they're only half cousins or some shit like that." He made the sound of a bomb exploding and then shrugged. "Oh well. Fuck it. I'm young, free and single again. Lock up your daughters, gentlemen, Romeo is coming home… one way or another."

That evening when all the men were sorted and resting back in their compound, Dean asked where the Prof had got to. Lofty, six foot six and fair-haired, was sat across the way, hunched over a deck of cards and about to deal out. He told Dean that if you couldn't see the Prof, he was normally in his pit, writing to his woman.

Dean was surprised. "The Prof's got a woman?" he asked.

It had been a good while since he had seen Andy hooked up. It had been all over Facebook when his ex had been doing the dirty on him. Andy probably would have found out sooner if he had taken more interest in the world of computers instead of reading all those books he had hanging around his house. It was only when he upset some slapper at a do months later by rejecting her drunken advances, that he heard what had been going on.

Dean looked around the room. He looked over at the photos above Spike on the wall. For a moment he thought he recognised the girl. He got up and walked across and asked to see one. Spike handed it over. "Not bad, eh?" he said, quietly proud of his blonde bombshell.

"How did you get hold of her?" Dean asked.

"Prof's woman," Spike said and took the photo back. "Why don't you ask him to get one for you?"

Dean was not amused. He kicked the door open and stormed out of his room and across the compound in search of Andy. He found him on his way back from a briefing with the CO about their upcoming operation. "Hey, Sarge."

"Fletch, heard you had come back to play with the big boys."

They walked side by side across the compound to Andy's little room. There was just enough room inside for a couple of rolls and Andy's was the closest to the door. Dean hovered in the doorway. He quickly scanned the area for the evidence he was after. He spotted the corner of a photo poking out from the pages of a book. He snatched the book up and deliberately dropped the photo out. He picked it up and saw the face of Sam. "So it's true," he said. "I wondered how you could get yourself a woman out here." He passed the photo to Andy. "You didn't. You nicked mine."

Andy put the photo safely away and turned to Dean.

"You never wanted her. If you'd really felt anything for her, you wouldn't have had two other women on the go at the same time."

"Well maybe I want her now."

"Too late, Romeo. That ship has sailed. She's mine now."

"And you're happy with my cast-offs?" Dean asked. "Not at all worried about whether you can fill my boots?" Andy glared at him and Dean held his hands up in surrender. "Hey, all's fair in love and war."

"Was there actually something you wanted, Corporal?" Andy said, with great restraint.

"Nope. Not a thing, Sarge."

Andy watched him until he was gone, then took a deep breath and took out the photo and smoothed the surface and reverently placed it back in his book. She was his now, his and no one else's. Three more days in this hellhole, he thought. Just three more days and he would be off on the long journey home and back to Sam.

He tried to imagine the moment when they would meet. Would she actually like him when push came to shove? Would she remember him? He wanted her, of that he was certain. She said she wanted to see him, he had got the message. All he had to do now was make sure he didn't blow it.

Two days later, he got her letter. She had been worried about him. He smiled. She had asked if there was anything he would like to do while he was on leave with her. Was she kidding? Absolutely. Several things actually, but he couldn't put any of that in a letter; she would probably run a mile. He chuckled to himself at her worries of being a disappointment to him – fat chance! But those last three words had him by the guts: 'Come home soon.'

Andy breathed deeply to calm his nerves. One more day, he thought, one more day. If he could make it through unscathed back to Kandahar, he was home and dry. He wondered if he could shave another day off his parents' visit. He would certainly try. Seven days was a lot to ask when there was a beautiful woman waiting for him back home. Maybe he could get away with five? It was time enough to get some scoff down him and get his clothes properly clean. He would, of course, have to sit through the usual round of 'we're glad you're back safe' from his dad, with heavy undertones of 'but wouldn't you have had a better time if you had gone over as an officer?' His father, he had learned across the years, had always been a disappointment to Andy's grandfather, a

Lieutenant Colonel - who had received the Military Medal, don't you know - failing twice to even get in. So he knew a lot about how to make someone feel worthless.

Andy's older brother had been protected from the pressures of living up to his father's expectations and had got out early. Simon was now earning megabucks in the city and certainly seemed to be the 'golden boy' in his parents' eyes.

Still, he would do his duty and check in for a while. But Sam would be waiting for him. For him. He should catch up on his sleep while he was at home, because sleep would be the furthest thing from his mind when he reached Sam.

He wrote back a quick note, wondering who would get there first: the letter, or him?

Chapter 6

Ten more days, Sam thought as she cycled into work. That meant five kid-free days with the shops open. Her dress was a little crumpled that morning, the iron being of low importance when unpacking the day before. There were bags under her eyes from the sleepless nights of worry: first with the move and then and perhaps more terrifyingly, with the impending arrival of Andy.

On several occasions throughout the day, Sam lost her train of thought and had to be reminded by one of the children, Jimmy being the most outspoken of the kids to come to her rescue. 'Miss Litton, are you dead?' was not a question she got asked on a regular basis.

On the days that followed, Sam started to make her house look more like a home. On Friday night she finished school and began making a list of everything that had to be done before Andy's arrival the following week. The hairdresser's was booked. Everything had to be waxed and as soon as possible - no pain, no gain. Fresh clean bedding was a little presumptuous, but… just in case. What was she thinking? This was going to be a first date. She shouldn't even be thinking about going that far yet; she didn't want Andy to think she was cheap. But was it actually a first date? And how far was too far when you had been conversing in letters for some time? She wished she knew the rules for something like this.

Sam arranged a night out with Kate and Chloe the night before he was due to arrive, for moral support. It was their night to be at the Crown anyway, so she had been pretty sure they would turn up. A new outfit for confidence and some new underwear, just in case, and last but not least she needed to get some good food in.

The nerves began to rise as she picked up her newly connected phone and rang Kate, eager for some reassurance. Kate answered and knew exactly the right words to put her friend at ease. It was a strange thing, the friendship between the two. They were different in so many ways, but they had always been there for each other. Most people struggled to understand why the two of them had remained friends for so long. They just had, and that was all they knew.

"It'll be your turn soon," Sam told her.

"I know. But if you think you're going to catch me worrying my arse off about what's going to happen when he gets here you've got another thing coming. I know exactly what we'll be up to. And so does he."

"Kate!"

"Don't tell me you won't be at it too."

"I have no intention of-"

"Have you booked in at the beauticians?" Kate butted in.

"Nnnooo."

"That means you haven't but you're going to do it yourself, Sam Litton, so don't you come all high and mighty with me you… tramp!"

Sam gasped.

Kate chuckled. "Well I for one intend to shag the poor boy's brains out. You've seen the picture of his body. One word: Yum."

"Oh you're incorrigible. How's Chloe doing with her guy, do you know?"

"No, I don't. We'll have to grill her on Thursday."

On Saturday morning Sam was a woman on a mission. She was out to find a new outfit to brighten herself up and some nice underwear in case things went well. By lunchtime she felt as if she must have looked around every shop, boutique and stall in town and still she had nothing to show for herself. On the underwear front, things had been a trifle easier: not too plain, not too tarty. It was a fine balance, but Sam was optimistic that she had got it right. Originally she had been aiming for just one set, but apprehensive of her ability to know when to wear it she decided that in this case more was definitely better. Holey faded knickers had no place in her life come next Friday.

Sunday morning was given over to beautification. Sam waxed and preened to within an inch of her life and then she cycled round to her parents for Sunday lunch and a nice calming walk. It was at this point she realised something else needed to be added to her list: she needed to keep her parents at bay. So she warned them that she would be incredibly busy with school reports and various other bits of paperwork she had neglected to do of late, so she'd have to see them again in a fortnight and neither her mum nor her dad turned a hair at this. Job done, she thought. Tick.

When she got back, Sam put on some Will Young and walked over to Andy's picture. He smiled back at her. But then the nerves began to kick in again. Just imagine if the worst did happen and he didn't like her, or they just didn't click, or worse still, if she didn't take to him? What would she do? She couldn't just say, 'sorry this just isn't working out for me,' and chuck him out, sending him back off to war. No, no, it had to work, that was all there was to it.

On Monday morning, Sam began to clean. Everything that wasn't hung up or nailed down was hauled along to the laundrette that day. Embarrassing nostalgia was hidden away and in between running clothes and bedding to and from the washing line, Sam did what she could to her little garden with the tools her dad had given to her to start out.

On Tuesday, Sam treated herself to an hour of pampering at the hairdresser's, and by the time she left she was feeling far more confident. It had been an expense that she wouldn't usually allow herself, but on this occasion she felt it was totally justified.

Wednesday was supposed to be the day set aside for filling her house with scrumptious food to feed her hungry soldier, but that had had to be put off until the afternoon, to allow Sam to pop back into town and search for that elusive new outfit. She braced herself for a second day of disappointment, but then came her break. The French market was set up in town and in it was a clothing stall for women. Sam hurried over and rummaged through the rails excitedly. Amazingly there were two dresses she liked, both in her size, one yellow and one red. She pulled them both out and wandered around looking for a mirror. She held them up and gazed at herself. While she was deep in thought, a woman walked over and stood behind her. "I think the gentleman would prefer mademoiselle in the red, non?" she said.

"The red?" Sam asked. "Yes. I think you might be right?"

"Absolutement."

Sam studied herself again. "Okay," she said, quickly glancing at the price label, "I'll take it. Thank you." Sam paid the lady for the dress and folded it carefully into her backpack. Then she scooted off home, ravenously hungry, as with all the excitement she had forgotten to eat any breakfast.

Pulling up outside her house, Sam noticed there was someone sitting on her doorstep. It was a man. She stopped the bike at the gate and got off, removing her helmet before she spoke. The man stood up and smiled and she realised who it was and was struck dumb.

"Hello, Sam."

Sam's heart almost exploded, it was hammering so hard in her chest. Her hands began to tremble and her mouth went dry. "You… you're early."

"Yes," he said.

"You weren't meant to be here until Friday. I'm not ready."

"Oh, sorry. I just thought… It was stupid. I'm sorry, I'll leave."

Sam's brain had stopped. She had no idea what to say to make things right. It was as if her brain was screaming inside her head, but nothing intelligible was coming out, so she said nothing, just continued to stare at him.

Andy picked up his rucksack and started to leave.

"No! No. It's all right. Stay, please." Sam stepped closer, her hands out to block his exit. "I just wasn't expecting you, that's all." She stepped past him towards the door and fumbled for the keys in her pocket. His body was only inches away from hers. She stepped inside and was greeted by an enthusiastic Humphrey. He yapped and jumped up at her, pleased to see her back, but Andy paused on the doorstep. "Come on in, please. I'm sorry, I must seem so rude. Don't mind Humph."

"Are you sure you wouldn't rather I left? I can come back on Friday if you prefer, or…"

"Stay," Sam said.

Andy held her gaze for a moment and then looked about him for somewhere to set down his things.

"Here, let me." Sam's body froze as in trying to help him with his bag, his arm brushed against hers. She breathed deeply and tried to hold on to her composure. Humphrey gave Andy a bit of a sniff and Andy patted him fondly, then Humphrey trotted back over to be with Sam. Sam showed Andy where to set his bag down, in an alcove under the stairs and walked across the kitchen. Busy, busy, busy, she thought. If she could keep herself occupied she might just get through this. The attraction on her side was no longer in any doubt at all. She was in bits around him already and he hadn't even touched her yet. But he was so calm and relaxed. Sam wondered if he was feeling anything approaching the level of nerves that she was suffering. "Coffee? Tea?" she asked.

"Er, tea, please." Andy stood leaning against the kitchen door-frame looking in and watching her as she clunked and clattered about nervously. He was taller than she remembered and his eyes seemed fathomless as they gazed at her. She couldn't look back, her nerves wouldn't let her. He was out of her league and probably far better than she deserved.

"Were you waiting long?" she asked.

"About an hour," he said.

"An hour? I'm so sorry. If I'd known I'd–"

"It's fine. It's a nice day. I didn't mind."

"God, I've just realised, I haven't got any food in the house to feed you. I was going to do that this afternoon, but–"

"I turned up unannounced. Sorry. If it helps, I'm not hungry."

"I might have a biscuit around here somewhere." Sam began to search high and low for something, anything to feed to Andy.

He watched her from the doorway.

"I've got some digestives." She looked around. "There's bread. I could make you a toasted sandwich, you've gotta love a Breville. Or a butty? I must have some bacon in here somewhere." Sam looked in the fridge and then opened and closed two more cupboards. "What about some…"

Andy moved inside and settled a hand on her arm. "I'm fine." His hand lingered and seared its mark on her skin.

Sam's mind was racing, her body felt like it was running a marathon and she was desperate not to look a fool in front of him. "I'm sorry; I talk when I'm nervous."

"I noticed." Andy smiled and let his hand fall away. Sam smiled back awkwardly. "Come on, let's get that tea poured. I'm parched." He helped Sam with the drinks and the two of them walked into the living room.

"I'm afraid there isn't much to sit on yet," she said. "I've only been in a couple of weeks. Do you want the futon or the beanbag?"

"The futon, I think," he said.

They sat down on the shabby old futon facing each other and started to talk and Humphrey settled down at Sam's feet.

They were still talking when Sam became aware of Andy's

stomach rumbling. Sam looked at her watch. "God, it's gone five, you must be starving."

"What about you?" he said. "Your stomach's been gurgling for hours."

"Has it?" she asked. "I hadn't noticed. I'll have to find you something to eat before you waste away. I'm afraid it might have to be a bit creative; there isn't much in the house. I hope that's all right?"

"No," Andy said. "It's not all right. I'm taking you out. I can't have you scurrying around waiting on me when I've turned up two days early. No, come on, we're going out. What do you fancy?"

"I thought you were dying for fish and chips?" she said.

"Yes, I was, but don't worry, I had that on my first night back at Mum and Dad's. It was the highlight of my visit there."

Sam gave him a chiding look.

"I don't mean it… much."

They caught the bus to the other side of town, to a little pub called The Dog and Duck. It was a quiet pub with a nice garden and good food, and there they talked some more. When the night's chill settled in, they went inside to a settee by an unlit fire and ordered another drink.

Little intimacies punctuated the conversation, like the touch of a hand, or one limb resting against another. Before Sam knew it, time had been called at the bar. She looked at her watch. "Good grief, we'd better get going if we're not going to miss the last bus."

On the way back to the bus stop, Andy reached for her hand and Sam gave it willingly. But when they arrived home, Sam began to talk faster again. She rabbited on about where they'd been and what Andy had been used to eating, while making them some more tea.

"Thank you for tonight," Andy said from his perch beside the door. Sam stopped and looked at him, her nerves jangling.

"I'll crash out on the futon, if that's all right with Humph?" he said. "You wouldn't happen to have a spare blanket or something, would you?"

Sam snapped into action. "Yes, of course. I'll get you some things."

Andy picked up her cup and handed it to her. "In a bit."

They finished their tea and Andy looked at her. "You look tired; beautiful, but tired. Perhaps we should hit the sack?" He took her cup and washed them both up. Then he walked out to get something from his bag in the hallway and came back in with a toothbrush, toothpaste and a small towel.

Sam locked up the house and nervously led the way upstairs. She found a spare pillow and a big blue blanket in a box in the study and took a sheet out of the drawer in her bedroom. She handed them over apologetically. "Are you sure you'll be all right on that old thing?" she asked.

"Absolutely fine. Don't worry about me. I can sleep on anything. I told you in my letter, didn't I?" He rested the bedding on the banister rail of the landing and went into the bathroom.

Sam walked into her bedroom and shut the door. Frantically, she got ready for bed. She waited until she heard the bathroom door open and then went out. It was a warm night, so Sam was wearing her short, white, cotton pyjamas and her hair was loose.

Andy stopped and looked at her. He took a deep breath. "Goodnight, Sam," he said. Their gazes held each other for a moment, Sam's heartbeat pounded in her head. Then he turned and walked away down the stairs.

Sam watched him go. "Goodnight," she said and then went into the bathroom to brush her teeth. When she opened the door again she came face to face with Andy. He was standing near the top of the stairs wearing only his trousers. His torso was bare, lean and muscular, revealing his strong arms. Sam froze, her rigid persona belied the turbulent emotion crashing around beneath.

Andy pointed to the pile of bedding still hanging over the banister behind her. "I forgot..."

Sam picked the pile up and walked the few steps over to where he was waiting and Andy climbed the final step to meet her. In such proximity, Sam could no longer think, nor move. The smell of him aroused her senses. It was a distant memory of familiar aftershave and the heat of a body. Her stomach trembled.

Andy took the bedding from her. "Goodnight," he said softly.

"Goodnight," she whispered. They stood there gazing at each other for a minute, sparks flying in all directions. Sam's heart was pumping faster now, her cheeks were flushed and her eyes bright, and then Andy went back down the stairs and Sam walked into her bedroom and collapsed onto her bed, screaming in silence.

God, he was beautiful. She was a good girl, she really was, but she had never felt so tempted as right at that moment and it was all she could do to stop herself from rushing down there and throwing herself at him. She rolled over. No, this was better. In a way she was relieved the pressure was off. At least if he got to know her better first he might more easily forgive her shortcomings later.

Sam prayed for a good night's sleep so that she might look her best the following day, but the gorgeous man sleeping only metres away from her was not conducive to a night of rest. Sam lay in her bed, craning to hear any sound from downstairs. He had been such a gentleman. He hadn't tried anything on. Or maybe he wasn't interested in her like that, now that he had actually spent some time with her? But surely it hadn't been just her that felt that charge between them? No. He had to have felt that. It was undeniable.

She tossed and turned for hours, worrying about how it was going and what would happen next, eventually falling asleep in the early hours of the morning.

When she finally emerged the next day, bleary eyed and straggly haired, she found the living room already packed away and Andy, looking fresh as a daisy, standing in the kitchen eating toast.

"Morning, Beautiful," he said. "Cup of tea?" Andy poured her a cup and popped another couple of slices of bread in the toaster. Sam sipped cautiously. "Bad night?" he asked, drinking back his tea and watching her closely.

How dare he look so gorgeous at this time of the morning after spending the night on her battered old futon? It just wasn't fair. She was the one who needed the help looking good, not him. He was looking as great as ever and she had had her worst night's sleep in years and had struggled downstairs looking like the bog monster.

"No, I'm fine," she said, too embarrassed to explain why. "You?" Great deflection, she thought. The very idea of admitting the truth, that knowing he was lying so close to her had kept her awake half the night was horrific. Maybe she was more awake than she felt.

"I slept like a baby," he said.

Okay, so he obviously hadn't been kept awake by the thought of her luscious body lying so near to his. Well, there was no need to rub it in.

"What have you got on today?" he asked. "Anything in particular?"

"Well, we are definitely going to have to go to Sainsbury's to get some food in. I'm going to need someone with strong arms to help me carry the bags back." She blushed, realising she had made reference to the muscles of his arms and looked at the floor.

"Okay. What else?"

"I don't know. What would you like to do?"

"I wouldn't mind seeing the park you cycle through. You know, the one you told me about in your letters." Humphrey barked as the word 'park' was mentioned. "Humph could come, couldn't he?"

Sam looked out of the window at the grey sky. "The old one? Yes, okay, maybe, if it cheers up a bit."

Sam marched Andy around Sainsbury's, reminding him that it was his fault he was being forced to do the shopping with her, and steadfastly refused to let him pay for anything.

Back home, she laid out a picnic on a rug on the living room floor, with cold beer and chunky sandwiches, fresh fruit and sausage rolls. If the weather wasn't going to play ball, then at least she had tried. She found Andy in the back garden on his phone. Sam opened her mouth to speak but Andy quickly put his fingers to his lips to stop her. She mouthed across that lunch was ready and he gave her the thumbs up. A few minutes later, he walked back in and his face lit up.

"Sorry about that. I told my parents I was just going home for a few days to sort out some things before I went back. Hey, you've done a picnic!"

"But I thought you said you didn't have to go back until after the weekend?"

"Yes, but they don't know that. Oh, wow. You have no idea how much I've missed fresh fruit," he said, quickly picking up a nectarine and biting into it.

"Beer?" she asked.

"Love one."

Sam took a swig from her bottle of beer.

"You drink beer too?" he said. "Beautiful, intelligent and drinks beer? You don't happen to watch football too, do you?"

"No. Sorry."

"Oh well, three out of four's not bad."

When they had finished their lunch, they sat and talked for a while before clearing away. Washing up afterwards, Sam looked out of the kitchen window at the sky and noticed that it was looking brighter.

It was a long walk from her new house back to the old park, but the weather was changing for the better and they were in no hurry. By the time they got there, Sam had warmed up enough to take off her cardigan and wrap it around her waist.

They walked through the park hand in hand as Sam described the things she had seen there. The ducks dozed on the banks of the pond, sleepy and full of bread, more of which lay scattered all around them.

"That duck looks a lot like you did this morning," Andy teased.

Sam looked over to where he was pointing and saw a tatty duck with feathers sticking out everywhere and its beak tucked in under its wing. She looked around and spotted a mother duck trailed after by four little ducklings. "Well I guess that must be you then, bossing the others around."

"I do not 'boss the others about.'"

"I bet you do." Sam laughed and Andy grabbed her and started tickling her. "No, stop!"

"Absolutely not. Not until you take that back."

Sam was breathless and wriggled to try and escape, but Andy was relentless. Humphrey joined in and barked at Andy protectively.

"Take it back. Come on, before I get savaged by a little white dog."

"No." Tears were welling in her eyes, she was laughing so much, and then she broke free. Sam ran with Humphrey alongside her, but Andy gave chase. He caught her with ease and pulled her into his arms, holding her against him. "Okay, okay, I take it back!" Sam gasped. A moment passed when Sam thought Andy was about to kiss her, but it passed and he released his grasp and took a step back. They walked on, hand in hand, when suddenly Sam remembered what day it was. She stopped. "Shit."

Andy looked amused. "You swore. Samantha Litton, you swore."

Sam blushed. "I'm sorry, but I just remembered that I'm meant to be going out with the girls tonight. It's okay; I'll cancel." She pulled out her phone.

"No, don't do that. Who are you meeting?"

"Just Chloe and Kate. It's our night to go singing down the Crown."

"Singing? Can I come?" he asked.

"You want to go to a karaoke night with three girls?"

"Do I have to sing?"

"Can you sing?"

"No, tone deaf."

"Then no, you don't have to sing."

"Will *you* sing?" he asked.

Sam thought about the words of the song she had been practising. She had been listening to Will Young over the past couple
of weeks and she had a mind to sing 'All Time Love'. It said the
words she wanted to say to Andy but wasn't brave enough to speak.
Was it too much to mention those words so soon? Would it scare
him off? Sam wasn't sure. She was happier right now than she
had ever been. Being with Andy felt right and she was afraid of
doing anything that might jeopardise that.

"We'll see," she said.

That evening, Andy and Sam arrived at the Crown and Anchor
and Sam lead the way through to the room at the back. She paid
the entrance fee and then walked inside. Kate and Chloe were
already there. They stood up, waving her across happily when
they saw her arrive. But their mouths dropped open in amazement when from behind her shadow, Andy emerged and smiled
at them shyly.

"Hello," he said. "Hope you don't mind me tagging along."

Kate was the first to regain her composure. "It's good to see
you again, Andy. Chlo, this is Andy."

Chloe closed her mouth and shook his hand. She turned to
Sam and lowered her voice. "Wasn't he meant to be arriving
tomorrow?"

Sam smiled and looked back at Andy with tender reproach.
"Yes, he was."

"I hope this is all right, me being here I mean?"

"The more the merrier," Kate said. "Are you going to sing?"

"No," said Sam and Andy together.

"That bad, eh?"

Andy turned and addressed the other two girls. "Apparently
Sam isn't sure whether she wants to sing tonight or not, which
would be a crying shame if you ask me. I was hoping you two
could help me persuade her."

"What have you been practising?" Kate asked. "She never sings unless she's practiced something a lot. Not like the rest of us. That's why she always gets the biggest cheer of the night."

"What about Will Young?" Andy asked.

Sam looked surprised. "How did you know I-"

"I saw the empty case beside your music system." Andy looked around. The room was starting to fill up. "It's popular here, isn't it?"

"It's the best karaoke in town," Kate told him. "They run a night every other Thursday. They've got the best selection and the best sound system of all of them."

"And believe me, we've tried them all," Chloe added.

Andy went to get a round in, and the moment he was out of earshot the torrent of questions began. The girls wanted to know when he had shown up, how it was going and how long she had with him before he had to go again. Sam tried to tell them as much as they needed to know, while still retaining her thoughts and feelings for herself.

Andy returned with his hands full of drinks and Kate excused herself. Sam studied her wonderful man as he talked easily with her friends. She was falling for him, hook line and sinker. She already knew deep down that he was going to be the big love of her life, the one all other men would be measured against, but was she going to be brave enough to sing him a love song after such a short time?

"So have they managed to persuade you to sing for me yet?" Andy asked her, waking her from her reverie.

Sam shook her head. "They've just been grilling me about you," she said.

Kate sat back down.

"Oh dear," Andy said. "Nothing bad, I hope."

"No you're okay. She didn't say much at all really. Nothing juicy, anyway. What have you done to her?"

Andy squeezed Sam's hand as it rested on the table. He looked into her eyes and spoke softly. "Not nearly enough."

Kate wafted some air about her face. "Wow, is it me, or has it suddenly got very hot in here?"

Sam blushed.

The host for the evening tapped the microphone and the room settled down. He welcomed everyone and read out the name of the first to sing. A rowdy group of thirty-somethings stood up to riotous applause and they walked over to the stage area and picked up their microphones.

One by one the groups, duets and solos took the stage to sing their hearts out, but Sam would not be moved. And then her name was read out. Sam's heart stopped. Kate grinned over at her and she knew who the culprit had been. She was far too scared to sing decently tonight. She knew he was worthy, but ideally she would like a few more months before she made such a bold gesture. But then again a few days was all she would have, for now.

Her body was cold. She shifted in her seat and a rousing cheer went up, followed by a chorus of 'Sam, Sam, Sam, Sam.' There was nothing for it. She had no choice.

"Go on, Sam. Your man wants to hear you sing. Get on up there!" Kate called over, winking at Andy.

Sam looked at him. He was smiling at her hopefully. She took a deep breath and stood up. Applause buzzed all around. She made her way to the front of the room and told the man the name of her song. Sam stood, trembling, in front of the room full of people, adjusted the microphone to her height and the music began.

Sam started to sing and the crowd hushed. The words flowed effortlessly from her lips. For a while she hid herself in the words of the song, but before the end she managed to lift her gaze and focus on Andy's face. She saw his reaction and knew that nothing had been spoiled. She finished and stood there in the spotlight of sixty or more gazes and the crowd erupted. Sam smiled and blushed. She set the microphone back in its place, thanked the man who organised the music and walked back to her seat.

Andy stood up and kissed her briefly on the lips in front of everybody there and Sam's whole body was tingling. A second cheer went up almost as big as the first and they retook their seats with Sam blushing profusely. Now Andy was not letting go of her hand. The crowd died down, ready for the next name to be read out. "You were amazing," he whispered.

Walking back from the bus stop later that night Andy held onto her hand. "Thank you for tonight," he said. "And for singing. You sang beautifully."

"It wasn't too soppy?" she said.

"No."

Back home, Sam felt tense. This was big and they both seemed to feel it. They talked about nothing much for a while, but when Sam went out to make them some tea, she could barely hold the cups for the trembling in her hands. She knew he was in the next room, waiting for her to return. She had never felt so totally insecure. Her pitiful experience with men consisted of one long-term boyfriend, with the physical side of things always leaving her cold, and a few brief disasters. Bugger, she thought, bugger, bugger, bugger. She was probably about to make a complete mess of things.

Andy appeared behind her and put his hands on either side of her body. "You're shaking," he murmured, his warm breath tingling the back of her neck. Sam couldn't say a thing. She couldn't even move. Slowly, Andy turned her around to face him. He held her head gently in his warm hands and tilted her face to his. "You're so beautiful," he said. Leaning closer, Sam felt like the moment stretched on forever, but then their lips met.

Fire blazed at his touch. Sam's pulse was hammering in her throat and her brain felt like it was close to exploding. She was running on instinct now. It was scary but exhilarating. Andy ended the kiss, pulled away and looked into her eyes. Sam could hardly breathe.

"I've wanted to do that for such a long time," he said.

"Really?" Sam barely whispered.

"What do you think?" Andy looked at her for a long moment and then leant in again.

Sam's trembling frame found strength in the powerful body that cradled it. His long deep kisses lingered in a way that made every nerve in her body spark. She was drunk and she hadn't touched a drop.

Andy pulled her toward him and his hands moved around her, exploring the curve of her hips and waist and awakening her skin where they touched. His lips slipped away from her eager mouth and traced a hot path from her ear, down the side of her neck, his tongue tasting her soft flesh along the way. Sam's head was in a whirl. She felt as if she could pass out at any second and then his lips found hers again and gave her strength.

Andy was her rock and she held on to him. Their bodies moved against each other closer and closer, their passion ever stronger as they strained to know more and more of each other. And then Andy broke away. He lifted her into his arms and effortlessly carried her up the stairs to her bedroom. Sam clung around his neck, feeling like a nervous child. He kicked open the bedroom door and strode inside, but once in there, he looked around at her small single bed and said, "I don't think so." Humphrey had trotted up behind them. "You can stay here though, Humph."

Carrying her straight back downstairs again, Andy let Sam down to the living room floor. He turned out the main light and switched on a lamp and from behind the futon he pulled out the sheet and the big blue blanket. In a flash, the futon was a bed. He knelt down and then reached for Sam's hand, pulling her gently down to be with him.

Andy's tempo changed. He was no longer in a rush. He kissed and caressed every inch of her, warming her body until her trembling subsided. Then her clothes were stripped away one by one until she was almost naked and then he too undressed.

Sam felt the wonderful heat of his skin as he slipped under the blanket beside her. Tentatively, she let her fingers explore his body as the last of her underwear disappeared. His kisses became deeper and more passionate, sending her senses to new heights. Sam's mind whirled at the intimate melody he was playing on her body. It seemed as if he had a map of all the switches in her body and he was turning them on all at once. She had never known anything like it. She needed to feel him closer to her, but Andy didn't seem to understand. He was licking, tasting and caressing every sensitive part of her body, places she hadn't ever known were so receptive, all except the one place she now yearned for. On and on it went and just when she thought she could take it no longer, he found her, and gave her exactly what she needed and it was magnificent.

Andy looked into her hazy eyes and hovered over her for a moment until Sam recovered her breath. "God, you're even more beautiful than I imagined," he whispered and kissed her some more. Gently at first, he teased her with lingering touches and deepening kisses. Sam found herself becoming far more confident. She rolled Andy onto his back and lying on top of him, she started to kiss and taste the delicious body beneath her. She explored him with her delicate touch and Andy groaned, straining with anticipation. He flipped her back over to lie beneath him and moved to lie in the valley of her thighs. Their gazes met for a moment and Sam pulled his face down to kiss her and she was lost.

Wave after wave of delicious pleasure soared through her body. Sam wanted everything he could offer and he offered so much. Finally, her body exploded and she clung to Andy and cried out as his body shuddered within her, and they lay, panting, intertwined and exhausted, neither having the breath for words, but blissfully happy in their own private world.

On Friday morning, Andy awoke to find Sam curled up with her head on the pillow next to him. It wasn't a dream. It had really happened. Sam was there beside him. He considered for a minute if he should tell her about Tenerife. But they were together now, and maybe the past was no longer important. After all those years of waiting, he finally had the woman of his dreams. That was how she had come to feel for him: like a wonderful dream, taunting him with a life he could never have. And it had been like nothing he had ever experienced. Andy was no stranger to the world of women, but nothing had prepared him for what happened last night. He had nearly lost control before he had even begun. She was breathtaking and she didn't even seem to realise it. If it hadn't been for that tiny little bed of hers, he might have ravished her completely. He thanked God that it had given him the chance to grapple back control and take his time.

The sun was shining on her face, making her beauty even more ethereal. He heard the post landing on the doormat and footsteps walking briskly away. Andy looked up and noticed the curtains still open from the night before. He looked back at Sam and couldn't help but touch. He couldn't tear himself away from her if he tried.

He stroked the back of his hand down the outside of her exposed arm and she stirred. Quickly he closed his eyes and pretended to be asleep. Sam opened her eyes and saw him. She looked around for her clothes, but there were none in reach. Andy smiled inside. He had already assessed the situation and knew exactly what Sam would be thinking. She looked at the time. The day had already started. Outside people were talking and driving up and down the street, only a couple of feet in front of the unclothed living room window. He felt Sam look around her as furtively as she could and then she seemed to fix on something. Very carefully she reached out across Andy to the top corner of the futon, but in an instant, Andy grabbed her, flipped her onto her back and pinned her down beneath him.

Sam gasped.

"Never make a move on a sleeping soldier," he said, smiling

down at her.

"I was trying to-"

Andy's head lowered and he started to kiss her. "What?" he muttered between kisses.

Sam moaned with pleasure and he sunk his body against hers. Lost in the moment, Sam seemed to temporarily forget about their lack of privacy. But not for long. She broke away. "The curtains are open."

Andy barely paused to speak, but continued to kiss her neck. "I know."

"People will see."

"Mmm, so what? Let them."

Sam wriggled free and hid under the covers.

Andy smiled broadly and spoke to the mound of blanket next to him. "So, what do you plan to do about this?" Sam was quiet. "I vote we stay under your lovely big blanket all day, having wild, uninhibited sex, until it goes dark and then you can sneak out without anyone noticing."

Sam's face popped out. She seemed to be considering this at first, but then her smile faded.

"No."

"Well unless you want to take the blanket and leave me here, on display in your living room, strutting about stark bollock naked…"

Sam gave him a look.

"No? Then *you* want to get out and run naked through the house yourself? Well I'm all for that. But I give you fair warning; I might have to give chase." He flashed her a wicked grin.

Sam let out a sigh of frustration and buried her head in the pillow. She rolled over and lay looking at the ceiling. "You could always do the chivalrous thing and pass me your T-shirt over there."

Andy considered this. The sight of this beautiful woman in his shirt would be a wonderful thing. But what was it worth?

Chapter 7

The sound of footsteps close by made Sam jump. Andy seemed to find the whole situation rather amusing. He offered Sam his T-shirt for the price of a kiss. Sam had experience of his kisses now and knew this to be a dangerous proposition if they were ever going to get out of there. She raised an eyebrow at him.

"I promise; just a kiss. I'll keep my hands behind my head." He raised his hands to the pillow.

Sam considered. She moved across his naked body under the blanket, kissing and caressing his chest and abdomen and emerged on the other side. She grabbed the T-shirt and quickly pulled it on and leapt up out of the way.

Andy looked at her incredulously.

"What?" she said. "You never specified where I had to kiss you."

Andy slumped over onto his front and thumped his fist into the pillow, groaning.

Sam smiled. "I won't be long," she said and skipped off upstairs to the bathroom.

By the time Sam got back down, the living room had been put right, a small pile of beautifully folded bedding poked out of the far side of the futon and Andy was standing in the middle of the room, wearing a pair of grey jeans and looking through a handful of Sam's CDs. "Tea?" he asked, holding out a cup for her.

Sam sipped her tea and moved closer to Andy. He wrapped a strong arm around her and she rested her head against his chest. She breathed in his scent. "When do you have to go back again?" she asked.

Andy almost choked on his tea. "Oh dear, was I that good?"

"No. I mean yes. It was… well, fabulous, but-"

"You can't wait to get rid of me." He chuckled, putting down his cup on the little table nearby. "I have to leave on Tuesday; if that's not too long?"

Sam shook her head and, putting her cup down too, she clung to him and he held her back just as hard. Sam wondered at how much he had come to mean to her in such a short space of time. "Just four more days," she said, pulling away and looking deep inside those inky blue eyes of his. "Well, we'll have to make the most of them, won't we?"

"My thoughts exactly. Come on, get that tea down you. We're off to buy a new bed."

Sam gave him a look and then realised that he was serious. "I can't."

"Of course you can. Now where's that place that delivers by teatime? What's it called?"

Sam was uneasy. "Andy, I really can't. I'm sorry, but I've already looked at them and they cost a lot of money. I-"

"Bugger the money. I'm paying. Now where is it?" Andy rifled through the Yellow Pages he found lying underneath the telephone.

Sam put a hand on Andy's arm. "I can't let you do that, Andy. It's too much."

Andy pulled her against him and spoke softly into her hair. "Sam, beautiful Sam, I work my butt off in the stifling heat halfway around the world under the constant threat of life and limb. But I'm happy, and you are the only one responsible for this. It has been your letters that have kept me sane while I've been out there. Let me do this, please."

Sam's eyes began to fill up, but she rapidly blinked the tears away, and after he had kissed her she was left with only bright, devoted eyes smiling back at him compliantly.

"Good. Then that's settled. Now get some food down you while I hop in the shower. I won't be long."

"Yes, Sir!" Sam saluted. She received a look for her efforts and she immediately acted contrite. Andy walked away, a smile playing on his lips and Sam sniggered and went to get some breakfast.

Sam followed Andy around the bed shop, as he asked her which beds she liked and they sat on them all. "What is it, Sam?" he asked when they were about half way round. "Are you still worrying about this?" Sam bit her bottom lip and looked at him through troubled eyes. Andy shook his head and smiled. "God, you look cute when you do that," he said. He patted the bed next to him and beckoned her to sit down. She sat. "Okay, is it the money or the fact that it's a bed we're buying?"

"Well, both really."

"Would you feel better if we said the bed was mine? Because I wouldn't be lying if I said I'd like to sleep in a sumptuous bed for the few days I have left over here. And then maybe, when I come back...?"

"I thought you said you could sleep on anything?" Sam said, afraid of saying anything about their future that might sound too needy.

"I thought so too, till I met your futon." He nudged Sam in the ribs playfully. "Now can we hurry up and find me a bed, or it'll be too late in the day to get it delivered by tonight."

Sam nodded, but then in lowered tones she said, "But can I just have it on record that the lack of sleep last night had nothing to do with my lovely futon."

Andy grinned. "Come on."

Another dozen beds were tested and finally they agreed on the perfect one. It had, by this time, passed midday and so Andy set about talking to the sales lady to try and persuade her to give him a same day delivery. Eventually, he landed a promise for later on that afternoon.

At about 4 o'clock, the doorbell rang and the deliverymen arrived with the new bed. Sam kept out of the way while two burly men lugged a double bed and mattress up her small staircase, along the landing and into her bedroom. After they had gone she went inside to take a look. Andy was busy screwing the base together.

"It's certainly bigger," she said. She looked closer. "Wait a minute; this isn't the mattress we ordered."

"Yes it is," he said.

Sam looked at him.

Andy held his hands aloft. "Okay, I ordered the nicer one. Shoot me. But it was so much comfier than the other one." He lowered his hands and looked at the expression on Sam's face. "Hell, I wouldn't want to come face to face with you in battle. Those searching eyes of yours would get me every time." He clutched at his heart and pulled her towards him. "Pass me that slat, would you?" Sam helped him put it together and they lifted on the mattress. "What do you think? Shall we try it out?"

Sam looked at the big bed and then stopped. "Bedding!" she said. "We need to get some bedding. None of my stuff will fit it."

"Bugger the bedding," he said, pulling her against him.

But Sam was firm. She shook her head. "We'll never get any sleep without some sheets at least."

Andy shrugged, not entirely sure sleep was on his agenda.

But Sam looked at him through large pitiful eyes. "Please. We'll have fresh bed linen, summer days and not a bagpipe in sight?"

Andy groaned and gave up the fight. "Oh, come on then. We can probably make Argos before it closes."

Sam beamed. "I'm ready."

"You're a bloody slave driver, that's what you are."

When the bed was finished, Sam stood back and looked at it. "There. What do you think?" she asked.

"It's a bed," he said. "You're not meant to look at it, you're meant to lie on it." He walked around and lay down on the bed. "Yep. It looks great from here." He patted the bed beside him and Humphrey hopped up. "Not you, you daft mutt. Come on, have a go."

Sam lay down on the big soft bed and smiled. "It's lovely and comfortable," she said.

Andy picked Humphrey up and plopped him down on the floor. "It is now. Go on, Humph, scat." Humphrey trotted off to the room next door to sulk and Andy got up to close the door behind him and found Sam getting up as well. He leant back against the door. "Oh no you don't. Haven't you heard it's unlucky to give someone a bed without christening it?"

Sam smiled and tilted her head. "Isn't that purses and money?"

Andy walked slowly towards her speaking softly. "Those too," he said, and took her in his arms and they christened the bed… thoroughly.

Later on, when they were lying together under the covers, Sam's stomach began to rumble. "Was that you?" Andy asked.

Sam was sleepy and tucked into his side, comfortable and warm. "No," she said into the pillow.

It happened again. "It is you." He rolled her onto her back to face him. "You need to eat."

"No," Sam protested, "I need to sleep."

Andy rolled his eyes, kissed her shoulder and slipped out of the bed to get dressed. Humphrey met him on the landing. "You hungry too, huh? Come on then." Humphrey trotted down the stairs following Andy into the kitchen and then watched as Andy searched around the cupboards until he found the tins. "Cesar?" he asked and Humphrey's tail wagged eagerly. Andy leaned down and grimaced as he picked up the slightly cruddy bowl and set about cleaning it thoroughly. When it was shining, he opened the tin and forked out some food. Humphrey pounced on it. "Well that's one of you happy, at least. Now let me see."

Andy spent some time clearing away all the new bed packaging and stacked all the parts of the old bed against a wall in the study. He hunted through the numbers on his mobile phone, in search of a pizza delivery service.

A little later they arrived, hot and steaming at the front door. Andy paid the deliveryman and then fished his little camera out of his rucksack. Grabbing some cold beers from the fridge, he went back upstairs, leaving Humphrey happily pottering around below.

Outside the bedroom door Andy put down the pizzas and beer and crept inside. He found Sam sleeping in their new bed and he felt more at peace than he had ever felt before. She was lying on her front, with her hair spread out all over the pillow and the duvet slung low across her back. Andy couldn't take his eyes off her. He took a photo, quickly, before she awoke. It clicked. Nothing; she didn't even move. He took a couple more just to make sure and then hid the camera away again in his trouser pocket, before going back outside to reclaim the beer and food.

Andy put the pizza down on the floor beside the bed and with a delicate touch, traced small circles with his middle finger across her naked back. Sam stirred. "Hello, Beautiful," he said.

Sam peered up at him and wiped a few stray hairs from her face. She smiled and then sniffed the air. "What time is it?" she asked.

"Nearly nine," he said.

"Nine? You shouldn't have let me sleep so long.

"I didn't really have a say in the matter," he said. "You were out for the count."

Sam slumped back onto the pillow and hid her face. "I'm Sorry. I blame that uncomfortable futon of mine," she said.

"Quite right too. Are you hungry?"

"Famished."

"Good. I hope you like pizza." Andy passed up the boxes and handed Sam a beer and then lay out on the top of the bed himself.

"My hero," she said. "Better mind the covers though."

"Sod the covers; I'm starving."

That night Andy and Sam stayed in, curled up together on the much-maligned futon with Sam's music playing quietly in the background. They talked and touched, leaving little room for air between them and wantonly living every moment within each other's lives.

The following morning they were woken by Andy's phone. Andy took the phone call downstairs and when he came up again, he was carrying two cups of tea. He suggested that they do something fun that day and Sam was definitely up for that. She had been worrying that she wasn't making his time back home much of a break. So far she had dragged him round shopping and little else. She nervously agreed to meet with some of his mates from the rear guard, who had not been sent out on tour, to go go-karting. Andy assured her that she would love it and promised to try and get at least one other girl for her to talk to on their trip. Sam expressed some concern that the other guys would not like an outsider tagging along, but again Andy told her not to be silly and sent her off to get dressed.

When she returned, Humphrey trotted in. "What do you think, Humph? Should I join in and make a complete fool of myself in front of a load of Andy's mates?"

Humph yapped excitedly and wagged his tail.

"Good man, Humph," Andy said. "That's settled then."

"I can't believe it. You've even got Humph on your side now."

Andy smiled, scruffed Humphrey's fur and walked outside to make some more calls.

It was a beautiful summer's morning so Sam made the breakfast and they ate it in the back garden. She handed Andy a plate of buttered toast and he mouthed a thank you back to her. Soon after, he put away his phone and tucked in. "Well it's all sorted," he said. "Steve's kids are at their grandparents' for the weekend, so they're both up for some grown-up fun. He and Helen will pick us up around twelve and drive out and we're going to meet Luke, Dave and possibly Tina at the track.

As it turned out, Sam needn't have worried. Andy's mates were a friendly bunch and she had great fun on the go-karting track. Tina and Helen in particular could not have been more welcoming and seeing Andy larking about with his mates and still being a great guy was just wonderful.

On the way back to the cars afterwards, Tina pulled Sam aside and told her how pleased she was that Andy had found someone nice like her. She said she'd never seen him looking so happy, and reassured her that he was definitely smitten.

"Do you really think so?" Sam asked. "I hope so."

"Of course he is. It's obvious. I haven't seen him this full of fun in - goodness - forever. You're really good for him, Sam. Poor thing had a rough time when his marriage fell apart - you know all about that, right? - But look at him now. So all's well that ends well, eh? How about you? Are you into him?"

Sam beamed, happiness shining through her eyes. She nodded. "Yes, I think I am."

"Great. I'm glad you said that, 'cause the amount of stick he's going to get from the guys when word gets out that the Prof has been walking hand in hand with a girl, as under the thumb as it gets, it had better be something pretty special."

Andy came up behind them. "And what are you two gassing about?"

"You, of course. I'm just doing my best to warn poor Sam off," Tina said.

Andy grabbed Sam to him and covered her ears. "Don't you dare."

Tina winked. "It was good to meet you, Sam."

"Yeah, you too."

The others said their goodbyes and went off to their respective cars.

"So, how did you like karting then?" Andy asked in the back of Steve and Helen's car on the way home.

"It was great. I was nowhere near as fast as you lot though."

Steve turned round from the passenger seat. "No, 'Driving Miss Daisy' here must have set a new record for the slowest lap ever."

Helen thumped him. "Don't you listen to the cheeky sod, Sam. A few more times out here and you'll be giving them a run for their money, I've no doubt."

"Why don't you challenge Steve to a rematch on your terms, say at the Crown and Anchor in a couple of weeks?" Andy said. "Sam's a great singer." Sam gave him a stern stare, but that only seemed to egg him on more.

"What? Like karaoke?" Steve asked.

"Yes, but she's not your average giggly teenage girl, or drunk middle-aged woman, Sam can really sing."

Sam felt herself blush and deep inside she was overjoyed at how proud Andy was of her.

"Can you? Can you really sing, Sam?" Helen asked.

"I sing, but I wouldn't say 'well'."

"Well I would," Andy said. "I'd say she was bloody fantastic." He leaned over and kissed her.

"Oh get a room, you two," Steve said, chucking an empty plastic drinks bottle into the back of the car.

Helen thumped him again.

"Ow. What was that for?"

"Leave them alone. It's young love. Just because you can't remember what that was like."

"No. I've had it beaten out of me, haven't I?"

"Oh, you love it." Helen briefly turned a warm smile on Steve before they pulled up outside Sam's house. "Here we go, folks."

Back inside, Andy announced he needed to run an errand for a mate and would need to be gone for a few hours, but he would be back later, in time to cook her dinner. Sam was curious as to why he had to leave, but not confident enough to question him further, so she pretended she was fine with it and while he was gone Sam popped round to her parents to see how they were doing.

Sam found her dad tinkering in the garage when she arrived. He welcomed her with a big hug and asked her what news she had to tell him. He was pleased to hear that her new man was unexpectedly in town and that everything was going well. He enquired about the prospect of grandchildren and Sam gave him the usual reproachful look and skipped off inside to find her mum.

Her mother was peeling potatoes in the kitchen when Sam walked in. They hugged briefly and her mum said what an unexpected surprise it was and how relieved she must be to be up to date with her paperwork again. Sam, thinking quickly, explained how her man had turned up unexpectedly and had been helping her with the shopping and tidying up.

"He sounds like a nice lad," her mother said when finally Sam paused for breath

"Oh he's so wonderful, Mum. He's everything I'd hoped he would be: he's kind and considerate, he's generous and he makes me laugh and he's… oh… he's just gorgeous."

"It sounds to me like someone is falling for him." Sam's smile almost split her face in two. "And does he feel the same way about you?"

"Maybe. Yes, I think so. I hope so."

"Well just be careful, love. You know what these soldiers are like"

"But he's not like that, Mum."

"Okay. So what have you done with him while you're round here?"

Sam had to concede that she didn't actually know.

"As I said, just be careful."

Sam sighed. "Okay, Mum."

Sam made sure she was back by five, but with no sign of Andy as yet she put on some Dido and slouched about in the living room. The day was hot, so she slipped off her shoes and brushed out her helmet hair and began to sing along. Humphrey retreated to the quiet of the back garden in the shade of the cherry tree. At some point Andy must have returned, but Sam hadn't heard him and it wasn't until she turned around, mid-song, and saw him in the doorway, watching her that she realised she was not alone.

"I tried the doorbell," he said, stifling a smirk. "I guess you didn't hear it. Who is this, by the way?"

Embarrassed, Sam turned it down and walked over. "Dido," she said.

"I got you something," he said. Sam took a step closer and looked at him. Andy reached into his trouser pocket and pulled out a long thin box. He held it out. Sam walked over and took it from him. "I hope you like it," he said.

Sam tentatively opened the box and inside she saw a delicate gold bracelet and in the centre was an oval plaque with an engraving of a bird on a rifle. Sam picked it out and looked up at Andy for an explanation.

"I tried to get you something to remind you of us, but I didn't want it to be too slushy," he said. Sam looked at the engraving. "It's you and me, see: the soldier and the songbird."

"It's perfect," she said and he helped her put it on. Sam stroked it into place. "I don't know what to say. Thank you. I love it."

"Are you sure? I can take it back and get you something else if you'd rather."

Sam pulled her wrist away. "Don't you dare." She reached up on tiptoes and kissed him with all the love and devotion she could convey.

"Right, let's get on with this cooking then," Andy said.

"You really don't have to, you know. I'll do it," Sam said.

"No you won't." Andy walked out to the kitchen and searched through the fridge and freezer for inspiration. Sam could hear a lot of cupboard doors opening and closing and then he stuck his head around the living room door and said, "How do bacon and egg butties sound to you?" Sam would have eaten barbed wire if he had served it up with that heart-melting smile of his. "Sounds wonderful," she said.

They spent the evening at home. They had each other for company and nothing else was needed. They talked and laughed and played Scrabble. The game ended in a draw as the board got tipped over during a wrestling match over a disputed word. Sam had never heard of the word, but she was convinced that even if it was a real word, it was unlikely to have both an X and a Z in it.

Sunday morning was a more subdued affair. Sam was painfully aware that this was her last full day with Andy before she had to go back to work and then he would fly back out to Afghanistan. Andy must have noticed a change in her, because he asked her what was wrong, but he seemed to understand her sadness even without her actually expressing it. It was amazing the words that could be conveyed in a simple squeeze of the hand. They both decided it was important to make the best use of the day.

The old park was a scene of idyllic English summertime. Families wandered through and spread out rugs on the ground. Children fed the ducks and chased after pigeons and the sun shone down warming rays on them all.

Andy and Sam walked among it, hand in hand, saying little. They had talked already about so much, all except the things that really mattered.

An ice cream van sang out from the edge of the park behind them and nearby children began to hurry towards it. Two of them ran past Sam and Andy, calling backwards for their slower parents to follow faster. The little girl noticed Sam and smiled. "Hello, Miss Litton," she said.

"Hello, Rosie. Hello Ron."

The parents walked passed and said hello and once out of earshot Andy turned to Sam.

"Miss Litton? I never really thought of you as actually being someone's teacher. Should I call you Miss from now on?"

"Only if you want me to thump you."

"Okay. Sorry, Miss." Sam thumped him and Andy laughed.

"You're not going to put me in detention, are you?"

"Only if you're very naughty."

Andy's face formed a mischievous grin and Sam thumped him again.

When they got back home, Sam sent Andy off to the garden to relax while she prepared the lunch. She turned on the oven and flicked the switch on her little radio, tuning it in. Sam chopped and peeled and tried to make everything as perfect as she could, singing along to the tunes as she went. The one o'clock news came on and Sam's tender heart stilled. Another soldier had been killed whilst serving in Afghanistan. He had been shot in an engagement while his troop had been on patrol, trying to clear an IED from a roadside in Helmand. The report said that two other soldiers had also been wounded and had been evacuated to the British field hospital in Camp Bastion. All relatives had been informed. Sam's beautiful, idyllic world crumpled around her. It was still happening out there, and any minute now Andy would be flying back to take up his role in it. She slunk down to the floor and hopeless silent tears began to flow.

A short while later, Andy's face appeared round the door. He stopped for a moment and assessed the situation. A jolly voice sang out from the radio, at odds with the scene within. No blood had been spilled and yet Sam was deeply upset about something. He walked inside and crouched down before her and gently put his hand on her shoulder. Sam did not look up. He said her name and lifted her chin to look into her eyes and there he saw a world of pain. "What is it?" he asked.

But Sam could not say. She could not even bring herself to speak the words.

"Was it something on the radio?" he asked.

Sam slowly nodded.

"About Afghanistan?"

Sam heaved a big sigh and nodded again.

Andy sat down on the floor beside her and she rested her head against him. "Was someone else killed?" he asked tentatively.

Sam could not even nod. She put her arms around Andy and buried her head in his neck, holding on for dear life. Andy put his arms round her and soothed her, stroking her hair with his hand. After a few minutes, Andy asked her if she remembered who the soldier had been, but she could not. She could only say he wasn't from 9 Rifles. After that Andy made Sam promise that once he was gone, she would not listen to any more news bulletins. Sam protested, drying her eyes and sitting up away from him. How else was she going to find out what was happening out there? But Andy was adamant. He would tell her anything she needed to know.

"You'll only worry otherwise," he said.

"You think I won't be worrying anyway?" Sam said as she fiddled with her bracelet.

"It's only the same amount of time as last time. You'll be fine."

"But it's different this time," Sam said.

"Why?" Andy asked.

"It just is." Why? As if he could even ask it? Was he being deliberately obtuse? She longed to cry out 'because I'm madly in love with you now, you idiot', because she was, she understood that now. She had to say goodbye to him in less than forty eight hours and the thought of it was killing her. She loved him so deeply, but she was too afraid to say so. He would surely run a mile if she were to gush all over him and then she would never see him again.

"Okay," he said. "But promise me you'll do as I ask. I don't want to think of you back here fretting every time you turn on the TV or radio."

Sam was quiet. "But what if you can't tell me you're all right," she said, unable to look him in the eye.

Andy thought for a moment. He nodded. "Leave that to me. I've got to pop back to the barracks at some point tomorrow. I'll give Miller's wife, Gina, your address and phone number. She'll know if anything bad happens with our lot. I'll ask her to keep you in mind if… She's a nice girl, Gina. You'd like her."

Sam nodded and then rested her head on his shoulder again.

"And maybe, if you can manage to put up with me for a bit longer, I could put you down as my next of kin on my next tour?"

Sam spluttered out a laugh. "Is that a soldier's idea of romantic?"

Andy's face fell. "Yep, sorry, that's as good as it gets." He turned to look at her and swept the last of the tears from her face. He smiled. "So do you think you could get on with making my lunch now? I'm bloody starving."

Sam smiled despite herself and leant against him. "Oh God, the potatoes; I didn't put them in."

Andy stood up and looked at the timer. "Chop 'em up smaller. They'll be fine."

Sam got to her feet. "Oh, my leg, it's gone dead."

"Well if you will pick the most uncomfortable place in the whole house to have your emotional meltdown."

Sam thumped him. "Oi."

Andy turned her radio off. "I'll put some music on, shall I?" he said and wandered off into the living room.

Sunday lunch was a quiet affair. Their bubble had been burst and reality had crept in. But lust was turning to love and the pain of separation was nibbling at their heels. They spent the rest of the day lounging on the grass in the garden, their bodies always touching and where they weren't together, that part of them ached.

A little bird fluttered down close by them and they watched it hopping around before it was startled by Humphrey walking over to see them.

"Look, it's a long-tailed tit. See. It's small, not much bigger than a wren really and with a long tail. There'll probably be more around if we stay still. And smother Humphrey, of course."

Sam chuckled. "So. You really do like bird watching. I had wondered."

Andy smiled. "Is it that sad?" he asked.

"Criminally. No, of course it's not."

Another one landed. "Look, on the fence over there. It's another one." Sam followed his direction. "It's got a little bug in its beak. It's probably taking it home to the nest. They'll have hungry mouths waiting for them."

Sam looked up. "If I was a bird, what kind of bird would I be?" she asked.

Andy made a point of considering carefully for a moment and then he said, "Great tit." Sam thumped him. "Okay, a song thrush, a song thrush," and he tickled her until she rolled on the ground begging him to stop, and then he kissed her.

By the end of the afternoon, clouds had made a barrier across the sky and the light was growing dim. Sam shivered. Andy suggested they make plans for the evening and Sam made arrangements to meet up with some friends down the pub later.

Their night was spent in patient love, no less passionate than before, but this time it held even more meaning. It was love and longing and desire, all rolled into one.

In the morning a reluctant Sam went off to work. But before she went she checked several times that he would definitely be there when she got back that evening. Andy tried to break the tension by teasing her about being a schoolteacher, but his efforts did little to ease the pain. Eventually he had to almost shove her out the door, or she'd have been late.

Sam cycled away, confident that the children would keep her mind occupied for the rest of the day. A near miss with a car helped to focus her attention on the job in hand, and before she knew it she was pulling up outside school, ready to start the day.

Melissa Andrews and her new pet stick insects came to her rescue. She had brought them in to show to the class and they sparked a great discussion and interest for the better part of the morning. Sam got them all writing about stick insects and then she let them draw a picture each – something she would not be doing again. They were named Sarah, Cynthia and Simon. Not the sort of names Sam had expected and she hoped that they hadn't been offended by a wrong gendered name, but then again she had no idea how you were supposed to sex a stick insect. Jimmy had panicked her half way through the afternoon, declaring that Simon was suddenly missing, but after a thorough search of the classroom, Melissa found that he was there after all and wasn't that amazing how good they were at camouflage? So with all the unexpected excitement and a bit of reading and maths, there was little time left for dwelling on the affairs of the heart.

It was by far the longest time she had spent apart from Andy since his arrival, and so it was with a real sense of purpose that she got her things together at the end of the day and sped off home.

Andy was waiting for her when she got back, with a bunch of red roses in his hand and a kiss on his lips. Then, from behind his back he produced two tickets for the theatre and handed them to Sam. He had somehow managed to get hold of some tickets for 'Much Ado About Nothing' that night, which Sam had heard had been sold out for months. Sam gasped. "But how…? I tried to get tickets to see this ages ago, but it was sold out."

"Ah, you obviously haven't got the knack."

"You mean you batted your eyelashes at the woman behind the ticket counter. I've seen you in action. I'm sure you could talk any woman into anything if you set your mind to it."

Andy laughed. "If only. I think usually I just bore them with logic until they give in."

Sam gave him a look. "Thank you," she said and kissed him.

Seeing Andy again after the break of a day was like seeing him anew. Sam could not believe that this tall, handsome, loving man with inky blue eyes was standing here with her.

The following morning Sam moved through the rituals of the day without a sound. There was nothing she could say that would make it any better. It was all she could do to keep herself together and not fall to pieces in front of him. Andy was quiet too. He had packed up his things and was ready to go. He had put his rucksack beside the front door and it stared at Sam defiantly. She looked at him, sipping his tea almost too calmly. Tomorrow he would be back there; back in harm's way, and all she could do was wait. Any minute now she had to say goodbye. She had to leave him and cycle off to twenty nine little faces and pretend that everything was okay; but it wasn't. It couldn't be, not for three more months. Three months of worrying and hoping and trying not to think about those horrible things that crept into the back of your mind when you weren't looking. A stiff upper lip had to be the only way, if you wanted to make it through with your sanity. Sam looked at the clock. It was twenty past eight; time to go. She paled. "What time is your taxi coming?" she asked.

"About ten minutes."

"I have to go."

"I know. I'll post your key through the letterbox as I leave. Go on now."

Sam rushed forward and hugged him so tightly, all composure lost. "Come back safe, won't you?"

Andy held her close. "I'll do my best." He prised her away from him. "Come on. You're going to be late."

Sam looked up. "We could always elope," she said, excited. "No one would find us."

"Sounds like a great idea." They kissed one last time. "Go on now."

Sam pulled on her helmet and opened the door.

Andy did not move. "I'll be seeing you," he said and Sam smiled and walked away. It was the hardest thing she had ever done. As her body mounted her bike and she rode away, her heart was crying out to run back to him. But nothing she could do would make a difference. He would still have to go, if not then, then soon. She cycled on with tears welling up in her eyes, and ached for the man that had come to mean everything to her. Please stay safe, my love, she thought when she reached the school gates, and walked inside.

As Andy climbed into the taxi and drove off back to barracks, he felt certain in his heart that this time he had got it right. He had found the woman who would stick by him through thick and thin, and nothing and no one was going to take that away from him again.

Chapter 8

Sam felt her loss keenly. Andy had only been with her for less than a week, but in that time he had managed to fill such a gap in her life, a gap that she had never even known existed, and now he was gone and Sam was left aching and empty.

A week passed in the shadows, with Sam battling against her will to listen to the news bulletins. She longed for word to come, to say that Andy was all right and still wanted her. Another week and Spike would be home and she would lose her best friend's support for a while.

Kate was so excited about Spike's imminent arrival that Sam felt quite jealous. Kate had all her time ahead of her but Sam's was now gone. She slept on the other side of the bed now, feeling closer to Andy as she lay there alone at night.

And then a letter arrived. Andy was safe. He was back with his group and all was well. Sam breathed a sigh of relief. She read the letter through again and was pleased to see he had written 'Love' at the end. Love from Andy. Was that real, or just a word? She scanned back through his old letters. Yes, he had used it before, but only once: in the letter where he had poured his heart out to her. It was real. Sam wrote straight back, telling him how she missed him and how much she wanted to be with him and ended her letter 'with all my love'.

Radio silence kicked in between Sam and Kate with Spike's arrival home, and for the following two weeks Sam's house seemed deathly quiet. And then Spike was gone too, and Sam was there to be a friend to Kate and help her through the melancholy.

Not long after, Sam heard a knock at the door. She wandered over and answered it. Dean Fletcher stood there in his uniform, a bunch of flowers in his hand and a sunny smile on his face. "Hello, Sweetheart, did you miss me?"

Sam was in shock. When she had last seen him, she had been sweet on him, it was true. But then he had gone… and… nothing. He had not sent a word or made a quick call. He had vanished out of her life, even before he had gone, if she was being honest. And yet here he was, all charm and dashing good looks, as if he had never been away.

"Well aren't you going to invite me in then?"

Sam panicked. She didn't have a clue how to handle this. She was with Andy now. Surely Dean had to see that he couldn't just waltz back into her life as if nothing had happened? She stepped aside and Dean handed her the flowers and walked in.

"Nice place you've got here," he said, peering around.

"H-how did you…?"

"Your mum," he said.

Tea, Sam thought. She would make some tea. She asked him if he would like some.

"Yeah, great."

Sam walked out into the kitchen and scoured her brain for what she should say. She poured some water into her vase and set the flowers in it to keep for later and then made the tea.

"So how have you been?" he asked as she passed him his drink and they sat down.

"Fine. And you? I mean, you know."

"Yeah. It was hardly Ibiza, but I'm still in one piece… so far." Sam smiled a weak, anxious smile. "Look, I'm really sorry I didn't write, Sam. Truth is I don't know what happened to your letter.

I must have lost it, or… I don't know, maybe someone nicked it, but… You know I would have written. I've missed you, Sam." Sam studied the patch of floor at her feet. "I did ask my Mum to get a message to you, but you never wrote, so I guess…"

Sam shook her head. "No."

Dean got up and, putting his cup down, he walked over to where Sam was sitting on the beanbag and knelt down before her. Humphrey, who had been lying under the window in the sun until then, sat up and began to growl. Dean looked across. "Still as grumpy as ever, eh? He's a tough nut to crack, that one, isn't he?"

Sam shushed Humphrey and he settled nearby, vigilant but subdued.

Dean resumed his purpose. "I've missed you so much Sam. Say you've missed me."

Sam braced herself. "Your mother said she'd met your girlfriend."

"What girlfriend? I don't have anyone else but you."

"But she didn't see me."

"When did she say this?"

"A while back. Kate overheard her talking to her mum."

"Oh, Katy? Well that explains it."

"What do you mean?"

"Well Katy's always had a bit of a thing for me, a bit embarrassing really. It wouldn't be the first time she's tried to wreck things up in my love life."

Sam was speechless. Everything that she thought she knew was called into question. First there was the implication that Andy might have stolen her letter from Dean. And now what Kate apparently said about his infidelity was in doubt. Had she actually two-timed her boyfriend, while he was out serving in Afghanistan, on the back of a pile of misinformation? Christ! He had to be lying. "Kate's my best friend. She wouldn't do something like that to me," she said.

"Hell, I know it isn't what you want to hear, Sam, but she's been playing you, sweetheart, and I won't have you lied to anymore. What did you think; that I just found myself another girl while I was out in Afghan? There aren't a lot of opportunities for nights out over there. Anyway you're my girl."

"She wouldn't lie to me," Sam said.

"Well either she has, or my Mum has. There is no one else. Are you calling my mum a liar?"

Sam stared at a spec of fluff on the floor and a small voice escaped her. "Andy said you did too."

"Andy? Who's Andy when he's at home?"

"Andy Garrington, your mate."

Dean sat back. "Mate? Hardly. He's a shifty bastard, that one. Anyway how did you manage to speak to him?"

Sam's skin crawled, desperate to flee her body. "He wrote to me."

"He did what? He wrote to you?"

"When I didn't hear from you."

"And how did he do that? I would have written, Sam."

"It had been a month," Sam protested.

"I was in the middle of a war zone. Pardon me if I don't think about you every day, when I'm being shot at and blown up by all and sundry." Dean took a deep breath and let it out. "I'm sorry. I don't mean to take it out on you. It's just... you come home after a long stint away and all you want to do is see your girl and you find she's been fed a crock of shit and thinks you don't care about her."

Sam looked up into sad blue eyes.

"Just tell me you still care about me Sam, at least, and then we can put all this behind us and move on. I don't think I could manage out there if I didn't have you back here thinking of me."

Sam could not move; she couldn't speak. She just wanted to find a big hole and curl up inside it.

Dean kissed her on the cheek. "You obviously need a bit of time to take this all in. I'll tell you what, I'll check in with my folks and spend some time with them and I'll come back on

Sunday night, okay?"

Sam looked up from her desolate position, battered and bruised on the purple beanbag. Dean's sad face smiled fondly down at her. He winked and then let himself out.

That night Sam was supposed to be going out with a recently bereft Kate, and Chloe, but she couldn't face it. She cancelled, claiming to have a really bad headache. She made a quick but cheery call to her mum and dad and then shut up the house for the night and just sat.

If Dean had lost her letter that would explain why he had written to his mum and dad, but not to her. But Dean obviously suspected it was stolen, so had Andy actually stolen it from Dean? And if so, how did she feel about that? Was that dishonesty, or devotion? And what about the other woman? Andy and Kate had both agreed on that part, but were they really unbiased? Worse still, if everything Dean had said was true, what did that make her? What did that make Andy? More importantly, did that mean everything she had made with Andy had been built on lies and deceit? However good it had been between them, Sam now felt riddled with doubt.

She walked upstairs to her bedroom and lay out on her double bed and stared at the photo of Andy, as if by staring hard enough, everything would suddenly become clear to her. Andy. But she loved him so much. He was everything she wanted in a man. He was just perfect. The words 'too good to be true' floated into her mind; that's how her mother had described him. What if her mother was right? Dean had said he was shifty and that was without even knowing she had got together with him. Oh, what did they know! Andy was heaven, her bit of heaven.

Sam really felt she needed to talk to someone, but who could she trust? Not Andy or Dean, that was for sure, and Kate was involved now too. Chloe was more Kate's friend than her own and that really only left her mum and dad, and the last time she'd come to them with her boyfriend troubles it had upset them more than she had ever been.

On Sunday evening, Sam was no better. The headache she claimed to have had the night before was now a harsh reality. She hadn't slept and she had barely eaten.

Dean arrived and kissed her briefly. "Hello sweetheart, have you eaten?" Sam shook her head. "Come on then, grab a jacket, we're going out."

Sam did not move. "I'm… not really that hungry," she said.

"Nonsense; everybody's got to eat."

Sam went along and picked at her food. She let Dean do most of the talking that night, which he seemed more than happy to do. Sam was on a different planet. She no longer knew who she was betraying with whom and it felt awful.

At the end of the evening, Dean dropped Sam back off at her house and walked her up to the front door.

"Are you all right, Sam?" he asked. "You just don't seem yourself tonight. Are you coming down with something?"

"Yes, maybe," she said.

"All right then, I'll leave you be. You get some sleep. Would you like to go out on Thursday night? I could pick you up around eight?"

Sam looked up. "I'm meant to be meeting the girls for a sing that night."

"Oh Christ, your karaoke, okay. What about Friday?"

"Yeah, maybe. I'll see how I feel."

Dean nodded and then he stepped closer and taking her in his arms he kissed her, passionately on the lips. Inside Sam's head her mind scrambled in panic, unable to respond. Dean stepped back and beamed at her. "Go on in and get some rest. I'll call you." He walked a few steps away and Sam called out.

"I can't, Dean."

Dean turned round.

"I can't. I'm sorry." There was a long pause. "I'm with Andy now. I'm really sorry."

Dean looked aghast. "You're kidding me, right? Sam?" He shook his head. "I thought you were better than that."

Sam watched him drive away and closed the door. She had expected a row. She had expected to be berated by him for her betrayal at least, but no. Sam thought she might be sick. How had this all happened? Only a few weeks ago she was the happiest she had ever been in her life, and now? Now she could barely put one foot in front of the other for fear of doing the wrong thing. She slumped straight down onto her futon and Humphrey hopped up and laid his head on her lap. Dean's face when she had told him. He had been devastated. God, how she hoped she had made the right decision.

The following day she received a letter from Andy. It was a loving letter and helped to ease Sam's conscience that she had made the right choice. He was a kind and generous man, the man she loved and the man she believed loved her. How they had got to that point was not important. Dean would get over her easily enough. There were always plenty of women willing to hook up with a gorgeous, fair-haired Adonis like him. If only she could feel Andy's arms around her and hear his calm, steady voice, she was sure she would feel much better. But he wasn't there and for now she was on her own.

Humphrey nudged her. Her stroking had ceased. "Sorry, Humph," she said and resumed her rhythm. "You love me, don't you, boy?" she said, picking up the remote and putting on the TV, hoping to find something to blot out the pain.

Thursday night at the Crown, Sam chose her words very carefully. Although she knew Kate would never betray her like Dean had suggested, she couldn't seem to get his words out of her head.

"Did you see Dean was home on leave?" Sam asked, as nonchalantly as she could manage.

"Yeah. Tosser's probably out shagging his way around town right now. Good job you're immune now, eh?"

Was that a little over the top for a neighbour? Sam wondered. Was it bitterness at his rejection? Had Kate tried to stuff things up to protect her? Or maybe this was just Kate? "Yes, I do believe I've had the shots now," Sam said.

"Chlo', how about you?"

"God, no. He's not my type. In fact I've had my eye on a gorgeous waiter at Dixie's. You know, the one who served the table next to us that time?"

"Really? But what about Karl?" Kate asked.

"Oh no, didn't I tell you? That's all old hat now. We're just good friends. He admitted to having another girlfriend back home. Anyway, it doesn't really matter. I was never as into him as much as you two were into yours. We still write, though. He's trying to get me to do something more than just eat at Dixie's. He says men aren't great at subtlety and he might not have a clue that I'm keen on him. He wants me to actually talk to the guy. Imagine that?"

"So have you talked to him yet?" Sam asked.

"No. It's costing me a bloody fortune."

Sam's heart just wasn't in it that night. She could not be persuaded to sing, however hard the girls tried, but she did enjoy listening to the others and when Chloe was out in the toilets later on, Kate leaned across and whispered to Sam. "What would you say if your best mate thought she might be pregnant?"

Sam gasped and her mouth fell open. "Pregnant?" she mouthed.

Kate's face was serious.

"But he's only just..."

"I know, but I was due on Tuesday and I'm never late."

Sam sat back. "Bloody Hell, Kate. What are you going to do?"

"I don't know. I think I'm going to keep it."

"What about Spike?"

"I'm going to do a test in the morning and then write to him." She grinned.

"You haven't done a test yet? So there's still a good chance that you're not."

Kate looked at her in earnest. "I am."

"Do you think he'll be happy?" Sam asked.

Kate looked down for a second. "I hope so. I like him a lot."

"Wow. Here comes Chloe. Have you told her?"

Kate shook her head. "Don't say anything yet."

The following night, Dean was back again. Sam answered the door and was surprised to see him standing there. He said he had just dropped by to check that she was all right after she had seemed so peaky the last time they'd met and Sam invited him in from the doorstep. He sat down and made every attempt to be friendly. He asked after her teaching and about her friends and to Sam, things had definitely eased between them. He obviously wasn't bearing a grudge and for that Sam was grateful. She asked him about Afghanistan and how it had been. Dean was pretty vague about the details, but she got the definite impression that all was not rosy within their group; some problem with a weak link was all he would say.

Dean noticed her bracelet and Sam fiddled with it uncomfortably. "It was from Andy," she said.

Dean nodded thoughtfully. "Yeah, that fits. Always flash with his cash, that one. Just be careful, yeah? I wouldn't want to see you hurt, Sam. I care about you too much for that."

By Saturday night Sam thought she was starting to get a grip on things and was feeling a little better as she rode the bus into town to get to her friend's hen party. It was Georgie's, one of the other young teachers from her school, and Sam was meeting them at the Dairy Maid, before hitting the nightclub later on. The end of term was in sight and the teachers were beginning to feel the holiday spirit. Not long to go and the pressure would be off and they could all put their feet up for the summer holiday.

Georgie was decked out in full Barbie Princess accessories and already incredibly drunk. The obligatory veil kept falling off her head and getting caught up in the sparkly earrings and wand, but that wasn't going to prevent her from having a good time.

The giggly party of slightly drunk women staggered en masse down the road to the nightclub just after ten. They collapsed into a corner, spreading themselves out over several seats, and ordered in another round of drinks. The DJ welcomed the bride-to-be over the speaker system and a big cheer went up from their end of the room.

Before long the club was heaving and dry ice began to hiss out across the dance floor. The girls found themselves having to shout to each other to be heard and a well-worn pathway became etched out between the dance floor and the bar.

Sam realised she had had enough to drink when she stumbled up a step and was caught by one of the friends. She decided it would be better to slow things down for a while and start to sober up. Rebecca, one of the party, tried to tell her something on the dance floor, but Sam couldn't make out what. She cupped her hand to her ear. "What?" she hollered.

"That guy over there is checking you out," she said.

Sam looked around. "What guy?"

"Over there. In the white shirt."

Sam looked harder and then she saw him. Standing at the edge, watching her carefully, was none other than Dean. She turned back.

"You've gone bright red. Do you know him? He's gorgeous." Sam nodded. "Watch out. He's coming over."

Sam's heart was thumping. She excused herself from the dance floor and made her way back to the safety of her group on the other side. But she was mistaken in thinking he would be so easily put off.

"Is anyone sitting here?" he asked, and a million fluttering eyes suddenly turned on him. Of course none of them minded in the least and Sam shrank back as far as she could.

The man was relentless. He charmed and flattered every woman at that table and soon no teacher was left on the dance floor. He never talked to Sam directly, but he held her eyes more than most and Sam was reminded of why she had fallen for him so many years ago. He stayed with them a lot throughout the rest of the evening, excusing himself occasionally to return to his friends and as the night went on Sam found herself growing more and more curious as to who else he was with and why he didn't want to talk to her.

Later on, as the night wore thin, she lost track of him altogether and decided to go looking for him herself.

As nonchalantly as she could, Sam wandered through the crowds, sticking to the dark spaces as much as possible. Completing a circuit with no sign of him at all, she decided she must have missed him somewhere. Sam refused to consider why she felt she needed to find him, she just did and that was all there was to it. So she began to double back, retracing her steps.

She was half way round when a hand reached out and grabbed her wrist, pulling her briskly to the side of the room. Dean held her against him, his aftershave wafting down around her and his warm chest within inches of her face. He let her pull away, still holding on to her wrist. He was well groomed, with a confident easy smile and in all that, he hadn't spilled a drop of his drink. "Looking for someone?" he asked.

"No," she lied.

"I don't believe you."

Sam was convinced her face must be crimson.

"You've been watching me all night," he said.

"I have not." Sam was mortified. "Besides, that's rich coming from a guy who's spent half his evening harassing my friends."

"Harassing?" Dean smirked. "I think someone wanted a bit of 'harassment' herself. You've been looking for me. I was watching you."

"No I haven't. I—."

"Yes you have. You're a bloody awful liar, Sam, and an even worse spy."

Sam tried to wriggle her wrist free.

"Oh no you don't," he said holding on tightly. "I didn't put up with all of those giggling plain Janes over there for nothing, Sam Litton. I wanted to see you."

Sam's insides battled to escape as her nerves began to jitter. "I want you, Sam. And you want me too. You know you do. That's why you haven't been able to take your eyes off me. Even now you're imagining what it would be like to press yourself up against me right here, right now."

Sam was outraged. "I am not!"

Dean smiled. "No? Pity, because I was." He leaned down and kissed her.

For a moment Sam fought to escape his clutches. She turned her face away and wriggled to free herself from his grasp, but her strength was no match for his and he seemed to know exactly where on her neck to kiss to weaken what little resolve she possessed after the amount she had drunk. "I want to feel your body against mine, Sam," he said, his hot breath against her ear. "Kiss me, Sam. Put me out of my misery and just kiss me." He guided her face to his and their lips were reunited.

Sam felt as if she had been drugged. Her body obeyed, sinking into the kiss, pressing up against him, but mentally she fought hard to set herself free. "Stop it, Dean. I can't. I told you." She caught her breath.

"The Prof? You're being faithful to the Prof? That's rich." He gave a short laugh. "If it was the other way around I'm damn sure he wouldn't be hanging around waiting for you."

"You're wrong."

"Am I? Who's known him the longest, then, Sam? Tell me, how much of his R and R did he actually spend with you?"

"A week."

"A week. And the rest?"

"With his mum and dad." Sam was feeling guilty about the kiss and resented this line of questioning.

"The Prof? Spend a week with his parents? Yeah, right! I

rest my case. If he was any good at his job I could let it go, but he's bloody dangerous. Lives depend on him out there and if he was anyone other than a Garrington he would never have made sergeant by now."

Sam was angry. She started to pull away, but Dean caught her hand again.

"I'm sorry. That was out of order. I've been drinking. Forget I said anything. Really, Sam. Don't let me ruin your night." He let her go and she hurried back round to be with her friends, but she did not enjoy the rest of the evening, merely sank herself in the drinks that were freely flowing.

At five o'clock the following morning, Sam awoke feeling distinctly fragile. Light was already pouring in around the one good pair of curtains she owned. She rolled over and groaned. Why did she always wake up so early when she had a hangover? At that moment she would have given anything to be one of those lucky people who could just sleep through the whole thing. She thought about the night before. Oh yes, Dean. She had kissed Dean. No, surely he had kissed her? But she hadn't put up much of a fight, had she? She groaned again. What the Hell had possessed her to go looking for him like that? It had been asking for trouble. She pulled her covers up over her head to hide. It must have been the drink, she thought. And in her defence, she had put a stop to it pretty quickly.

As she cowered beneath the covers, hiding from the trials of her complicated life, words began to filter through her hazy mind. She pushed them away. Two paracetamols and a glass of water later, Humphrey wandered over, obviously disturbed by the noise so early in the morning. Sam let one arm dangle out of the bed and stroked him feebly. Humphrey's tail wagged eagerly, but to no avail and in the end he wandered back off to his bed.

A gruelling hour crawled passed and still Sam lay there, waiting impatiently for either her painkillers to kick in, or sleep to come. What had Dean been saying about Andy? He had as good as said he was no good at his job and endangering the lives of the other men out there. How could he say such a thing? And to imply Andy would never be faithful to her… well… that just wasn't true. But he did have a point about Andy spending a week with his parents. He had also taken quite a few calls, from whom? She had never thought to ask while he was with her. One he had said was his parents, but then she only had his word for that. God, what was she thinking? Andy was hers. It would be too cruel to play with her heart like that and not feel the same way she did and he was not a cruel man. But what did she know? She had only really known him a week. Tears began to slip from her eyes. She tried to remember their time together, but the memories were distorting. Her beautiful man was slipping away and Sam felt the shadow of desolation cross her path. Her insides lurched and she leapt out of bed, desperate to reach the bathroom before she heaved.

On Wednesday evening, Kate arrived at Sam's house. Chloe had given her a lift across town on her way to the gym. Sam let her in and knew immediately that there was good news to be had. Kate was shining as brightly as the sun. Sam talked as she poured Kate some mint tea and then settled her on the beanbag and took up position on the futon opposite her.

"Well?"

"Well what?" Kate asked, fooling no one as to her delight.

Sam gave her a look. "You're busting to tell me something. Is it about Spike?"

"He rang!"

"When?"

"Today. I had to come round and tell you."

"And?"

"He's over the moon."

Kate was so excited that Sam couldn't help but be excited too. "Kate, that's wonderful news. I'm so pleased for you."

"I'm so happy. He's going to be with me and we're going to

have this baby together, like a proper family." Tears began to streak mascara down Kate's face. Sam went over to Kate and hugged her. Then, when Kate was composed again, she fetched a tissue for her eyes and enquired about how she was actually feeling in herself. Kate complained about her aching bust, but apart from that she said she was fine. And then Kate asked about Sam and Andy.

Sam wasn't ready to face that whole can of worms just yet. She wasn't even sure in her own head what was going on with Andy and Dean. All she was knew was that the weight of the worries she was carrying was dragging her down to a place where she didn't want to be. Andy's letters had been less fluid since he had returned to Afghanistan, but was that part of being back out there, or something to do with her? Or was she just over-thinking the whole thing? So she just said, "Fine," and left it at that.

A few days later, Kate rang Sam to tell her Dean had gone back out and that for once he'd seemed less cocky than normal, so things were looking up. Unfortunately for Sam, this message had the opposite effect to the one Kate had expected. Sam asked her if she knew if Dean had got a new girlfriend in tow for his second stint, fishing to see what she could find out. But Kate said apparently not and that he'd got quite shirty with her when she'd teased him. She did say, however, that she had seen on Facebook that he'd been spotted snogging some trollop in Club Seven the previous weekend, but again her reassurances were lost on Sam.

Sam asked who else might know about that and if the source was definitely to be trusted and Kate told her she couldn't remember quite, but she was pretty sure it was some of the girls from The Patch. On the other end of the line Sam winced and died a little inside.

On Monday evening a letter came for Sam. She picked it up off the mat as she walked in the door and was saddened to realise that she was no longer ecstatic at the sight of it. What she felt now had been spoiled by a strong dose of suspicion and guilt. She took off her things, made herself a cup of tea and then wandered into the living room to sit down and open it.

Dear Sam,

How distant you seem to me out here. You could almost be on another world. I miss you. The work out here is hotter than ever, even getting up to fifty degrees today. Come midday it was only the mad dogs and us Englishmen left out in the sun.

I hope you and Humph are both well. You would have loved the kids we met yesterday. We had to visit a school that was rebuilt under our protection and only reopened a few months ago. The children were all so happy and glad to be there. They all wanted to shake our hands. I wish you could have seen them.

There's a big operation in the offing. We'll be moving out to join another platoon on a long op, but it's not certain when as yet, so I'm not sure when I'll get a chance to write to you again, but I will be thinking of you, always.

I long for shady lawns and ice-cold beers, and you.

Write soon,

Andy

PS Is my bed missing me yet?

He sounded so sad. When he had been with her, he had felt like the love of her life and she had been so happy every minute she had spent with him. But then he had gone, and there was Dean: the Adonis she had long held a torch for, who, by fair means or foul, had lost her, but who now made her question everything she believed to be true. She wondered again how she could actually get to the truth. If only she had a contact on The Patch, but Andy only gave her details to them, not the other way around, and now it was possible the same people who had met her with Andy had seen her kissing Dean! Sam gazed in desperation towards the heavens. Why her? Why did nothing ever go right for her? Maybe Chloe's chap could shed some light, but then what on earth could she say? 'Which of your mates is a bastard?' No, this one she was going to have to work out for herself.

She looked back at the letter. Well, she thought, if he's going to be too busy to write to me, then he's going to be too busy to read, so it won't make much difference if I wait a few days before writing back, just in case anything useful comes to light. There were only three more days before the summer holidays. Then she would be free to spend her time how she pleased. But two days after that, Kate rang with some awful news.

Chapter 9

Dean had been shot. Sam replaced the handset and slumped down onto the floor. He had been hit while out on patrol and had already been flown home to England. His parents had gone up to Birmingham to be with him, and suddenly Sam knew where she had to be. She dashed off a quick note to Andy.

Dear Andy,

Dean home injured. I have to go. I need to make sure he's all right. I'll write again when I can. I can't believe it. Stay safe.

Love from Sam

She knew it was far less than he deserved, but right then she could manage no more. All she could think about at that moment was Dean.

The last day of term passed in a dreamlike state. Sam cruised through her usual routine on autopilot and at the end, when the bell rang and everybody started to leave, she realised that she could barely remember anything that had happened there that day.

Most members of staff were meeting at the local pub for a drink to celebrate the end of term, but Sam could no longer join in. Instead she cycled straight home and got herself ready for the following day.

On Friday morning, the first day of the summer holidays, she was on the train as soon as the rush hour had passed, arriving in Birmingham before lunch. Sam could not remember where Kate had said Dean had gone, so she just found the taxi rank and explained her situation to the chap in the front of the queue. The language barrier was a bit of a problem at first, but before long they seemed to understand each other and she was cruising through the streets of Birmingham on her way to find Dean.

She was deposited on the pavement in front of the most awe-inspiring building Sam had ever seen. It was huge. It looked almost space age, like something out of one of those American dramas she had occasionally caught on TV, not English at all. She thanked the taxi driver and hesitantly walked in.

After explaining her situation to several different people, Sam finally arrived outside the ward. She stopped. Her heart was thumping like a steam train at speed and her hands were sweating. She looked around and found an intercom. She pressed the button and a voice answered. Sam said who she was and who she had come to see. Silence. Up until this point it had never even occurred to Sam that she might not be allowed in. "Wait there, please," the voice said.

A few moments later a woman came out and introduced herself. It was Dean's mother. Mrs Fletcher asked if Sam was Dean's girlfriend and Sam wasn't sure how to answer. "I'm not entirely sure," she said. "How is he?"

Mrs Fletcher looked at her for a long moment, as if weighing her up, and then she mellowed. "He'll be okay. How did you hear, may I ask?"

"Kate told me. Your next door neighbour?"

"Oh, yes."

"Will I be able to see him?"

Dean's mum smiled sympathetically. "I'm afraid you can't just yet. He had to have a second operation this morning on his leg, so he's sleeping right now. Just his father and I are allowed at the present, but there is visiting this afternoon if he's up to it. Are you on your own?"

Sam nodded.

"Then why don't you go off and get something to eat, have a wander round and get back here for about two and we'll see how he is then."

Sam had to know how bad it was. "His leg? How bad is it?"

Mrs Fletcher was serious. "He's still in one piece; that's the main thing," she said. "He took a blow to the head, but that seems to have settled down now. He was lucky, I suppose."

Sam nodded. Mrs Fletcher gave Sam directions to the hospital canteen and went back inside.

Sam wasn't hungry, so she walked back outside for some fresh air and to calm her nerves for a bit.

The weather was kind outside and she walked around the grounds of the hospital and arrived at a cool grassy bank at the side. She sat down and applied her mind to people watching for a short time. They came in all shapes and sizes. There were old couples with sticks walking up to the hospital with a resigned air; worried parents with young children huffing and puffing at the world in general and in amongst them all were men and women of the armed forces in all different uniforms walking purposefully through, immaculately turned out and polite.

When her stomach started to rumble, Sam wandered back inside and walked around the hospital shop, looking at the magazines and cards on the racks. She bought a quiz book and a tuna roll and attempted to focus her mind on whiling away the time, but it was no good. Her nerves were twisting her insides and she could think about nothing else than seeing Dean. Finally she threw the remains of the roll in the bin and walked outside, back into the fresh air, and paced about the grounds, walking up and down the various pathways and checking her watch impatiently until it said it would soon be two.

Outside the ward, Sam hovered, her nerves threatening to choke her. At five past two, Mrs Fletcher came out. She smiled. "He's awake," she said, "and very eager to see you." She held out her hand and Sam followed her through. Outside his room, they stopped. Mrs Fletcher turned to Sam. "Are you ready?" Sam nodded. Mrs Fletcher squeezed her hand for a moment. "I'll take you in and then, if you like, his dad and I can pop out and get some fresh air and give you two a bit of time on your own."

Sam shook her head. "No, please. I don't want to turf you out-"

"Nonsense. Dean would never forgive us." She smiled and pushed open the door. "We're coming in. You'd better be decent."

Apart from getting there, Sam had given little thought to actually speaking to Dean and she hadn't expected him to look so good.

Dean was resting back, his bronzed lean body set a striking contrast against the crisp white sheets. His left leg was covered in bandages, with the sheet draped around him to the waist. All this exposed flesh and his sleep-ruffled hair made him more endearing than ever. He was a little thinner than she remembered, but considering everything he had been through he was looking inexcusably good. He smiled and Sam was lost for something to say.

"You remember Sam, Mum? She used to play round Katy's house years ago. Remember? I got into trouble for squirting her with the hose over the fence that time."

"Oh yes! Sorry Sam, I didn't recognise you. It's my age. You'll have to excuse me."

Sam was staring at Dean in wonder. He remembered. Until then she had had no sign from him that he had ever remembered her from back then and he seemed to know it.

Dean beamed, obviously pleased with himself. "Well don't stand on ceremony, Sam, sit down."

Sam blinked and looked around for a seat. She went to sit down on the chair furthest from the bed.

"No, you take this one, dear," his father said, getting up from the chair on the far side of the room, next to Dean.

Sam moved awkwardly round and sat down where she'd been put.

His mum and dad nodded to each other and then smiled at Sam. "We'll be back in a bit. You two have a nice chat now," and then they were gone.

So she was actually there, with Dean. Suddenly Sam could not think of a single thing to say.

"You're not afraid to be left alone with me, are you?" Dean asked, obviously amused at her discomfort. "I'm not exactly in a position to be a threat right now." He indicated his bandaged leg.

"How is it?" she asked.

"Not so bad. It could have been worse."

Sam nodded thoughtfully. "What happened, or would you rather not-?"

"No, it's all right. We took fire while we were on patrol, that's all. They must have been lying in the fields waiting for us. If the Prof's team had been where they were meant to have been they would have spotted them, but there you go. At least I've still got ten fingers and ten toes. Smithy got it worse than me." He paused and looked at the expression on Sam's face. "Sorry. I forgot you and he…"

"No. It's fine."

"No. I shouldn't have said anything. Forgive me." He moved his position within the bed and his discomfort showed.

"Is it hurting?" Sam asked.

"No. Not really. I'll be up and at 'em again soon. Got to get back out there, haven't I? The lads'll be missing me."

Sam was astounded. "What?"

"Well, probably not this tour."

Dean tilted his head slightly and his eyes searched her face for a moment. "So what are you doing here then, Sam?" he said.

Sam was speechless. What the Hell was she doing there? Ever since she'd heard about Dean's return home she had been desperate to see him, but now she was actually there, what did she expect to happen? Her mouth moved in silence.

"I'm sorry; that was rude. I'm glad you came, really." He held out a hand and took hold of hers. It stayed there, caressing hers, and if Sam's head had found thinking difficult before, it was definitely in trouble now.

"I had to make sure you were all right," she said at last, when the silence between them had stretched on long enough.

"And am I?" he asked, gazing at her steadily.

Sam felt uncomfortable. She nodded.

Dean smiled. "Good. I've missed you, Sam."

Sam's insides squeezed so tightly she could barely breathe. Then, as if coming to her rescue, a nurse from the ward chose that moment to come in. Dean broke away.

"Corporal Fletcher, you're looking a lot better. How are you feeling?"

"Just dandy, thank you ma'am," he said, turning on his usual charm.

The nurse moved alongside him and wrapped a cuff around his arm. It started to inflate and Dean began to talk. The nurse popped a thermometer in his mouth and smiled at Sam. The machine whirred and made a series of beeps and clicks and the nurse wrote down her findings. She checked the leg below the bandage and enquired after his level of pain. "I think you're up to putting some clothes on now, aren't you, Corporal? Especially with a lady present." She opened his cupboard and took out a neatly folded khaki T-shirt. She handed it to him and Dean put it on. "Much better," she said, and with that she disappeared again as quickly as she had arrived.

"There's no slacking in here, is there?" Sam said.

"No. You wouldn't pass me that water over there, would you?" He pointed to the jug of water and glass on the table that had been wheeled out of the way when the nurse came in.

Sam looked across the bed and, leaning over him, she picked up the water and glass and began to pour some for him. A muffled groan escaped him and Sam realised she was leaning her stomach against his bandaged leg. She pulled away instantly, mortified by what she had done. "Oh, God, I'm so sorry. Are you all right? Should I get a doctor?"

Dean tried his best to placate her. "I'm fine, honestly, Sam. Don't make such a fuss. I'm okay, really."

How stupid could she have been? How thoughtless? She apologised profusely. Dean patted the bed beside him.

"What? No. I'm not allowed to."

He gave her a determined look. "Sit."

Sam sat down, careful not to press on anything.

Dean took both her hands in his. "I'm fine. Relax." Sam took a deep breath and let it out. "Better?" he asked.

Sam nodded. "You're sure you're okay?"

"Sure," he said. "But I can think of something that would make me feel better." His eyes sparkled, daring her to ask.

Sam didn't take many seconds to understand his meaning, but decided to brazen it out. "I'm not sure you're up to anything like that, soldier."

"I was only thinking of a cool flannel," he said. "What were you thinking of?"

Sam was mortified and blushed from head to toe.

"Well I'm game if you are," he said. "But we'd better be quick; my parents will be back any second."

Sam gasped in horror and tentatively thumped him on the arm.

"No? Oh well, your decision." He chuckled. "But I'll take a kiss." He pulled her to him, releasing her hands to rest against his chest and taking her head in his gentle grip. Sam's brain was screaming out to break free, but her body was bending to another's will and suddenly she was kissing him.

As the burden of guilt caught up with her and the heat of the kiss intensified, Sam pulled away.

"I'm sorry, Sam. I had no right to kiss you like that. It's just when I'm with you I fall under your spell and I just can't help myself. You have my permission to wallop me if I try to do anything like that again. You will come and see me again, won't you? It would really help me if you did."

Sam said she'd see if she could manage it, but she couldn't promise anything and a moment later there was a knock on the door and Dean's parents were back again.

The four of them talked pleasantly for a couple of minutes, then they said their goodbyes and Sam and Dean's parents walked together out of the ward.

On the way down the stairs Mrs Fletcher asked Sam if she was staying in Birmingham for the night. They had been up for two days to make sure Dean was going to be okay and satisfied he'd live; they were going back home tonight. Outside, Sam pulled out her mobile and rang her mum, who agreed to fetch Humph and keep him until Sam got back, but she was not at all sure she was happy with the reason why. Uncomfortably, Sam ended the call and gave Dean's mum the nod to call their hotel and check the availability for that night. Sam shared a taxi back to the hotel on the Hagley Road and said goodbye to Dean's parents.

"Thank you for today," Sam said.

"No, thank you. It's a hard thing to have your own flesh and blood injured so far away from home. We can't be with him every second of the day, more's the pity. So it's a real comfort to find out that there is someone else who cares so much about him. He's really taken with you, you know. I'm so glad he's got you. Watch out for him while we're away, Sam." His mum kissed her on the cheek and his dad smiled and said goodbye. "We'll see you back home soon, yes?" Sam nodded and waved them away.

In her room, Sam busied herself looking around, checking out the facilities. The bathroom was clean, if a little tired. The bed was dressed in neutral colours with just a splash of burgundy here and there. There was a tea tray on the desk, with a pair of cups and saucers on it and, to Sam's delight, two tiny packets of shortbread biscuits. The full-length curtains at the back of the room were open and Sam walked over to have a look out at her view. The car park. Oh well, she thought, she wasn't exactly there for the scenery and at least it was quieter around the back than the front by the busy main road. She pulled the curtains closed and sat down on the bed.

Sam felt like an onlooker watching at a distance, observing a young woman getting herself into something she was not prepared for. What was she doing in the middle of Birmingham, spending money that she could ill afford, to see a man that was once her boyfriend, but not anymore?

Dean's parents had been so happy she was with him, as they had assumed she was. They had been so kind and welcoming, had made her feel one of the family even. Dean himself had seemed more genuine than ever that day. Sure, he larked about and tried it on, but he seemed to have really been pleased to see her. What if he'd been telling the truth all along? It was hard to believe that Andy could be the predatory animal he was being painted as, but it wouldn't be the first time she had been mistaken in her choice of men. She thought of her mum and dad and had to speak to them.

Her mum answered the phone. "Sam, where are you. Are you okay?"

"I'm in Birmingham, in a small hotel a couple of miles away from the hospital. Is Humphrey with you yet?"

"Yes. He was a bit miffed at first, but your dad fed him a whole handful of those treats he likes and he's almost forgiven us now."

"Oh, he could string that one on forever," Sam said, chuckling at Humphrey's manipulative behaviour.

"So you didn't really say before, what on earth are you doing in Birmingham?"

Sam paused before answering. She knew how it was going to look. "I had to come and see Dean," she said.

Sam's mum was silent.

"He's been shot, Mum. I couldn't not go."

"And Andy? Is he shot too? I mean he is your boyfriend now, isn't he?"

"It's complicated, Mum," Sam said.

"It sounds it." There was an awkward pause again. "So when are you coming home?"

"Tomorrow. I'm going to see Dean first and then get the next train back home."

"I hope you know what you're doing, love."

"It'll be fine. We're just friends. Look, I've got to go, Mum. I'm running short on credit. I'll see you tomorrow night, okay?"

Sam ended the call. Who was she kidding? If there was one thing she wasn't it was 'fine'. She had kissed him. It had not been a timid peck on the lips, but a long delicious dance with the devil. It was exciting and terrifying all at once and though racked with guilt, it left her wanting more. And Sam was under no illusion; more was definitely going to be on offer. It was going to be up to her to stop him, but when the time came, would she? Or even, should she?

Chapter 10

With all the sounds of the city outside and the weight of the doubt on her shoulders, Sam did not manage to get much sleep that night. She almost picked up the phone at one point to talk to Kate, but the voices inside her head whispered words of caution. Kate would tell her not to go back. She would tell her not to believe him and to run home as fast as she could. But Sam was drawn to him, by whatever force was controlling her now, so she pushed it to the back of her mind and locked it away. For now, this was what she had to do.

Sam was free for the morning, so she took a cab into town and wandered around, making the most of being in a big city. As she walked among the crowd, Sam's phone began to bleep. She checked and found a text from Kate. **Where r u?** Sam put the phone back in her pocket. A couple of minutes later it went again. **Call me.** Sam hesitated. Her fingers hovered over the buttons to call, but she fought the urge and put it back in her pocket. Again it beeped. **Don't u dare do anything stupid.** Sam turned her phone off and found a gigantic HMV to take her mind off things.

After finding a Burger King, Sam wandered back up to the station and took a train to the University stop and asked some students for directions. She walked past the medical school and down a long hill to the hospital at the bottom. She stopped and looked at it. The day before it had seemed immense, but now, a little more at ease, she could regard it with an appreciative eye. It was beautiful really, as modern buildings go. Maybe in a few years it wouldn't look so good, but new as it apparently was, it was shiny and clean and looked spectacular with its sweeping arc, like a wave of silver down one side.

Outside the ward, Sam checked her watch and drummed her fingers impatiently. Three minutes to go, she thought. She walked over to the window and looked out. Someone else arrived behind her and she smiled politely. They pressed the buzzer and were let in. Sam walked over and announced her arrival and the door was opened for her too.

There was laughter coming from Dean's room as Sam approached along the corridor. She knocked and poked her head around the door. Dean beckoned her in and the other soldier noticed her and wheeled himself out, greeting her politely as he passed.

Dean looked a whole lot brighter than the day before. His hair was groomed and he was dressed now in shorts and a t-shirt. He was lying on top of his covers when Sam arrived. "You're looking better," she said as she walked inside the room.

"Hello Sweetheart, what a treat to see you again. I was hoping you'd come back. You didn't travel all the way back up here again today, did you?"

Sam smiled. "No. I spent the night at the hotel your parents were staying in."

"Just to see me?" he asked, a big grin on his face.

Sam rolled her eyes. "Well they do have a very good HMV here." He looked gorgeous, but suddenly Sam panicked. She felt the colour drain from her face and thought she was about to be sick.

"Are you all right?" he asked. "You look as if you're going to faint, or something. You're not squeamish, are you? The smell in these places can get you like that."

Sam sat down on a chair. "No. It's not that."

"Then what?" He paused. "You're not up the duff, are you?"

Sam was shocked. "No!"

Dean's eyebrows rose. "You're sure?"

"Yes," she said firmly.

"Good. The last thing we need is another little Garrington running around messing everything up."

Sam looked at him.

"I'm sorry, Sam, but you have to be able to do better than him. I mean, he's already screwed up one marriage. If you can only get a woman by stealing someone else's then it's a bit crap, you've got to admit?"

Sam felt uneasy. "Whereas you tend to have them lined up, forming an orderly queue, waiting for you."

"Well they can wait all they like; only one woman is here with me." He was looking straight at her, a serious expression now set on his face.

Sam blushed.

"I don't care how he tricked you into believing I didn't want to write, Sam. It's not important. All that matters now is that you're here again, with me. I don't know what I'd do if I didn't have you to hold on to."

Sam found it increasingly hard to hold his gaze. "How's your leg doing?" she asked.

"It's a bit sore where you leant against it yesterday, but…" Dean rolled up laughing as the expression on Sam's face fell. "It's fine, Sam. I'm only kidding. Honestly."

Sam got up from where she was sitting and marched over and thumped him.

"Ow!"

"That's not funny. You deserved that," she said.

Dean laughed. "They're moving me out onto a four-bedded bay sometime this afternoon, so I'll soon have witnesses to all this abuse."

"You won't get the chance; I'm back off home after I leave here today."

Dean stilled. "Well then I'd better make the most of you, hadn't I?" He pulled her slowly toward him and stopped only millimetres away. "This is the point when you are supposed to stop me, Sam." But Sam did not say a word, only leaned in the last little bit and kissed Dean delicately on the lips. But Dean was not in the mood for delicate and he pulled her firmly up against his good side and held her there in an ardent kiss for several more minutes. Dean's hand slipped down toward Sam's breast and she pulled away.

"What's wrong? I thought… You seemed…" Dean shook his head. "Tell me what you want, Sam. I'm no good at playing games. You travelled all this way up to see me and… you didn't tell me to stop."

Sam was a mess. "I know. I'm sorry. It's all my fault."

"I wonder how many other hearts you've broken along the way with that kiss?"

Sam looked at him. Other broken hearts? Had she broken his heart? Sam was shocked.

"What? Did you really think I cared so little?" He shook his head. "You're one in a million, Sam, and you don't even know it."

A nurse knocked and walked in. "I'm very sorry, but I'm going to have to cut visiting time slightly short today. We've got some men arriving soon who are going to require our full attention. We're going to have to shuffle round a few rooms. I'm sure you understand." She smiled apologetically and a moment later Sam heard the same two knocks on another door and the sound of sirens in the distance. She looked at Dean. He shrugged.

"I'd better be off then," she said and picked up her bag from the floor beside her chair. Dean looked sad as she went to leave. Sam held his hand and squeezed it. "I'll see you soon, soldier," she said and walked out of the ward and back up to the station on the hill, with a convoy of three ambulances passing her on the way.

The train journey back home was a moment of calm for Sam. The steady rhythm of endless miles of scenery floating past let her empty her mind of all her troubles and forget about things for a while.

Back home she was faced with a decision: collect Humphrey and face her mum, or stay by herself again and put off the evil hour until the morning. Sam had no wish to talk.

On the doormat lay a letter from Andy. She reached for the emotion she usually felt when a long blue envelope arrived on her mat, but all she felt was guilt. Sam unpacked her bag and made herself a cup of tea and some toast with Marmite and took the letter into the living room to sit down. Then, tentatively, almost afraid of the words it might convey, Sam opened the letter.

Dear Sam,

I am so sorry. Dean was my responsibility. I let you down. I wish there was some way to change what has happened, but please believe me that I did what I could. That it was not enough is the burden I will have to live with.

If you can get a message to him and Rifleman James Smith, injured in the same exchange, let them know we are thinking of them and wish them a speedy recovery.

I love you, Sam.

Andy

That was it. She checked the date. It must have been written about the time Dean was shot. A large expanse of empty blue paper stretched out before her. Sam did not know what to think. Was Andy actually apologising for Dean being injured? Had it really been his fault? And if so, had Dean actually been telling the truth all along? It had all gone on too long. Sam decided it was time to bite the bullet. So, weary as she was, she got out a bluey and wrote straight back.

She read it back. It *was* all over the place, but then so was her head. Hard as it might be, she had to send it. At least this way she would know, one way or the other, where she stood.

She rang her mum and arranged to pick up Humphrey in the morning and settled herself down to watch some mindless TV.

Days ticked by with no word from either of them. Sam thought Dean might have called from his hospital bed and although she prayed for the letter to arrive from Andy that would answer all her fears and put her mind to rest, none came. Sam felt as if she was floating through a kind of limbo. She should have been enjoying her holiday, away from the work and the kids, but instead she was frustrated and tattered. Every drop of a letter on the mat, every phone ring, every knock at the door had her jumping in her skin.

A fortnight later, Sam was round at Kate's. Kate was not enjoying the first stage of pregnancy and was in full morning sickness mode. On the plus side, her mum had just about come round to the idea of a new baby in the house and the tension between the two of them of the past few weeks had settled. Kate was feeling grim and the weather outside was dull and grey. She had propped herself up against the open window to get a bit of fresh air when a car pulled up next door and Dean got out. "Hello, hello. What have we got here?" she muttered, turning to look across at Sam.

Sam got up from the bed where she was lounging and wandered over to see what was going on. She followed Kate's gaze and looked down.

"It's lover-boy back, complete with crutches and heroic limp."

Sam had heard nothing from Andy since she had confronted him in her last letter. She was starting to think that that was it for them. Surely Andy's silence on the matter was as good as an admission of guilt? She suspected so. Sam stood behind Kate and watched as Dean moved slowly up the drive. He looked up and smiled. "Hello, Gorgeous," he said. Mr Fletcher looked up and greeted the girls too.

"Are you two my welcoming committee?" Dean asked.

"You wish. I live here, remember," Kate said.

Dean looked straight at Sam.

"Oh, her." She moved out of the way, back from the window and Sam stepped forward. From behind Sam, Dean could hear, "Romeo, Romeo, wherefore art thou, Romeo?" Sam looked back and threw a cushion at her friend, then turned back to Dean to see him rolling his eyes in amusement.

"Thank you, Katy!" he called out and winked. Then he walked inside.

Sam sat down again, on the beanbag this time as Kate had stretched herself out across the bed. She sighed.

Kate looked at her carefully for a minute. "Oh go and see him then if you want. You're no bloody good to me like this anyway."

Sam shifted on the beanbag. "I can't just go round there. Besides, he's only just got home."

Ten minutes later, the doorbell rang and Kate's mum made a big fuss of him, calling the girls down to see him.

"Hello, Katy. How's the bump?"

"You know?" she said.

"I think the whole of Afghan knows by now; he doesn't stop bloody talking about it."

For once, Kate really did glow.

"And what about you, Gorgeous? How have you been?"

"I'm fine, thanks. How are you? You're looking good."

Dean smiled.

"I mean well. You're looking well." She blushed furiously.

"Yes. I am. I've got a lot of exercises to do every day and a bit of walking. In fact, would you mind coming for a walk with me now… if Katy doesn't mind?"

"Take her," Kate said. "She's all yours. Mad cow would only sulk if she didn't anyway."

"Kate!"

"Good. We'll see you in a bit then."

"Don't keep her out too late," Kate called after them.

To Sam, everything seemed to have changed. The Dean that had gone off to war was a completely different man from the one who had come home. He was attentive, considerate, and romance blossomed. Sam had no reason to doubt him. As the weeks went delightfully on with no further word from Andy, Sam began to realise she was falling slowly back in love with Dean.

Sam spent a lot of her time round at Dean's house, staying for meals with his parents and becoming, to all intents and purposes, one of the family. The experience she had shared with his mum and dad seemed to have given them a bond they appreciated. But Sam's parents were still struggling to understand how her heart had been changed so drastically and whether this man, charming as he was, was really the right one for their daughter. Unfortunately the tension between Sam and her parents rippled under the surface and festered over the summer, unwittingly driving her closer to Dean.

Before she knew it, the school term had started again and Sam was thrust back into normal life. Lesson planning and spelling tests returned to fill her days, and soon after, Dean got a date for his rehabilitation.

Chloe, who had been notable by her absence of late, called her when Sam was round at Dean's one night. She wanted to invite Sam out singing. "I'm sorry, Chlo, I can't," she said, "Dean's taking me out to dinner on Thursday night." Sam smiled across at Dean, playing snooker with his dad in the back room.

Chloe suggested Sam bring Dean along too. Sam called out the suggestion to Dean, well aware of the reception it was going to receive.

Dean pulled a pained expression. "I can't," he called back. "I'm allergic."

"Heathen," Sam scolded.

"But we haven't seen you down there in ages, Sam. We miss you," said Chloe.

Sam felt bad that she hadn't been able to see Chloe in weeks, and asked about 'Mr Dixie.' Chloe told her that dream had ended, but also that there was a new man in her life and Sam listened attentively. Then she said something that threatened to rock Sam's cosy world.

"Listen, Sam, you know Karl still writes to me every now and then?"

"Yeah."

"Well, I just thought you should know he said something about Andy being sent home injured."

"No, that was Dean. Besides, Andy hasn't written to me in ages. And Miller's wife, Gina, would have told me if anything bad had happened. I think he just realised I was on to him."

"Oh. You're certain? It's just that I was sure he said Andy. How is Dean anyway?"

Sam called across to Dean. "You haven't heard anything about Andy being injured, have you?"

"No. Not a thing. Why?"

"Oh, no reason." Sam told Chloe how Dean was getting on and then suggested she give Kate a ring and try to get her out of the house for a while.

On Thursday evening Sam had just finished getting changed when the doorbell rang and Humphrey began to bark. Sam hurried down the stairs, twisting her hair up into a clip and shooing Humphrey out of the way to get to the door. She greeted Dean and he stepped inside and kissed her. Humphrey growled. "Damn dog still hates me," he said.

"Don't take it personally. He's like that with everyone." Well, she thought, not quite everyone.

Dean took Sam out to a fancy restaurant and wined and dined her until late into the evening and then they got a cab back to Dean's parents' place. But before they arrived back at the house, Dean stopped the driver and told Sam to get out. Sam protested that she was wearing high heels, but Dean was not taking no for an answer. He walked with her to the edge of the park and they found a bench under a street lamp and sat down. He put his crutches down beside him and took her hands in his.

"Sam, you know you mean the world to me. My parents love you, more than they love me, I think. I know I'm about to go off and leave you again, but this time it will only be for a few weeks and I promise I'll call this time. I'll be back before you know it."

"I know-"

"Wait. I haven't finished. What I'm trying to say is… I want you to marry me."

Sam was stunned. "I… we've only been with each other a month or so."

"I know it seems quick, but we were together before I left. We don't have to get married straight away. It doesn't matter how long we wait. I want you, Sam."

Sam was speechless.

"The lads will be back in a few weeks. It would make me so proud if I could say you were mine when they got home."

Sam's brow twitched. "So this big rush is just to show off to your mates, is it?"

Dean looked annoyed. "That's unfair, Sam. Maybe if you don't feel the same way, you should tell me now."

Sam filled with guilt. She had jumped on him full of suspicion and had hurt his feelings. "No. You know I do. I'm sorry. I didn't mean it. You just surprised me, that's all. What will our parents say?" she asked, stalling for time.

"I couldn't care less. But maybe you don't want to make a decision without talking to your mum and dad first?"

Of course she could make important decisions without speaking to her parents. "No," she said.

"Okay, so what's it to be, Sam?" His dazzling blue eyes gazed longingly into hers. "Will you marry me?"

Sam's brain was screaming inside her head, trying to process what was going on. Was this what she wanted? Was she completely happy with Dean? A tiny corner inside her warned of danger, but it was drowned out by the innocent girl she still was deep down, who longed to be loved and to do the right thing. "Yes," she said, before she even knew the words were out.

"Yes? You'll marry me?"

Sam nodded, swept up in the moment. "Yes!" she said.

Dean wrapped her up in his arms and kissed her happily. He hugged her to him and then, from his pocket, he produced a ring. It was in an old box and he held it out with great awe. Sam took it and gingerly opened the lid. It was a thin gold band with a heart shaped ruby and a diamond on each side. Sam looked up at him. Dean took the ring out of the box and slipped it onto her finger. Amazingly it fitted. "It was my grandmother's," he said. Sam regarded the ring on her left hand. "If you don't like it we can get another one," he said.

"No, no; I love it. It's beautiful. Thank you."

Back at the Fletcher household that night, all was well with the world. Dean's father congratulated them both and went to fetch some champagne. His mother was crying happy tears. She said she had known they were right for each other when she met Sam in the hospital at the beginning of the summer. After several more drinks, Dean reluctantly called Sam a cab and waved goodbye as she rode home, glowing with happiness, back to her little house and her loyal dog, Humphrey.

The following night they broke the news to her mum and dad. The reception it got at her house could only be described as 'strained'. It was embarrassing for Sam to let Dean see the reserve her parents felt toward their happy announcement. Her mum asked her to help her get the drinks and Sam walked into the kitchen behind her mother, aware that she was about to be grilled.

"But you've got to admit, Sam, it is all a bit quick. It's not like you to rush things that are as important as this. It's not like choosing a pair of shoes. This is forever."

"I know, I know; but it means so much to Dean to be with me when his regiment come home and I don't want to disappoint him."

"Forget about his disappointment, love, you need to be absolutely certain this is what you want too. Is it, Sam? It seems like only a few weeks ago you were head over heels over that other guy… Andy. What happened there? You never did say."

Sam shrugged. "He wasn't the guy I thought he was. Anyway, he stopped writing when I called him out on it."

"Called him on what?"

"Oh, you don't want to know. Anyway, it's all over now and I'm back with Dean and I'm happy."

"Are you? Are you really, Sam?"

Sam hesitated and then nodded solemnly. "Yes,"

Sam's mum looked at her thoughtfully. "Well I have to admit he's a charming lad." She smiled and hugged her daughter. "Well if you're certain? Come on. Let's get in there before they die of thirst."

Back with the men, Sam's mum asked if they had given any thought to a date. "What about Christmas?" Sam said looking up at Dean.

Dean almost choked on his drink.

"You can't organise a wedding in that space of time," her mother said.

"It doesn't have to be that soon," Dean assured her.

"Next summer, then?"

"Dean took a deep breath and let it out. "Er… yep… okay."

They made a toast to the following summer and it was settled. Mr and Mrs Litton asked for a closer look at the ring and heard from Dean about its history, after which the tension seemed to ease a lot.

Within the month, Dean was back from his rehab and walking without crutches. He still had exercises to do each day and a bit of a limp, but he was looking a lot happier.

The regiment returned and Kate was buzzing with excitement and looking forward to introducing her bump to its dad. Sam had mixed emotions about their return and felt unable to accompany Kate to the reunion, just in case she bumped into Andy. Dean was, however, happiest in the thick of it. He spent a good deal of time with his mates and had an appointment with the army doctor with a view to re-joining his group. He even moved back into quarters as soon as he was able.

A party was arranged, to welcome home all the men and women who had been on tour, and Dean was eager to show Sam off. Kate was going to go along for a bit, but she needed too much sleep at her stage of pregnancy to stay out too late, so Sam arranged to meet her there. Sam was a little anxious, but realised it was a good opportunity to get to know some of the other wives ahead of time, so that when she officially became one of them she would have some friends already. She just hoped meeting Tina and Helen again wouldn't be too awkward.

The night arrived and Sam's dad dropped her off at the entrance to the barracks, where Dean was waiting for her. Sam had spent half the afternoon making sure she was looking her best for Dean that night and she was anxious to make a good first impression.

"Wow, you certainly scrub up well," he said and Sam was pleased. "Come on. I want to show you off."

Sam followed Dean into the building and they arrived at the Mess, which was already humming with music and chatter. The room was rectangular, with a bar along the short end beside the door. In the far corner were tables set out with piles of plates and cutlery, but no food as yet. The lighting was dim and the room was already quite full.

Dean whisked Sam around, introducing her to all his mates and showing off her ring to their partners and although completely out of her comfort zone, Sam did her best to get along with everyone she met. But as the evening wore on, she began to feel unfriendly gazes staring in on her. She spotted Tina and Helen and excused herself to wander over and see them, but the greeting she got was not the one she had hoped for. In fact her reception was distinctly cool, from Tina more so than Helen. Sam tried her hardest to be jolly and fun, but in the end she just came out and asked them what it was that she had done to offend them. Tina wandered off to get another drink and Sam turned her worried expression on Helen. Helen said she'd better talk to Tina and the pair of them stood there in silence until Tina walked back over towards them.

"Sandy's just arrived, Helen, better late than never. I'm going to go and say hello. You coming?"

Helen looked briefly at Sam. "Wait, Teen. Sam wants to know why we're pissed off with her."

Tina turned her searing gaze on Sam and thought for a moment. "Okay, Miss 'I've got a sparkly new ring', tell me this: how many times have you been to visit Andy since he got home?"

Sam couldn't believe it. Was that all that this was about? She had come here with another man. Really? Sam looked from one to the other. "But we're not together any more. Why would I?" The two women were unmoved. Sam looked around to see if she could spot him. "For heaven's sake, they've only been home a couple of weeks." She looked round again.

Tina and Helen looked at each other and then back at Sam. "What? You're not serious. You think he'll be here?" Tina said.

Sam was confused. Surely Andy wouldn't let the thought of bumping into her stop him from coming, would he?

"She does." Helen looked serious. She looked back at Tina and then again at Sam. "You don't know, do you?"

"Know what?" Sam asked, worry starting to grip her.

"He was injured back in the summer, Sam. He was flown home to Birmingham… July, I think."

Sam felt her heart freeze.

Helen quickly guided her to a chair to sit down. "Nobody told you?"

Sam shook her head.

"Not even Romeo? I would have thought they'd have been in there at about the same time."

Sam looked up. "What…?"

Tina pulled up a chair beside her. "It was an IED. He was with Miller when it went off."

She shook her head. "What…?"

"It's pretty bad, I'm afraid. He's lost his right leg below the knee, and an injury to the right arm, but it's the infection they've been battling with. The poor guy's been in and out of a coma for weeks."

Sam's body began to shake. "But he said that someone called Gina would call me if anything happened."

Tina looked at Helen. "Gina?" Helen put her hand on Sam's shoulder. "Gina is Miller's wife. Miller didn't make it. I guess she had enough on her plate. I'm sorry."

Sam was in a living nightmare. Tina sat down too. "Shit, so

you thought he'd just stopped writing to you? Fuck. Didn't you hear it on the news?"

Sam shook her head. "I went to pieces on him when he was home on R and R. He made me promise not to listen to any of it while he was gone. That's why he arranged for Gina to let me know if anything happened."

"I'll get you another drink," Tina said.

Whispers began to spread around the room and Dean looked over. Tina noticed and said quickly to Sam, "He's still in the hospital if you want to go and see him. Heads up, here comes trouble."

Dean crouched down in front of Sam. "What's up, Sam? People are beginning to think you're up the duff."

Sam looked at him.

"You're not, are you?"

She painted on a brave face. "No. I'm just feeling a little unwell, that's all. I think I should go home."

Dean looked at first relieved and then crestfallen.

"It's okay; you stay. I'll get a taxi back. You have a good time. I'll be fine."

On the way out, Sam passed Kate and Spike on her brief trip out to the party. Kate was on cloud nine showing off her very own engagement ring, but she was quickly subdued when she saw Sam looking so pale. Sam congratulated her and said she would be fine but agreed to let Kate call her in the morning to make sure she was okay and they hugged and parted company, Kate, with huge smile and sparkly ring went forward into the jolly throng, and Sam outward into oblivion.

They met up the next morning at the old park near Kate's place. Sam had a proper look at the ring. She admired it from several angles and then she told Kate her news. Kate seemed surprisingly glad at hearing such bad news, but she explained she now understood why Sam had been getting so much bad press on Facebook lately.

"I've what?"

"For once I didn't like to say anything and I knew you weren't into all that, so I thought what you didn't know wouldn't hurt you. I'm sorry."

Sam thought about it for a minute. "I've got to go to him, Kate."

"Of course you have. Is there anything I can do?"

"Do you think you could babysit Humph for the night? He'll be no trouble and I'll bring you back some yummy cookies from the little kiosk I discovered in New Street Station."

"Okay, Sure. I can throw up anywhere. Can Spike stay?"

"Yeah."

"Great. Nighttime sex, what a treat. I'll give him a ring."

Sam rolled her eyes. She waited while Kate spoke with Spike and then Kate closed up her phone and looked at Sam. "Spike's going to drive you up. He's been wanting to go and see some of the guys up there anyway. He can take you up and bring you back all in the same day. I don't suppose we can have your house for the night anyway?"

Sam gave her a look.

"No, okay, maybe not."

Sam thanked her and raced home to get ready.

At half past eleven Spike arrived outside her house to take Sam back up to Birmingham and she emerged, deep in thought, but ready.

Chapter 11

The journey up to Birmingham was awkward, to say the least. For the most part the two of them sat in silence, listening to the radio, but every so often one of them would make a comment, or ask a question. Sam discovered that Andy had probably been in the group of casualties admitted on the day that she was last there. She asked Spike why, if he had known about Andy, he hadn't let her know? But he said he had asked Kate to find out from her how Andy was getting on and Kate had told him that she was getting back together with Dean and Sam knew Spike was a guy of few words at the best of times.

Outside the ward, Sam waited for Spike to bring her some news. Time ticked past as she awaited her fate. What was she going to say? Would she even get the chance to speak? Andy might not be fit enough to see her, or maybe he wouldn't want to? Andy had been hurt far worse than Dean and yet in his hour of need she had abandoned him. Sam felt lower than the heel of her shoe.

At last a nurse came out to meet Sam and they sat together and spoke. "So you're the elusive Sam," she said. "We've waited a long time to see you." Sam had not thought it was possible to feel any worse. She hung her head. "Sergeant Garrington has been calling for you ever since he arrived, but nobody knew who 'Sam' was. We thought at first it was one of the other lads, or a brother or someone, but his family and the other men from his regiment who were here at the time didn't know anyone called Sam. But now the mystery is solved." Her face became serious. "I have to warn you, if you haven't seen him in some time, he may look a lot different from before. He's lost a lot of weight. He's been battling a series of infections ever since he arrived. His right side is scarred with the injuries from the blast and I'm afraid he lost his right leg below the knee, but he was protected from the worst of the blast by the soldier he was carrying. It may be all a bit of a shock, especially as Corporal Drury tells me you've only just heard about all this. He's pretty sleepy on the whole but he's awake at the moment. Would you like to go in?" Sam took a deep breath and nodded.

The nurse led Sam through the ward, past the room where Dean had been. She paused as she passed it and the nurse turned and looked at Sam's face. "You know I thought I recognised your face. You were here a couple of months ago visiting the lad in there, weren't you?"

"Dean."

"Yes. Left leg bullet wound, wasn't it? How's he doing?"

"Fine," Sam said, her chest tightening as she spoke.

On they went to a room that was far more high tech and expansive than the other one. They used the hand gel as they quietly entered the room. Another nurse was already in there.

"This is Sam," the first nurse announced softly.

"*The* Sam?" the other asked.

Sam nodded, staring over at the patient in the bed. "I think so."

A groan emanated from the sleeping figure and everyone turned to look. The first nurse took Sam over to the bedside and touched Andy on his good arm.

"Sergeant Garrington, you've got a visitor here to see you."

Sam looked at the pale thin man before her, pink scars healing down the right side of his head and chest and a right arm enclosed in bandages. His hair, which had been shaved around the wounds on his head, was growing back again now. He had lost part of his ear and his right cheek held a dent where a chunk of flesh was obviously missing. He opened his eyes and looked at her. At first there was nothing, but after a moment or two his features seemed to come to life. Inky blue eyes focussed in on her and Sam was devastated. Until that moment it had all seemed so unreal that none of it had quite sunk in. Slowly his lips formed a single word. "Sam."

Sam stepped closer and placed her hand on the bed beside him. "I'm here, Andy. I'm here now."

The nurses across the room were smiling back at her and nodding their encouragement.

Andy's hand moved and Sam reached out and took it. He squeezed tightly and tears sprang up into Sam's eyes. She fought them away and smiled back at him. Sadly she reached deep inside herself but could find nothing of worth to say. "How have you been?" Hell, was that all she could come up with? Her face fell.

Andy attempted a smile. "I've… been… better."

"Does it hurt?" she asked.

"Not too bad. Still got ten and ten."

Sam looked over at the nurses, concerned. She recognised this expression.

One of the nurses walked over and put a gentle hand on Andy's shoulder. "Andy. You lost your right foot, remember?"

Andy rolled his eyes and nodded. "Fifteen out of twenty's not bad."

Sam smiled. "It'll do for starters."

"How's Dean?" he asked. "And Smithy?"

Sam fiddled absentmindedly with her ring. "Fine; both of them, I believe."

"I'm sorry," Andy said.

"What for?"

"I promised you, before we left." His eyes closed.

"Promised what, Andy?" Sam asked. Things were getting hazy

now. What she thought she understood was starting to make no sense at all.

His dark blue eyes opened again. "Promised to keep him safe. I'm sorry."

Sam dredged back through her memory. Surely he wasn't talking about the promise he made that night after bowling. That was just a throwaway comment, nothing really. Had Andy taken his promise so seriously? It seemed he must have felt responsible when Dean had got shot.

The nurse who had been hovering nearby walked over to them. "It must be a huge relief to have your fiancée back again, Sergeant? I'm sorry, but I couldn't help noticing the lovely ring." She beamed at Sam.

Sam felt her world implode. It turned upside down and she was left alone in the middle of it. It was too late to slip the ring off now. He had heard it. His hand gripped tighter. The nurse, obviously realising she had made a horrible mistake, withdrew to a safe distance.

In silent plea Sam looked back at Andy and his eyes tore her apart. "Andy… I… If I'd have known you were in here you couldn't have kept me away. I didn't know. Nobody told me. I had no idea. You have to believe me."

Andy turned his face away. His eyes closed, but his hand would not release its grip. After a moment or two he turned back toward her. "I don't believe you."

"It's the truth, honestly."

"And you missed me so much… you… shacked-up with some-body else? Who is it?"

Sam could not bring herself to say his name. His hand squeezed a little tighter.

"Dean."

Andy's face turned away and his hand let go. Sam pulled her own hand free and rubbed it with her fingers. She apologised again, but her words fell on deaf ears. Andy said nothing. Sam stood beside him, not knowing what to do. She asked him if he wanted her to leave, but still he said nothing, so she moved around the bed to the side nearest the door and glanced at the one nurse still able to look her in the eye. "I think I'd better go," she said.

Then he spoke again. "Better off with him now anyway," he said. "Not a lot of use like this."

Sam looked across at the saddest eyes she had ever seen. And then they closed. She hovered, not knowing which way to turn. He turned his face back away from her again. Sam approached the bed. "Don't say that. I'm sorry Andy." She was too afraid to touch his damaged side, so she walked back round. "Andy. Please. Don't push me away."

He closed his eyes without looking at her once and turned his face away. His croaky voice strained to call out, "Nurse." One of the nurses walked across the room. "No more visitors."

Sam was escorted through the ward to the corridor outside. The nurse apologised for the other nurse's lack of discretion and Sam reassured her that she didn't blame her. It had been bound to come out in the end. She led Sam into a quiet room and sat her down, and there Sam let go of her tears.

In the conversation that followed it came to light that Dean definitely had been there at the time Andy had been brought in and had been one of the ones asked about the name Sam. He had denied all knowledge. Andy was also thought to be something of a hero. The nurse didn't know all the details, but she believed he had saved several lives and was trying to save one more when he got caught in another blast.

The nurse offered Sam a cup of tea, but Sam thanked her for her time and understanding, dried her eyes with some of the tissues in the room and then made her way back to the entrance where she had arranged to meet back up with Spike.

If Spike noticed Sam had been crying, he didn't say a thing. Most of the journey back was passed in silence, Sam's head replaying every agonising second of the day over and over again.

When Spike dropped her off at the end of the journey that evening, she leaned back in through the window of the passenger seat. "You will let me know how he's doing, won't you? I know I messed up, Spike. I know."

Spike looked at her for a moment and then nodded.

The following nights passed in torment as Sam tried to make sense of what she had learned. Her days stretched out, towering before her like a mountain that had to be climbed and she was approaching it on her own. Dean wasn't free and that was okay by Sam. On Sunday night she rang Kate to tell her what she had found out. Kate was very understanding and agreed to dig around and see what she could discover by any means at her disposal.

The nurse had told her there was an officer in the camp who dealt with personal and family matters and who may be able to help her. With Kate on her side, Sam managed to get hold of Tina's number and rang her to see if she thought it might be of any use. Tina arranged an appointment for her with the Family Liaison Officer up at the barracks on Friday afternoon and wished her luck with it.

The kids got away with murder for the rest of that week, as Sam's distracted mind wandered at every opportunity. By Friday morning, she could no longer eat. In her head she knew that everything was wrong, but what she was actually going to say to some huge scary officer was less secure. 'My boyfriend lied to me. Please make everything better?' No, that wasn't going to cut any ice. Everything she could come up with sounded either petty or bitter. In fact it was only her desperate need to know the truth that kept her from turning round at the gate and running as fast as she could in the opposite direction.

She left school at lunchtime for her 'dentist's appointment' and rode her bike out to the army barracks on the outskirts of town. She arrived at the main gate and gave her name to the guard. First hurdle over; at least she was expected, but now there really was no going back. The guard directed her to where she needed to go and Sam parked her bike and walked into the building. Inside, Sam found a long corridor. She walked along to her right, but then her memory went blank. Fortunately a passing soldier kindly escorted her the short distance further to the FLO's room and left her there.

Sam knocked on the door and a man opened it and shook her hand. He was fortyish, Sam suspected, immaculately dressed in his khaki uniform and had a kind face. That Sam had not expected. He had a quiet way about him that helped to put Sam at her ease and he had already been informed of the names of the two soldiers who were concerned in the matter. He had a file on each out on his desk in front of him. Sam felt like she was ten again. It was like she had been in trouble in the playground and had been sent in to see the headmaster. She looked about her nervously. The walls were clear except for photographs of different collections of military men. Behind the officer, on the wall, was a big time planner, and his desk was clear except for the files of the two men.

First, the officer took her name and contact details and then he looked at her expectantly. After a moment or two he must have sensed Sam's discomfort and got the ball rolling. As Sam tried to get across what she believed had been going on that summer, the officer listened patiently. From his expression Sam began to realise that she was not making much sense.

"Miss Litton, I'm sure there is some fundamental problem at the heart of all this. Why don't you just start at the beginning and tell me what's been happening. Don't worry, I am very difficult to shock or annoy."

Sam had little dignity left to lose, so she took a deep breath and began again. When she had told him everything she thought relevant, Sam sat back and braced herself for his scathing response. The officer had been taking notes on the way through and he perused them silently as Sam became more and more anxious.

"Miss Litton I have something I think I had better read to you. It concerns Sergeant Garrington and you may find it answers a lot of your questions." He pulled out a piece of paper and cleared his throat. "This is a copy of a letter of recommendation regarding Sergeant Garrington's actions on the day he was injured. I think you will find it rather illuminating."

"Sergeant Andrew Garrington of B Company, 9 Rifles is an extremely capable and natural soldier and he has led his men with the utmost skill and dedication while on operations in Afghanistan.

On the 18th July 2010, Sergeant Garrington was part of a patrol sent out to secure the route east of the base in Southern Helmand when his team came under fire. Rifleman Smith, the point man for this operation, was injured, as was Corporal Fletcher. Sergeant Garrington quickly moved the rest of the men under cover and ordered a fast evac. He then organised and executed an ambitious counter-attack and with his men now in a better position to return fire, he ran back into open ground, under enemy fire, to personally extract the wounded men.

On 23rd of July 2010, Sergeant Garrington's section came under fire once again in an ambush just outside a compound they were investigating for reported Taliban activity. The section was driven back to the west of the compound where they took casualties from two IED explosions. Lieutenant Durbin was injured in the explosion and radio communication was temporarily lost, leaving Sergeant Garrington to lead the assault. He calmly took control and rapidly secured a safer position for his men. Then, without thought for his own safety, he ran each injured man from the line of fire back to cover and organised their field medical attention until a medical evac could be established.

Four men were brought out and each time Sergeant Garrington ran back for another and then, on his final run, with Corporal Miller over his shoulder, a third IED was detonated, killing Corporal Miller outright and seriously injuring Sergeant Garrington.

I believe that without the selfless acts and courageous spirit shown by Sergeant Garrington that day and the quick thinking leadership he has shown on both these occasions, quashing the enemy assault, many more lives would have been lost and it is for this reason that I am recommending him for the honour of receiving the Military Cross."

He paused for a moment and then looked up at Sam. "It was signed by Lieutenant Durbin, Sergeant Garrington's CO that day." He put down the piece of paper and looked at her.

Sam felt the full force of his words piercing her body like a knife. Her guilt grew as she sat there, contemplating the lies and deceit that had put a wedge between Andy and herself. "I can assure you we do not take this sort of thing lightly here, Miss Litton. A soldier bringing into disrepute the name of another, especially when that man has actually saved his life will not be looked on kindly. I can see that you will need some time to come to terms with this news, but I may need to call on you again, if you would be kind enough to oblige? As for the rest of it, I'll leave that with you. I'll be in touch."

Sam nodded again, thanked him and wandered back out to her bike. She cycled all the way home, giving herself plenty of fresh air and time to think.

The following day Sam met Dean in town as planned. They were browsing around Waterstones when Sam's phone went off. She whispered down the phone and Kate answered. "Sam, can you talk?"

"Not really."

"Is he with you?"

"Yes." Dean was looking across at her, a questioning look on his face. Sam mouthed the word 'Kate' back to him and he seemed content.

"Give me a ring when you're free. I've got some news from Tina you might want to hear."

"Okay. Thanks. Bye." Sam put away her phone and looked

across at Dean. How could she have been so foolish? She shook her head and decided then and there that she would never ever fail a good man again. She did not disclose her findings of the day before, but tried as much as possible to act as if everything was normal, and Dean did not appear to notice. She wasn't ready to confront him yet. Sam wanted as much evidence as she could get before she took up that fight.

That night Dean cried off again and Sam rang Chloe. Swearing her to secrecy, she let her in on what was going on, just in case she had any means of helping Sam put it all together. They arranged to meet up again on Thursday night.

On Tuesday evening Sam cycled out to see Tina. She was a little nervous as she arrived at her house, after the welcome she had received the last time they met. Tina opened the door and invited Sam in. It was small inside, the same layout as hers, only much lighter and more modern. There were pictures of her man around the walls in various exotic locations and an ironing board out in the living room. Eastenders droned on in the background, but Sam paid little attention. Tina switched it off and heaved the laundry basket out of the way.

"Is Dave around?" Sam asked uncomfortably.

"No, you're quite safe. They're busy tonight. But Helen wanted to join in, if that's all right with you?"

Sam nodded. "Of course."

Tina sent a quick text and a few minutes later, Helen appeared. Tina made them all some tea and they sat down at the dining room table giving Sam the distinct impression this was not going to be a friendly chat.

"Kate tells me you're trying to find out about Andy," Tina said.

"And Dean," Sam added.

"Hmm. Well I can help with Andy. I've known him a good few years. I was friends with his wife before too."

Sam was listening intently.

"What can I tell you? He's a great bloke, Sam, but then you

knew that already; at least you seemed to for a while, until old Romeo stuck his oar in. I'll tell you, if I wasn't happily married to Dave I'd definitely be fighting you for Andy right now."

"It's true," Helen added.

"He's a good guy, quiet but, you know, deep. I think he went to university like lots of the officers, but he wanted to start from the bottom and work up. So he became a squaddie and a good one he was too."

"What happened with his wife?" Sam asked.

"Claire? Poor sod was besotted with him to start with. But something wasn't right between them. Claire said once that she felt as if she was a constant disappointment to him. I don't know; I only ever heard her side of it. It wasn't that he criticised really, just didn't engage. I think she just gave up trying in the end. After barely a year of being married, she was off behind his back, trying it on with half the regiment. Just wanted some attention, I think."

"It was her then?"

"Well, yeah, in a way I guess. Why?"

Sam shook her head sadly. "It doesn't matter."

"You thought it was Andy?"

"No, not really, but-"

"Romeo bullshitted you, did he?"

"Well…"

"No. Andy's as solid as they come. It was Claire, or rather *them*. Oh, I loved her to bits; she was a right laugh, but I don't care how difficult he was to live with, he didn't deserve that."

"So what happened in the end?" Sam asked.

"I don't remember exactly, but someone blabbed as they always do. He confronted her with it one night and she blew up and stormed out of there. A few days later she walked back in, collected her stuff and she was gone. That was the last I heard of her." Tina took a swig of her tea.

"How did Andy take it?"

"He was crushed. Refused to talk about it, of course; just sort of closed off. He was never the same after that, until you showed up." She looked at Sam's face. "I'm sorry, Sam, but we could all see how happy he was with you. It was just great to see him looking so relaxed and having fun again."

"So what exactly went wrong between the two of you?" Helen asked. "If you don't mind me asking?"

Sam's lips moved, but no words came out. She shook her head. "I just don't know anymore." Tears threatened to spill down her face, but Sam refused to let them. She didn't want anyone's sympathy. She didn't deserve it and she very much doubted she would get it round here. She had brought this on herself.

Tina offered her the chocolate Hobnobs and Sam took one and began to eat it. She told them both how the summer had gone, just the bare bones of the time-line and they listened intently, gasping and cursing at appropriate points, until she reached the point where the three of them met at the homecoming do.

"Did you try to see him?" Tina asked.

"Yes, of course, I was up there the very next day. But it was a mess." She told them about the nurse and the ring and about Andy's reaction to the news.

"Shit," Tina said. She reached for another biscuit.

She told them how he had been calling for her all that time and nobody had known who she was.

"Well, he's a very private person," Helen added.

"But the worst of it was Dean was there at the time. He was asked."

"Bastard!"

The three women sat in silence, sipping their tea, taking in the events laid out before them.

"So what are you going to do?" Tina asked at last.

"I'm still working on that."

"But you're surely not going to marry him?" Helen said.

"I don't think that would be wise, do you?" Sam said. "But I'm not quite ready to deal with him yet. There are some things I need to work out first. You won't say anything, will you, either of you? I don't want anything getting back to Dean before I'm ready."

The two women swore to secrecy. "How long have you two been together, anyway?" Helen asked. "It just seemed like it was very quick."

"Oh, I know. I guess this time it started when he was sent home injured."

"I thought so."

"But we were going out before he was sent out there, for a couple of months."

"But a while back, 'cause it was a girl called 'Jules' wasn't it, Teen, at the pre-deployment bash?"

They looked at Sam's face. "Oh. Well I suppose he didn't get the nickname 'Romeo' for nothing. Are you all right, Sam?"

Sam assured them that she was gradually learning to detach herself from the things she was learning. It was all coming at her too thick and fast to keep up emotionally.

In the blink of an eye, a bottle of wine appeared on the table and a few moments later three glasses arrived next to it. "Not for me," Helen said. "I've left the kids with repeats of Ben 10. I'd better be getting back. But you two go for it. In fact have one for me an' all." She wished Sam luck and hurried home to her children.

"Well I'm in," Tina said, filling up their glasses and without a moment's hesitation Sam picked up her glass too and started to drink.

The next morning Sam stood up in front of twenty nine infants with a horrible hangover. She couldn't remember how she had got back home the night before. But her bicycle, lying flat out in her front garden, made her think that possibly she had managed to cycle home. She was secretly impressed that she'd even made it back in one piece.

Quiet study was the order of the day, with chanting of times tables and music put on the back burner for a while. At lunchtime,

Sam popped out to the local shop and stocked up on sweeties and the afternoon flowed far more easily, with prizes awarded for the quietest at sums, painting and writing on offer.

That night Sam tried hard to give herself a night off. She tried to focus on something else, but like a child on Christmas Eve, the more she tried not to think about it, the more hopeless it became.

On Thursday night at the Crown and Anchor, she updated the girls on what she had learned. "All I need to find out now is how it all started in the first place," she said. She had been so busy telling the girls about the new developments that she had failed to notice the serious expressions on their faces, but now she was finished they became obvious to her. "What? What's wrong?" she asked. "The baby?"

Kate calmed her. "No it's not the baby, don't panic."

Sam looked from one to the other. "So… what is it then?"

"Tell her, Chlo."

Sam turned to Chloe and the familiar lick of dread she was learning to recognise was toying with her again.

"You know Karl was bunked in with Spike and Dean at the beginning of the tour?"

"Yes."

"Well I met up with him the other day, just as friends, and well, after a lot of badgering, he finally admitted he was in the room when the whole letter incident had happened. It seems Dean had said something about you being… dull or something and he couldn't really be bothered to write to you because he had two other hotter women writing to him already."

Sam flinched.

She turned to Kate. "Apparently, Andy was trying to stand up for you when Dean shoved your letter at him and said he obviously cared more about you than Dean did, so maybe he should write to you instead. But Andy wouldn't take it. So the bastard went and offered it around to everyone else, and when the rest of them had the good sense to stay out of it he chucked the letter on the floor at Andy's feet. And so Andy took it. I guess he didn't tell you all that because he didn't want to hurt your feelings."

So there it was; the last piece of the jigsaw puzzle. It all fitted into place and the picture was complete. She had been well and truly conned by a man, the man to whom she was now engaged.

Chloe and Kate looked at each other and back to Sam. "Are you all right, Sam?" Chloe asked. "Sam?"

Sam had reached her lowest ebb. But from where she stood, the only way was up. "I will be," she murmured. The two girls sat nervously for a few minutes until Sam returned to them. But now Sam was alive. She had flashes of fire in her chestnut eyes and she was raring to go. "Chlo, put me down for a song; 'I will survive' should just about cover it. Who wants a drink?"

As Sam marched off to get the drinks, Chloe turned to Kate and asked, "Do you think she's going to be all right?"

"Yes," Kate said to her. "But I think we've seen the last of our little church mouse. That there's a woman on a mission. I've never seen her like that before."

That night Sam went home to her cosy little house and Humphrey and for the last time, she decided, she would let in the self-pity and allow herself to cry, but no more. She was done with crying. What was needed now was action.

Chapter 12

The following weekend Sam arranged to meet up with Dean. He arrived half an hour later than expected, leaving Sam dangling in anxious limbo. He casually wandered in, oblivious to the gravity of the situation. Sam stood tall. Dean tried to kiss her, but her frame was unyielding.

"You all right?" he asked.

"No. No, I'm not."

"What's up? I've not forgotten your birthday, or something, have I?"

"Do you even know when my birthday is, Dean?"

"'Course I do it's er…"

"Yeah. That's what I thought. Tell me, what was the first thing that attracted you to me? Just off the top of your head."

"Well, you've got nice tits."

Kate let out a short breath.

"What is this? Why am I getting the third degree? Is it your time of the month or something?"

Sam had never felt so close to physical violence. "You don't know a God damn thing about me, do you, Dean? I bet you couldn't even guess at the music I like or the things that make me happy. You just got that ring on my finger and checked out. I don't even know why you wanted me to wear it in the first place.

165

You don't love me. You never have. I'm just the sucker who fell for your charms and took all the crap that you fed her, wrecking up my chance at happiness and causing pain to the man I loved in the process."

"If you loved him so much, why did you come back to me? Because you wanted me, Sam. You always have. Why shouldn't I steal you back from him? He stole you from me in the first place."

"Stole? You abandoned me."

"And good old Andy just swooped in and picked up the pieces. You are kidding me right?"

"He's more of a man than you'll ever be. You're a liar, Dean. You manipulate people without any thought for the consequences. I don't know what I ever saw in you, but I'm definitely over it now." Sam pulled the ring off her finger and held it out to him.

Coldness closed in around the features of Dean's face and Sam remembered his threatening strength. She held his gaze, though she was shaking inside.

Dean took the ring. "Don't worry; I wouldn't marry you now if you paid me," he said. "And if you think the Prof'll have you back after all this you're kidding yourself." He looked at her, scornfully appraising what he saw. He laughed. "You're pathetic."

"I *was* pathetic, you're right. But not anymore. Get out of my house, Dean and get out of my life."

Dean laughed again; he obviously felt no remorse. He enjoyed playing with people's lives. Sam stood her ground before him and he finally turned and walked away.

Humphrey barked at the receding figure in a final show of defiance, and that at least made Sam feel a little better. "You never did like him, did you, Humph?" she said, patting him on the back after it was all over. "Don't worry; we won't be seeing him round here anymore."

And so step one was done. A tiny weight lifted from Sam's shoulders, but the bigger task, the part she was dreading, was yet to come. Sam still had to bare her soul and grovel on her knees to Andy. She didn't fancy her chances of forgiveness much, but she knew she had to try. She owed him that much at least.

She didn't write that night. This was not something she felt she should rush. It was important and though she felt things needed to be said as soon as possible, it all needed careful consideration. She thought about the right words to say for several days and finally, she felt able to put pen to paper.

Dear Andy,

I know I'm probably the last person you want to hear from right now, but there are things that need to be said.

I'm sorry, so very sorry, for everything I put you through. I can't begin to imagine the Hell you've been through these past few months and the fact that I let you down when you needed me most is something I'm obviously going to have to live with.

I was weak, I know that now. I allowed another to cloud my judgment and I turned my back on what I should have known was good and true. You were the love I had waited for and I was too naïve to have strength in my conviction. This will never happen again.

It was very hard to see you so low in hospital and to feel the pain I had inflicted on you. Or maybe I am too full of my own self-importance in that? It might well be that my part in all this was but a mere drop in the ocean of the turmoil that you have endured of late and if so, please forgive me these ramblings. I only mean to convey how ashamed I feel about the way I have behaved. You deserve so much more.

As for me? I intend to try and prove myself worthy of your friendship. If you would allow me to write to you again, as I

*did before, I promise I will be there for you if ever you need
me. I have changed, and I am truly sorry.*

Please write back.

Hoping this finds you well.

Yours sincerely,

Sam Litton

A few days later Sam was back up at the barracks, signing a
statement for the FLO. She felt no regret. Sam shook the officer's
hand and walked away with her head held high. She had done the
right thing by everyone. If Dean never had any comeuppance he
would never stop playing with people's lives, and this way Andy
would be recognized as the wronged party, leaving her with the
satisfaction of putting the record straight.

A fortnight later Tina rang to let her know she'd found out Dean
had been put on report and was being disciplined for misconduct.
She asked if Sam had received any news from Andy and Sam told
her that she had written, but as yet had had no reply. Tina agreed
to keep in touch and was keen to know if Andy ever wrote back.
Not long afterward, Sam wrote again.

Dear Andy,

*I'm sorry you don't feel able to write back to me, but I hope
it is not because you are too unwell. Better that you are
improving but cannot forgive me than you are physically
unable.*

*Life with me is pretty much back to the way it was when we
first met. I still cycle to school every day and try and make a*

December came and with it a rapidly arranged wedding. Kate
had suddenly decided that her baby had to be born within wedlock
and in her highly emotional state, Spike agreed to bring things
forward just to keep her happy.

Sam was to be the only bridesmaid, having shunned the title of
'maid of honour' because it made her feel too old. She thought it
might be a difficult day, with her link to the men more complicated
than ever, but she hadn't bargained on inadvertently upsetting the
bride as well.

Kate stood in her bedroom, trying her best to hide her
expanding waistline under an off-white, high-waisted, layered dress.
She turned this way and that in front of the mirror, obviously
dissatisfied with what she saw. Sam walked up behind her. "You
look lovely," she said.

Kate took one look at Sam and burst into tears. The flowing,
low-backed, burgundy dress emphasised Sam's slimmer than usual
figure. "It's not fair. It's my wedding day and you look so slim

and elegant." She sniffed in a big breath. "I'm the one who's supposed to look elegant today, not you."

"But Kate, you look amazing."

"I do not; I'm fat."

"You are not fat. Come here." She pulled her friend into her arms and hugged her. Sam looked around for a tissue and offered it to Kate, then guided her over to the bed and they sat down. Kate dabbed at her eyes. "You're beautiful, Kate. There's a life growing inside you. That's amazing. You are protecting Spike's baby with your body. You're nurturing it and feeding it and keeping it safe until it's ready to come out. There are lots of poor women out there who would give their right arm to be able to do that, so don't let me hear any more of your 'fat' talk. You look amazing and Spike is going to be blown away when he sees you. The man's besotted with you - Lord knows why! - so pull yourself together and get down there and snaffle him up."

Sam fetched the flowers and set the small tiara on top of Kate's head, and Kate started to feel like the princess she had wanted to be. With a quick check on her make-up, she turned to Sam and beamed. "Ready."

At the reception after the service, Sam was approached by several of the lads from Dean and Andy's regiment and although she appreciated all the charm and flattery she received that day, she was not inclined to take any of it seriously. It was nothing more than talk and she really wasn't interested.

Dean approached her at one point in the evening and commented on how well she was looking. Sam was pleased to realise that the man who had held such power over her for so many years no longer sent shivers through her, and actually looked far more bland than she remembered. She looked at him objectively, as if she were seeing him for the very first time, and all she saw was a man, quite nice looking, but nothing special compared to the company they were in. He remarked that she seemed to have changed and Sam was left in no doubt that he saw this as a good thing. She thought at one point that he had actually started flirting with her! She *had* changed, she knew it and it was definitely for the better, just sadly a little too late.

Tina found her. "Well, if it isn't the avenging angel."

Sam gave her a stern look. "How are you doing?"

"Good, thanks. You and Dean have had a major shake-up, haven't you? I've not seen him trying this hard since… God, I don't know if I ever have."

"What are you banging on about? We're over; you know that."

"I know, I know, but now it's all topsy-turvy. You're so 'hey boy, kiss my feet', and he is *so* drooling over you. It's quite a change of face, you've got to admit?"

"Don't remind me."

"He didn't give you the time of day when he was your fiancé and now you've ditched him and reported him, he suddenly can't get enough of you."

Sam looked around to find Dean and true enough there he was, still looking at her. She turned back to Tina. "Men; I'll never understand them."

"Speaking of which… any news?" Tina's tone was more subdued now.

"From Andy? No."

"You know he's off to Headley Court this week?"

"Yes, Helen told me. I'm glad he's on the mend at last."

"Well, he's a stubborn bugger; it should stand him in good stead for his recovery."

Sam smiled sadly.

"Come on, come and meet Michelle. She's a great laugh. You'll love her."

That night Sam wrote again.

Dear Andy,

Kate and Spike got married today. You would have loved it.

Kate looked amazing in her long floaty dress and Spike looked every bit the dashing soldier.

In the reception after, Lofty and Dave started stripping off to that song from The Full Monty – hysterical! – don't worry, Tina broke it up before they got indecent, so no elderly aunts were offended. They all miss you, although they don't say as much, well not to me anyway, but I hear them talking.

I thought of you today. Can I say that? Wondering if we would have made it. I like to think we would. But it's hard to see such happiness in others when you've gone so wrong yourself. If you only listen to one word of this letter then let it be this: I'm sorry.

It's getting cold now. It must be late. They tell me you're off to Headley Court soon, so I will send the next letter there.

Keep fighting, my love.

Never give up.

Affectionately,

Sam

A week later she wrote again.

Dear Andy,

Well I have a settee now. You should see it; it's dark green and so comfortable and soft. I haven't been able to part with my old futon, though. Too many good memories.

School is manic. Twenty-eight over-excited children on the run up to Christmas, don't you just love 'em? It's definitely time to break out that rifle!

Today Katy Pearson spilled red paint all over the new carpet in the reading corner and then managed to walk it half way round the classroom before I virtually had to rugby-tackle her to the floor to get her to stop. Fortunately no angel wings were splattered in the fiasco, or the Nativity may have had a far more Quentin Tarantino look to it.

I miss you. Happy Christmas, my love. I wish I could be there with you and take away some of your pain. I wish the thought of me was more comforting to you. You know I hold you so close to my heart that sometimes I think I can hear yours beating.

I'm glad you are starting to mend. I only wish I could mend the pain I caused you too. But maybe that is hoping for too much. Wouldn't it be wonderful though if we could meet again one day and smile?

Please write to me. If you can. But if not, just be happy.

Yours always,

Sam

But still she heard nothing.

Andy received her letters without emotion. They were met with an indifference that might befit a bill or insurance quote. He filed them away beside his bed and carried on reading his book. Andy was sore from the exercise he was doing there. He had suffered a considerable amount of muscle wastage from his injuries and the resulting weeks in and out of consciousness. His joints were stiff from lack of use and his bones stuck out in places where once they had been covered with toned flesh. It was a long road ahead; he understood that, although every day he battled against the frustration. He was going to have to work hard to regain the physique he had had before the blast.

Andy's stump ached. He thought about his leg and looked at it dispassionately. It had been five months since the blast. His external scars had all healed now, but there was still such a long way to go.

His gaze flickered toward the drawer where Sam's letters lay and he drew in a calming breath. Sam was no longer important in his life. She was a part of the past. She had disappointed him, like all the others. His life had changed now. Living so closely with men who had lost much more than he, Andy was brutally aware that it could have been worse, but even so, his life would never be the same again. He was not the man he once was, in so many ways. Who in their right mind would want him now?

Andy closed his book in irritation. Concentrating had been hard for him of late. He hauled himself off his bed and into his wheelchair, but a crashing sound nearby alarmed him and suddenly he was back in the heat and dirt, under fire and afraid. The world rushed in to choke him and blood was running down his face. What was happening? Where was Miller? The pain, the pain was overwhelming, pain like he'd never experienced before. He cried out and started to shake uncontrollably. His hands went to his face and he felt the dent in the right side of his cheek. He screamed out again and a nurse was by his side. Gently calling his name, she calmed him with a cool gentle hand, easing his fears with her softly spoken words. His eyes focused in on her and he was back in Headley.

The nurse offered him a drink of water and passed him a towel to dry his face. The nurse sat and talked to him for a while until he was calm and then she left him alone. He was on his own now. That was just the way it had to be. He dragged his hands across his face and sucked in a deep breath. Get on with it. There was no room in this world for self-pity.

Later that evening, Andy wheeled himself round to spend some time with the guys. They were good for each other's morale, he knew that. Unless you were completely determined to be miserable while you were surrounded by a load of other lads going through a similar ordeal, you were almost guaranteed to find someone who would make you grateful for the life you still had. For Andy, he always carried his motivation with him. Miller would never get his chance to rebuild his life and his wife and children had to live with that for the rest of their lives. Andy owed it to all of them to fight for every day that he had.

Christmas arrived, and apart from the activities being replaced by physically challenging games, and party hats being worn at the Christmas table, life in the military establishment continued to resemble the routine that its residents had grown accustomed to and relied upon to get through each day.

Letters arrived from family and friends bringing smiles to the faces of those they loved, but in Andy's bed there were few smiles to be had. She had gone off with another man, like Claire had before her. He had thought Sam was so perfect. He'd thought she was his soul mate. He had longed to find her again all those years, all the time thinking of how his life would have been different if he had been with her, only to have his illusions shattered. Why? What purpose had it served? No, he must not think of her, not as anything more than an old injury. That's all she was now, another injury he had to overcome, and overcome it he would, given time. Why she still felt the need to write to him, Andy had no idea. He wished she wouldn't. But of course she knew nothing of his life. She was not a part of his life anymore. There was no one left to disappoint him, or let him down now. He was better on his own.

Mr and Mrs Litton's Christmas passed more soberly than usual. Sam was a quieter, more thoughtful version of the daughter they had known before and as the New Year rolled past, Sam's parents wished for her the happiness she seemed to have held so briefly the previous year.

The spring term was the easiest part of the year for Sam. Gone was all the fuss of Nativity and harvest festival, and reports and sports day were not yet upon her. She had time to catch up with her paperwork and get down to some really productive time spent with her class.

Kate had moved into a little house on The Patch and was busy nesting, preparing for the arrival of her baby, leaving Sam pondering on the bizarre twists in life. Less than a year since she had had the discussion about what each of them had wanted out of life, so much had changed and now they both had the opposite of what they had wanted. The only consolation to her was that at least Kate was happy with the way things had turned out.

As the spring approached, Andy learned to walk on his new foot. He built up most of the muscle that he had lost and worked hard to pull himself out of the quagmire of darkness that had threatened to engulf him. Now he was focused, a picture of capability and routine. He fixed himself targets and drove himself hard until he achieved them. His health continued to improve, as did his fitness. He was back at the barracks and making the most of the facilities available to him. His life was in order, his kit was crisp and his mind was focused on his recovery and to the outside world, all seemed well.

Sam heard that Andy had returned to barracks. He was not yet back to full capability and no one really knew if he ever would be. She was anxious not to bump into him when she went out there to visit Kate, but returned each time almost disappointed that she never actually did. Her letters continued, writing faithfully every week, bringing him her news and her thoughts, but she never had a reply.

Kate's baby arrived, weighing in at 7lb 5oz and with a fine pair of lungs. Sam went to visit Kate in the hospital the day after she gave birth. She peeped round the corner and was beckoned in by Kate. Spike stood up and kissed his wife. "I'll leave you two to it for a bit," he said. "I'll get a coffee and make a few more phone calls. Okay?" Kate smiled and nodded and he walked around her bed, gently touched the cheek of his sleeping baby and looked back at Kate fondly before walking out.

As the door closed Sam turned to Kate. "How are you? How was it?" Kate pulled a face.

"Well it ain't no picnic," she said and then smiled across at her newborn babe. "But she's definitely worth it."

Sam looked at the sleeping baby and then turned to Kate. "You've had a baby. You. You've got a little girl." She shook her head in amazement.

Kate grinned. "I know. How mad is that? I always thought you would be the first for all this lot." She heaved a big contented sigh. "Still, I'm sure I can get you fixed up with one of the lads. They're a good lot, you know."

Sam looked at her in horror. "No, thank you. What are you going to call her?" She nodded at the baby.

"Ellen. Ellen Sophia Drury."

Sam repeated the name. "Yes, that's a good name. Can I hold her?"

"Absolutely not. This is the longest she's slept since she was born. I'm making the most of it." Sam's face fell. "You can have first squeeze when she wakes up, I promise." Kate winked. "Go on; let me get you a guy so you can have one yourself? You're not getting any younger, you know."

"Thanks a lot. I'm not that old. I'm only two months older than you, remember."

"There is one really hot guy Spike says is a decent bloke. He only arrived a couple of weeks ago. He's single."

"Not interested."

"Why not? You're not still flogging that dead horse, are you? Forget about him, Sam."

"I can't."

"Has he ever written back to you?"

"No."

"Well then?"

Sam shook her head.

"It's just such a waste, Sam. I want to see you as happy as I am, that's all. You're a lovely girl, although it pains me to say it." She grinned. "There must be loads of guys out there who would kill to go out with you, I'm certain."

Sam shook her head again.

A door slammed further up the ward and Ellen stirred. Slowly her little dark eyes opened and Sam's face lit up. "Go on then. You can pick her up."

Carefully Sam scooped up the wobbly bundle into her arms and held the baby close to her. She leaned her cheek gently against baby Ellen's soft head and melted. "Oh, she's just beautiful, Kate. She's perfect." She held her back to gaze at her face and spoke in doting words to her, filled with love for the tiny child.

Spike walked back in, carrying a banana milkshake and slice of cake for his wife.

Kate gasped. "My hero," she said. She asked Spike to find her phone from her locker and set it up to take a picture. "Get a picture of Ellen and Sam, before she starts to cry, will you, hon'?" Spike took a couple of photos and handed the phone back. "You're a natural, Sam," she said and Sam blushed. "Forget about him, Sam. Move on. Get yourself a good man and have some babies." She squeezed Spike's hand.

Ellen began to fret and Sam handed her over to her mother, who was eager to hold her again, and sat down. She could never make Kate understand how she felt about Andy. There were no words to describe it. All she knew was that she would not give up on him. She couldn't. Not unless he told her to, and as yet she had heard nothing. But sitting there, watching Kate with her new little family, she was suddenly faced with the harsh contrast between their two worlds. Inside, she could only cry a little as the reality of her having a loving husband and child of her own seemed ever bleaker.

Andy sat in his house on The Patch, dishing up his evening meal. He ladled out some stew into a large bowl and dolloped a pile of mashed potato close by. The cutlery clanked against the bowl as he carried it over to the coffee table in front of the TV. He sat down, picked up the remote control, flicked through the channels and settled back into the armchair. He lifted up his dinner to begin to eat and the doorbell went. Irritated, he paused the TV and put down his bowl.

Tina stood before him in a brightly coloured vest top and jeans, her circlet of tattoos on display. She stubbed out her cigarette and walked in. Andy was taken aback. He turned and looked at her standing in his living room waiting for him, and closed the door. "Come on in," he mumbled. "I was just sitting down to eat."

Tina looked round and saw his food on the coffee table beside her. She nodded, unmoved.

Andy looked at her. "What's up, Teen?"

Tina looked around, avoiding his gaze. "I wanted to talk to you about Sam," she said.

"Sam? Why?"

"She's a lovely girl, Andy. You were good together. Why can't you give her another chance?"

Andy's mood darkened. "I'm sorry. That's none of your business."

"But you were so happy. She's good for you."

"Stay out of it, Teen, I'm warning you."

"Don't be so bloody stubborn."

"Does Dave know you're round here doing this?" Andy asked.

"What's that got to do with it?" Tina countered.

"As I thought. Teen, do me a favour, keep your nose out and let me get on with my life my way."

"But this isn't a life. This-", she gestured at his clinically organised, Spartan house, "is existing. Christ, you were a different guy last summer, so full of life. You were actually fun."

"Well, being blown up and spending months in a hospital can do that to a guy."

Tina was duly humbled, for a moment at least. "It sucks, I know, and I'm sorry, we all are, but you've got to move on, you know?"

"You don't know what you're talking about." Andy was starting to lose his rag with her.

"I know she screwed up. She knows it. But she loves you, Andy. Lord knows why."

"I think you'd better leave." He held out his arm toward the door and stared her down.

Tina stayed where she was for a second and then walked up to him and lowered her voice. "She's a lovely girl, Andy, but she won't wait forever. She fucked up. She gets it. But you'll lose her for good if you don't do something about it soon." She paused for a second, while Andy stood his ground, his jaw clenched hard.

"That already happened. Or did you miss it?"

"Dean? But that was over months ago. As soon as she found out the truth."

Andy hadn't been aware of this, and the realisation smarted.

"You should see her, Andy. She's changed. Hell, half the regiment was after her at Spike and Kate's do. And she just smiled sweetly at them all and walked away."

Andy looked away.

"She wouldn't have any of them."

He looked back.

"She wants you. Think on it, Andy," she said, walking past him and out of the front door.

The door closed and Andy remained where he stood. Who was she to go raking up the past and blaming him? Sam was the one who had walked away. He took a deep breath and let it out. His eyes closed. Move on, he thought. He looked down at his dinner and found he had lost his appetite, so he walked out to the kitchen, put his bowl on the side and grabbed a beer from the fridge.

As his head tipped back to swig the beer, he caught a glimpse of the pile of letter on the side. They were high up on the top of his bookcase, pinned under a heavy crystal decanter, half filled with whiskey and gathering dust. He paused for a second with the bottle in his mouth and then took the swig. Bloody women, he thought.

Easter arrived and Sam was weary. She had been writing to Andy every week for five long months with no reply. She had finally come to the conclusion that she had lost. Andy obviously wanted nothing more to do with her and for her fault in that, she could only apologise so many times. She penned one last letter to him, a farewell, and then with a heavy heart, she posted it and sadly whispered goodbye.

On Easter weekend, Sam's dad drove round to collect her and Humphrey to spend a few days at home. Sam was feeling tired out and had happily accepted the offer of a few days of mothering.

Mrs Litton poured Sam a nice hot bath and unpacked her things into her old room, complete once again with her old bed. Then she took Humphrey down into the living room and tried to settle him down in his basket, but he appeared to be clingier than ever.

When Sam was out of the bath and into her pyjamas and fluffy socks, her mum sat her down in the living room with a cup of tea.

"You've been working too hard, Sam," her mum said. "You can't go on like this. There'll be nothing left of you."

"I'm fine, Mum. It's been a long term, that's all."

"I don't know love. Are you sure there's nothing else? You look to me like you've lost weight."

"Maybe a little."

"You've got to find time to eat, love. Promise me you'll take better care of yourself. You're not still pining after that soldier of yours, are you?"

Sam was taken aback. She had not told her mother about writing to Andy.

Her mother seemed to sense this. "I met Kate the other day when she was visiting her mum. Isn't that baby adorable?"

"Yes, she's gorgeous." Sam would have words with Kate the next time she saw her.

Mrs Litton waited for Sam to speak. "Well?"

"Not any more, Mum. I did, for a long time, but I've accepted now that he's not going to forgive me."

Mrs Litton looked at her daughter with her heart aching. "One day he's going to realise what a mistake he's made, Sam. Are you all right?"

"Yes, I think so. I will be." Humphrey hopped up on the couch next to Sam and nuzzled in beside her and for once, Mrs Litton did not object.

"You spoil that dog," she said, affectionately.

"I know." Sam hugged Humphrey to her.

"Do you see much of Kate now she's up at the barracks?" her mum asked.

"A bit. I brought some photos with me, in case you hadn't seen her."

"Where are they?" her mum asked. "I'll fetch them."

Sam described where to find the pictures and her mother brought them back down and passed them over. The bundle included the picture of Sam and Ellen that Spike had taken on Kate's phone and they'd printed out for her.

That evening Sam and her mum sat together on the couch and watched an old episode of Morse while her dad read in the armchair nearby. Sam didn't make it to the end before she drifted off to sleep and when it was over, her dad helped her up to bed, kissed her on the forehead and tucked her in, with Humphrey cuddled up close by.

It was the following Thursday before Sam won the battle to return home. Her mother had seen how exhausted she was and insisted she stay to let her get some rest, but with the new term looming, Sam needed a bit of time to prepare. She did promise, though, that she would try to eat and rest when she needed to and with those conditions firmly understood, her dad drove them back home.

A few weeks later, Chloe rang around to try and organise a night out singing for Sam's birthday. Sam hadn't sung for ages and their girly nights out had seemed long gone, but she agreed and with a new sense of excitement, she began to practise a song to sing on the night. Kate was eager to go out too, having not been on a night out since Ellen was born. A few nights before, Kate was feeling awake and strong and she resolved to try to bring Andy round. What better birthday present could she get for Sam than Andy? She asked Spike to watch Ellen. Spike did his best to try and talk her out of going round to Andy's, telling her to leave the poor chap alone, but Kate was not going to be easily dissuaded. She was determined to make Andy see reason, and if physically shaking him was what was necessary to make him see sense then that was what she was going to do.

Chapter 13

Andy sat in his living room sipping a glass of red wine and reading his book. The doorbell went and he checked his watch. Eight thirty. He got up and answered the door and found Kate for once without the baby. "Hi, Kate. Everything all right?" He was concerned. Visits out of the blue without a smile were never good news. "Is the baby okay?"

"She's fine. Spike's got her."

"Do you want to come in?"

"Could I?" Kate walked inside and looked around. She had not been inside Andy's house before. For the most part it was like all the others, but in his, there were few of the comforts of home the rest of them could boast: photos, pictures, cushions and knickknacks. Andy's house was bare and functional. There were seats to sit in and curtains to close, but the personal touches, the things that make the house a home were missing.

Andy followed her inside. "What's up then, Kate? It must be important to drag you out at this time of night."

"It's Sam."

Andy's frame tensed. He clenched his teeth and took a calming breath. "What is it with you women? Why can't you just let things be? It's over." He made a move toward her, intending to herd her rapidly back out of the front door.

Kate held up her hands to stop him. "Look, Andy, I'm not going to give you the hard sell, I know Tina's already tried that. I just wanted to give you a chance, if you wanted one. I thought that if you knew Sam was going to be at the Crown this Thursday night for the karaoke, then you might just happen to be there. It's her birthday."

Andy straightened and looked at her with a guarded expression. The pain told him his armour still had a chink in it and he would give anything to find out how to close that gap.

"I thought you might like this. It's a photo of Ellen." She put the photo down on his coffee table.

Immediately Andy leaned down and noticed it was Ellen being held by Sam. He handed it back. "No thank you. I don't need any photos of her. I remember quite well what she looked like."

Kate looked at him for a long moment. "Well, I've told you now. That's all I came to do." She smiled briefly and then walked back out toward the front door. Andy walked after her. Kate opened the door and without looking back she said, "We'll be there around nine, if you change your mind." Then she left the photo beside the front door and walked out.

Andy closed the door behind her and leaned his forehead against it. He looked across at the photo despite himself, and standing up straight he held it up and looked at it. Big chestnut eyes full of love smiled back at him and the pain soared again. Sam was holding baby Ellen against her shoulder; her fingers gently cradling the baby's head as her smiling lips rested delicately against her. She appeared to be tenderness personified. And then he saw it. The bracelet he had given her all those months ago, when he had thought her the best thing in the universe, was once again lying against the soft, pale skin of her delicate wrist. He was transfixed. He stared at her, aching for the woman he had once loved. He leaned back against the hallway wall and thumped his head backwards hard. His forehead crinkled as his eyes begged to look away, but there was nothing else around his house half so compelling.

The months of torment threatened to sweep back over him, pulling him down, but with a deep breath he found the strength to pull away. Quickly he hid the photo up on the top of the bookcase, where it found its home, concealed within the pile of her letters already lying there. Then he straightened his clothing, pulled back his shoulders and returned to his book in search of the sanctuary he sorely needed.

When Thursday evening came, Sam was more than a little tempted to cancel. She was weary from the day and had little energy left to spend the evening out singing, much as she had missed it. But she got herself ready and called a cab, and before she had time to change her mind she was outside the pub on a warm spring evening.

Kate was inside already, excited to be out on her own for a change and she squealed with delight and ran over when Sam walked in. She hugged her and then spun around and pointed out all the decorations. "What do you think?"

Sam looked around the room. In the corners of the room were bundles of balloons and streamers strung out across the room either side of a large banner. It read 'Happy Birthday'. "It's fantastic, Kate. Did you do all this?"

"I had a little help." Kate nodded over at the staff behind the bar and then turned back and reached out to the table nearby and picked up her present. She thrust it at Sam. "Happy birthday, hon'. I hope you like it."

Sam took the present and smiled. She unwrapped it carefully. Out of the sparkly purple paper slipped a hard-backed book. Sam turned it over and read the covers. Then she flicked to the front and searched down the list of contents.

"It's not much, I'm afraid. You know how things are. Baby stuff is so expensive. You wouldn't believe it."

Sam looked up and beamed at her. There was another book too. The first was a volume of poetry and the other was about birds.

She turned them over in her hands and looked up. "Christina Rossetti," she said. "Thank you, they're perfect. I can't believe you remembered." She hugged her best friend again.

"Right. Let's get this party going. What are you drinking?"

Sam walked over to the table and took off her coat.

"Wow, you've lost weight, you skinny minnie. You'll have to tell me how you do that."

"Oh don't you start."

"What? What did I say?"

Sam heaved a big sigh and sat down. "I'm copping it from my mum about not taking care of myself. The teachers at work are convinced I've gone anorexic." She was getting more and more stressed.

Kate held up her hands. "All right. I'm sorry." An awkward moment passed when Kate didn't know what to say. "You're not, are you?"

"No!"

Kate went to get some drinks. When she got back, Chloe and Jake, Chloe's new boyfriend, were there and a few other friends that had come to celebrate Sam's birthday were with them. Together they made a rowdy lot in the corner of the room.

From out of nowhere, Chloe produced a cake and a great cheer went up. She put it down in pride of place at the centre of the table and smiled at Sam. It had been made in the shape of a huge microphone, with one end covered in chocolate sprinkles and the other a slim black string of icing, trailing away like a wire. On the top was a single, rather large, silver candle. Kate borrowed a lighter from a woman at the next table and lit the candle in the middle. Suddenly a large plume of sparks shot up and everybody cheered and sang Happy Birthday to her. Sam gazed in delight as her friends enjoyed themselves and when it had burned out, a chant of 'cake, cake, cake,' started up, Sam asked the barman for a knife and the cake was duly cut and dished out among her friends.

Soon the room began to fill and the night really got started.

As they settled in, Kate turned to Sam and told her she had put her name down for nine o'clock, but didn't know what song she wanted to sing. Sam made a little sigh. "I guess it'll have to be-"

"Dido?" Kate finished.

Sam smiled. "Who else? 'My Life', I think."

"Okay, I'll let him know. Back in a minute."

As nine o'clock approached Kate became increasingly distracted. She checked across at the door every couple of minutes, hoping to see if her efforts were going to pay off, and then Sam got up to sing and a ripple of applause went up. Kate checked back at the door. Nothing. Then, just as she was about to turn back, he appeared. Quickly, Kate looked over at Sam, but she was already up at the microphone and had started singing.

Andy watched as this fragile woman began to sing. Her beautiful voice called out to him across the space between them but his feet were rooted to the ground. All the emotion he had hidden away for so long flooded back through him and his chest heaved with the effort of drawing breath. Was he really risking undoing all the good work he'd done, just to see her again? She was singing Dido, of course. Who else? She sang to him of being herself and living life her way, and his stomach clenched. Had she known he was going to be there? He steadied himself on his crutch.

As she finished, the room erupted and Sam smiled shyly. Yes, he could do this. He would walk right over and tell her how beautifully she had sung and she would smile up at him with those loving brown eyes of hers and he would know, know if it was right. But then she returned to her table and a guy stood up and put his arms round her and kissed her and sat back down with his arm still hovering around her. Andy cursed. What had he been thinking? Of course she had moved on. That was obviously why he hadn't received a letter from her in a couple of weeks. He caught Kate's eye and scowled. He was a bloody fool. He glanced briefly back toward Sam and stormed out as fast as his aching leg would carry him.

Kate got up and rushed to the door, suddenly aware of how it must have looked. Trailing out in his wake, she searched around the front bar, but he was already gone.

Sam, tired out after her performance, sat back in her chair and did her best to catch her breath. She began to hiccough. Her friends found this very entertaining, but Chloe was concerned. "Are you feeling all right, Sam? You've gone awfully pale." Several of her friends offered to get Sam another drink, to drive away the hiccoughs, but all Sam really wanted to do was go to the toilet, and so she pushed them off and stood up. Suddenly, she collapsed. Her body crumpled to the ground with a sickening thud.

A few moments later, Sam came round and was confronted with a sea of faces looking down at her. They swam before her, the noise tangling around her senses like cobwebs. Somebody called for the music to stop and she heard Kate shouting for someone to call an ambulance.

Sam began to get up. "No. I'm fine," she said. "I don't need one." Kate knelt down beside her and helped her up to a nearby seat. "See? Just a bit of a headache, that's all." She gently touched the side of her head where she had landed.

Kate was not convinced, but it was enough to satisfy the rest of the crowd and soon the singing continued as before. Then, just as a song came to a quiet part, Chloe said, "You're not pregnant, are you?" a little too loudly, and half the room turned and stared.

"I think you have to have sex for that," she said, and a titter spread around the neighbouring tables.

Chloe was mortified and mouthed over 'sorry'.

"I still think you need to see a doctor," Kate said. "You haven't been right for weeks."

Sam nodded, "I will. I'll ring them in the morning, I promise." She had had her head in the sand for too long now. She was well aware that something was not right, but deep down she feared it was something very bad and the thought of finding out frightened her more than not knowing. She looked at Kate. "But I think for now I'd better get myself home to bed."

"Absolutely not. I'm ringing your mum and dad. You're not going home on your own after a do like that."

"No, don't. You know what they're like. Mum'll only worry and fuss and Dad will get all edgy. I just want to go to bed. Please, Kate."

Kate looked at her for a moment and then agreed to ring Spike to arrange for him to pick them both up and stay with Sam for a bit, to make sure she was all right. Everybody agreed it was for the best to get Sam home, and wrapping up the last of the birthday cake, they wished her better soon and Kate and Sam went on their way.

Kate wasn't happy leaving Sam on her own that night, but Sam insisted they leave, and Kate's maternal instinct urged her to see her baby girl safely back in her cot. Sam said she would ring if she felt ill again and would call the doctors in the morning to get an appointment.

The following morning, Sam was still not right. Kate rang her and insisted that if she was determined to go into work, then she should at least take a cab to school. Sam rang the surgery in morning break and got an appointment for the following week. The day ticked by in ever slowing minutes. Finally it was the weekend and she was free to catch up with her sleep.

When Sam failed to show up for lunch on Sunday, her mum began to get very concerned. She tried the phone, but there was no answer on her land line and her mobile went straight to answerphone, so in the end, with the dinner smothered in foil on the dining room table, she got in the car and drove around to Sam's house.

As she approached the house, she felt a surge of terror rise up inside her. She knocked on the front door. There was no reply. She knocked harder, but still no answer came. Fumbling inside her bag, Mrs Litton found the spare keys and opened the door. She called out. Sam's things were there. Her coat hung up beside the door and her keys and purse were on the table in the hallway. She rapidly searched around and then hurried upstairs.

At the bedroom door she knocked and paused. "Sam?" she called out, and then with no reply, she crept inside. In that moment all else paled around her and her stomach wrenched. Lying there on the bed was her beautiful daughter. She rushed over and tried to rouse her. Sam stirred a little, but would not wake. Her lips were cracked and her eyes sunken. Mrs Litton reached for her phone and with trembling hands managed to type in the three digits.

When the ambulance was on its way, Mrs Litton rang her husband. She could barely speak for the trembling in her voice. But theirs had been a long and happy marriage and little needed to be actually said. She arranged to meet him at the hospital and then she waited, unable to move from her daughter's side until the siren blared outside the house and a knock battered hard on the front door and she was obliged to let go of her hand and step away.

In the early hours of Monday morning, Sam came round in a hospital bed. She looked around her. Her left hand was connected to a drip and to her right sat her mother, her head nodding awkwardly to one side in a high-backed chair. She looked some more and saw her father slumped in an armchair against the wall. It was dark in there, but Sam could see well enough. Somewhere beyond her vision she could hear a single set of footsteps, walking quietly around. Sam stirred her aching body and her mother was immediately alert. She tried to speak, but the effort was too much. Heavy sheets weighed her body down. Only her hands had enough energy left to speak. Sam squeezed her mother's hand and tried to smile. She tried to speak again and her mother leapt up and was by her side with a small plastic beaker of water. Sam took a couple of sips and rested back, exhausted. How had she got there? She could not remember.

"Darling, how do you feel?" her mother asked, her eyes weary with concern.

"I've felt better." She nodded towards the beaker again and her mother helped her to take a few sips. "What happened?"

Her mother sat down and held onto Sam's hand. "You didn't show up for Sunday lunch," she said.

Sam was confused. The last thing she could remember was her party on Thursday night. "But…?"

"I don't know how long you'd been there, but you looked awful." Fresh tears sprang up in Mrs Litton's eyes and her voice began to quiver. She sniffed in a large steadying breath. A soft snort from behind her chair helped to break the tension in Mrs Litton's voice and she smiled and then quickly whipped round. "Your dad! Pete. Peter," she called out softly, but with urgency in her voice. Mr Litton awoke. "She's awake."

Mr Litton got quickly to his feet and in a moment he was by Sam's side. "Sweetheart, we've been so worried about you. How are you feeling?"

Sam smiled up at him, her sense of security growing. "I'll be all right, Dad. I just feel like I've been run over by a steamroller right now, that's all."

Her mum looked out of the room towards the corridor and saw a nurse walking by. "I'll go and tell them you're awake," she said.

Sam looked at her dad. He was always the one to tell her the truth. Her mother meant well, but Sam knew she would say whatever she thought Sam wanted to hear. "What happened to me, Dad?"

Mr Litton sat in the chair beside her and held her hand tightly in his. "You were dangerously dehydrated, love. It seems you got so weary that you forgot to drink and then it just snowballed. You gave us quite a fright."

"So I'll be all right when I get some fluids into me?"

Mr Litton paused, his face taut with the effort. He took a breath to speak but at that moment Mrs Litton came back in with the nurse, who was pleased to see her. "You're looking better," she said and began to check Sam's charts.

Sam looked around. "What time is it?"

The nurse looked at her watch. "Just after three," she said. "How are you feeling?"

The next time Sam opened her eyes the sun was shining in around her hospital room.

"She's awake again. Hello, Princess." It was her father's voice.

Sam focussed on her dad. He was hovering beside her, clutching her hand and looking older than she remembered. She made a weak smile. "Hello, Dad." Her mother was by her side a moment later. Sam turned her head. "Mum."

Mrs Litton smiled, but her eyes betrayed her. "Would you like some water, darling?" she asked.

Sam accepted gratefully. She looked around and then suddenly panicked. "What time is it?"

"Just gone eight thirty. Why?" her dad asked.

"School."

Her mother patted her hand. "Don't you worry about any of that. I'll give them a ring in a minute. I've got to ring Jude from next door anyway; she's got Humphrey." Sam was confused. "She was an absolute star yesterday. When you were rushed in here, she drove all the way in to collect your door key and then drove off to get Humphrey and took him back to her place. I told her I'd ring and tell her as soon as there was any news. The doctors should be around soon. Are you hungry? I'm afraid you've missed the breakfast trolley. I could get you something, though. It shouldn't be too difficult. One of the nurses said there was a little kitchen around here to make toast. Or I could find you a yoghurt?"

Sam stopped her mother's nervous chattering. "I'm fine, Mum. I'm not hungry."

Mrs Litton fidgeted.

"How are you feeling, love?" Mr Litton asked, diverting Sam's attention for a moment. He placed a reassuring hand on his daughter's shoulder.

Sam considered this for a second. "A bit better."

There passed several days of blood tests and scans and finally the doctors came in to deliver the verdict. Their faces were serious and as Sam waited, in those few moments before she heard the truth, a shiver of dread washed right through her and left her paused on the brink, awaiting her fate.

The junior doctor kept his eyes averted, watching only his senior colleague and the pattern on the floor. Sam's parents were with her for the meeting but as the news was delivered, Sam lost focus on everyone else in the room and suddenly she was all alone.

As if they knew what was coming, her ears forgot to hear and her mind began to wander. She knew it was important and that she should be listening to every word they were saying, but in that moment, Sam was riding a wave of surreal calm, watching over her world through a hazy film and only the odd word or phrase managed to find their way through her invisible shell to penetrate her bubble.

"I can see you need time to take it all in, Sam. I'll leave you with your parents for now. I'll come back when I've finished my rounds." He looked at Sam's mum and dad. "Mr Litton, Mrs Litton, I'm sorry I couldn't bring you better news. Have a think, all of you. I'll be back in an hour or so to answer any questions." He shook their hands and saw himself out.

Over the following twenty four hours, Sam began to understand her diagnosis. She was in the advanced stages of an atypical lymphoma; the bulk of the tumour was expanding rapidly through her chest, compressing her heart and lungs. The doctors had advised immediate action with aggressive therapies, but from the looks on their faces, Sam realised that her chances weren't good.

The next few weeks were filled with injections and treatments. Kate was there almost every day. Several times she brought up the subject of Andy, but Sam was not willing to discuss the matter further, telling Kate to let him be. Various family and friends came to see her, each time with more concern on their face, until one day, when every inch of her body was aching and all she wanted to do was close her eyes and sleep, she quietly thought to herself, 'Is this it?' She felt sorry for the things she would miss out on, mostly having children, but she was not unduly sorry to be going. She was tired now. Her only fear was how it would happen.

Mr and Mrs Litton tried to chivvy her along with fighting talk and when they feared Sam was not listening, in desperation, they called Kate and asked for advice. Kate arrived on the ward less than an hour later and was met by Sam's dad. He pulled her to one side and gently told her about the precarious situation Sam was now in. Kate began to shake. Tears filled her eyes and Mr Litton reached for a tissue from his trouser pocket. "Now, now," he said, patting her gently on the back, "we're not ready to give up yet. We're going to fight this thing, aren't we? We need Sam to stay strong right now, which means we have to stay strong for her." He looked Kate in the eyes.

Kate sniffled and dried her tears. "Absolutely." She shook herself and took a deep breath. "Sorry, it's just… she can't…"

"I know. You're a good girl, Kate. If you can think of anything we could do or say to give her something to fight for - anything at all - then you've got to let us know. But I'm sure seeing you will do her some good. Are you ready?"

Kate nodded and then followed him in. She tried to be jolly while she was in with Sam. She showed her pictures of Ellen and told her stories of how she was getting on, but that night, when Ellen was in bed, fast asleep, and Kate and Spike were finally alone, Kate broke down in tears and sobbed. And when she finished crying, Kate realised there was only one thing better she could do for her best friend. She was going to go round and make that stupid, stubborn man swallow his pride and make peace with her friend. If Sam was out there fighting for her life, it was the least she could do.

Kate found Andy on his way out. She walked up the short

garden path and met him as he stepped out of the door. "Andy, have you got a minute? We need to talk."

Chapter 14

Andy was concerned by Kate's complexion. He faltered. "Are you all right?"

"Can we go inside?"

"I was just…" he looked at his watch and then back at Kate's blotchy face. "Okay, but I can't be too long. I'm meant to be meeting a friend at eight." They walked inside. Andy asked Kate to take a seat and he sat down opposite her. His attention was secured. Kate seemed to take a moment to consider how she was going to approach this. She fiddled with her fingernails.

"What is it, Kate?"

Kate took a deep breath. "It's Sam."

Andy immediately stood up. He had had it with the women on The Patch. Their endless digs and interfering were getting beyond a joke. "He sucked in an impatient breath. "Look, I've told you before–"

"Sit down, Andy!"

Andy was taken aback. He knew Kate was no shrinking violet, but this was forthright, even for her. He hesitated and then retook his seat and after a moment, he lifted his gaze to Kate's eyes and she continued.

"She's ill, Andy, seriously ill."

Andy didn't know what to make of this.

"I know the pair of you are history; this isn't about that. I just thought if you could forgive her… go to her and just talk, maybe… it might give her a little… peace. She still feels something for you, I know she does."

Give her peace? What was Kate talking about? It sounded as if she was nearly dead. A chill crept silently through him. "When you say ill… how ill actually is she?" His voice trailed off to barely above a whisper.

"They said they're doing all they can, but…" Kate's composure began to break. "For Christ' sake, she still loves you, Andy. God knows why, after all you've put her through!"

"All I've put her through? You're having a laugh! Anyway, you're wrong."

"Wrong? She writes to you for months on end with nothing in return. If that's not love, then-"

"She stopped."

"When?"

"About a month ago. She got another bloke."

Kate seemed surprised. "What? No. She said so?"

Andy was still.

"Andy?"

He looked up at her; guilt shading his eyes.

"Well, what did she say?" The silence between them rang out bells of warning. "You haven't read it, have you?"

Andy swallowed. His chin lifted slightly in defiance. "I didn't need to. I saw her. On her birthday."

In all the turmoil of the past few weeks, Kate had quite forgotten about that day. "That? That was nothing. That was just Mike, an old friend of Chloe's. He has always had a bit of a thing for Sam, but she's never been interested. Hell, he was drunk as a lord before he even got there."

Andy looked at her for a long moment while he battled with himself over the idea of letting Sam back into his orderly life. He looked up and then walked over to the pile of letters and lifted them down from their perch high up on the bookcase. He placed them carefully on the coffee table, the dust marking where his fingers had been, and stared at them. He was afraid. Like searing a wound: you knew it was going to hurt like Hell, but without it, you were just going to rot or ebb away, and Andy needed to heal.

Kate looked at him. She picked up the pile, thumbing through them, and was shocked. "You haven't opened any of them!" she said. She looked up and found Andy motionless, staring at the letters on the table. "You haven't read a single word she's written." She shook her head in disbelief. "Not one. All those months she wrote to you and you couldn't even tell her to go to Hell." She checked through the pile and handed across the last letter written.

Andy took it and stared.

"You can't, can you? Not even now." She shook her head and stood up. "When are you going to stop blaming everyone else for the things that go wrong in your life and start facing them like a man? You're weak, Andy. I thought you were better than this." She shook her head in disgust. "She's better off without you. Forget I said anything." And with that, she strode out of the house, leaving Andy dumbstruck at the coffee table, facing a mountain of words he had fought so long not to hear.

He replaced the top letter gingerly, as if even touching them would do him harm, and straightened them up into a neat pile. He stared at them. What was she talking about, weak? That woman had no idea how strong he had had to be just to keep Sam at arm's length. He had seen her several times around The Patch and always made a conscious effort to stay hidden in the shadows. Andy's body remained still, trapped in the undercurrent of a turbulent mind for some time. Finally he reached out and drew the letters closer. Then he put them into chronological order and began to read, from the beginning.

The first one stung, but he was still holding strong. The second and third were read, every word seeping into his soul. Sam asked for forgiveness, for understanding, each time apologising without reservation for everything she had put him through. Not once did she try to pass the blame onto someone else. This was a journey he had started now, and he knew he had to finish. He rang his friend and claimed sudden illness, freeing his evening for the purpose in hand.

Each new letter became more like a diary. She was talking to him of her life and dreams. Her hopes and fears were his to know. She trusted him, though he had never given her any reason to believe he even cared. He knew full well where a good deal of the blame for her actions had lain. She had been weak, he could not deny, but she had herself been used. He sat back and regarded the pile of letters still unread with the sickening fear that he may have been a stubborn fool and let the love of his life pass him by. Deep down he hoped there would be some small sign within her letters that he had been right in turning his back on her all this time, but he was now increasingly afraid there was not.

Sam wrote about experiences she had enjoyed and would have liked to have shared with him and about how very much she missed him. She told him every time she heard news of how he was doing and how proud she was of him receiving his Military Cross. Each letter ended with a wish for his health or his life, or his future.

I find myself thinking back to our days together, as if in a dream. And then I wake and you're not there and my heart aches just a little bit more.

Think of me when you need a friend. I will always be there for you, if you need me.

I miss your hand in mine.

When I walk through the park I think of you and I hope that you will find happiness again as full and wonderful as I found with you.

In the later letters, Sam also wrote of her fears about her health and as Andy reached the first of these he was gripped by the realisation that had he been with her, or even heard her words through the letters at the time, maybe he could have done something about it.

I worry sometimes that I may not be very well, but then I think of all you went through and I give myself a stiff talking to and soldier on.

I am tired tonight, so I will not write for long, but I heard today that you are starting to walk again. I am so pleased for you.

She had obviously been following his recovery closely and asking after him.

I'm afraid, Andy. I think I might be really ill. I know I should see someone, but I'm not as strong as you. I don't think I could cope. Tell me it's all in my mind. Maybe it is. If you do ever read this…

She had suspected. Of course she had. She had no proof that he had ever heard a word she'd said.

…which by now I doubt you ever will, then you might think I am losing my mind. Maybe I am. But you have not once told me to leave you alone. Perhaps you still feel something for me, however small? I only hope you do not think so little of me that you toss this straight in the bin and leave it to rot on a rubbish heap for eternity unread. Or maybe that would be wise, considering my endless ramblings. I'm sorry.

I am so tired. I ache all the time. I'm sorry to complain, but I'm afraid this is not just a virus. My friends think I'm anorexic after all the stress of the past year. Don't laugh. If they only knew how much I liked my food! Oh well, at least if my teaching career gets too much I can always switch to the catwalk! Don't make me laugh, my chest hurts.

Andy discovered that she had begun to read poetry, as she told him of each poem she had read and what she thought of it. She wrote at length about baby Ellen and how beautiful she was and how she hoped more than anything to have her own children one day. Yes, thought Andy, she would make a wonderful mother. Andy realised that towards the end of her letters she must have been certain she was no longer being listened to, as she unburdened her worries to him, her ever silent best friend. What better friend to have than one who never judged, or criticised?

As he opened her final letter, dated the 10th of April, he finally found out why she had stopped writing.

Dear Andy,

My dearest confidant of nearly five months, I shall miss writing to you. But I know now that you are fully recovered and must assume therefore that you either cannot bring yourself to reply to me, or you are using my letters as firelighters. Either way I suppose I must learn to take a hint, for both roads lead to my getting burnt.

What we had, if only very briefly, was beautiful to me. You will never know how sorry I am for how it ended and for not being there for you while you were going through your private Hell.

I am too tired now to fight any more, so I am releasing you from the burden of my expectations. My heart may take a little longer to heal, but I will get there. And I am patient.

I have found something you may know well, but it says with far more eloquence the words I have wanted to say to you:

Farewell! Thou art too dear for my possessing,
And like enough thou knowst thy estimate,
The Charter of thy worth gives thee releasing:
My bonds in thee are all determinate.
For how do I hold thee, but by thy granting,
And for that riches where is my deserving?
The cause of this fair gift in me is wanting,
And so my patent back again is swerving.
Thy self thou gav'st, thy own worth then not knowing,
Or me to whom thou gav'st it, else mistaking,
So thy great gift upon misprision growing,
Comes home again, on better judgement making.
Thus have I had thee as a dream, doth flatter,
In sleep a King, but waking no such matter.
William Shakespeare

It only remains for me to say... I love you.

Think of me sometimes with kindness and try not to judge me too harshly. I was weak, nothing more, and I have paid the price.

Goodbye my love. I wish you every happiness.

Yours always,

Sam x

As he finished the final letter, Andy looked over to the photograph lying on the table, no longer hidden within its papery bed. He picked it up and stared at it and as the beautiful smiling face of Samantha Litton, tenderly holding a baby, wandered into his breaking heart, his body filled with pain and long-imprisoned tears were finally released and began to flow.

Andy spent a long while wallowing in the misery caused by his foolish pride and his stubborn refusal to hear her words. He had punished her for not being the woman he had built her up to be. For years he had held her up as an example of perfection. She could have done no wrong. Each time Claire and he had argued he had reflected on how things would have been different if he had had Sam by his side - and then she had proved herself to be just as bad.

Minutes turned to hours as he sat in his living room, turning over in his mind all the events that had brought him here, and finally Andy realised where he had gone wrong. He had built Sam's pedestal up so high that Claire hadn't had a hope of climbing it. He had gradually learned to block her out of his life. No wonder she had sought the company and affection of other men. He had been the downfall of his own marriage. All those years of blaming Claire when it had been him all along.

Sam had come close to perfection, but in not letting her truly in, he had given her space to harbour doubt. Why hadn't he told her about their holiday all those years ago? He could have explained to her how precious she was to him. Even when she cried on his shoulder at the thought of losing him he had kept her from knowing his heart. She had known how much more he had meant to her then, why couldn't he have told her he understood. The pain he had felt when he'd found out she was with another man spoke all too clearly of how close they had become. He could have told her he loved her, because he had. He did. From the very first moment he had loved her. And still, she had never heard those words pass from his lips. He read through her letters again… and again.

Andy swiped the tears from his face and rubbed his damp fingers through his hair. He looked around for his mobile phone, but in the mess he had created, it wasn't readily to hand and so he stormed out of the house and around the corner to Spike and Kate's.

Andy hammered on the door impatiently, eventually rousing a rather disgruntled Spike. Baby Ellen was screaming in the background.

"What the fuck's going on?" Spike asked.

Andy peered around Spike's shoulder to look for Kate.

"It's gone eleven!"

Andy was aware he must be disrupting their life, but this was important. "Look, I'm sorry, Spike. I just need to speak to Kate. It won't take long." His frame moved uneasily, as he shifted his weight to try to see past him.

"Have you been drinking?"

Andy shook his head. "Not nearly enough." He called out. "Kate?"

"Keep your voice down, will you."

Kate appeared at the back of the hall, a screaming baby over her shoulder. She looked at him and in that moment, he could see that she understood. "It's okay, Spike. Take her, will you? I'll be up in a minute." She passed the baby over and walked inside and Spike took Ellen back upstairs. She stopped inside and turned to him.

Andy could not find the words he needed to say. He couldn't bring himself to ask what he desperately needed to know. He was afraid. His mouth moved in silence as his eyes spoke volumes. Kate invited him to sit and he did as he was told. Cots and push-chairs and soft toys littered the living room. He moved a couple of fresh muslins to one side.

"You've read them, haven't you?"

Andy nodded and searched her face for the forgiveness he so desperately needed.

"Right." She shook her head sadly. "What a bloody waste."

Andy looked her in the eye, his mouth ajar.

"You want to know everything?"

He nodded. "Yes."

"It's lymphoma. I don't know much about it, but it's a type of cancer."

Andy felt the pain soar.

"They've only just found it and it's big. They've started her on some treatment, but…" Briefly she let her head hang down and then rallied her courage and looked him in the face, more kindly now.

"But she will be okay?" Andy asked.

Kate smiled sadly. For a long moment she said nothing. "They don't know."

For a few minutes neither of them spoke. In the distance, Andy could hear the floorboards creaking in a rhythmical pattern and the muffled whimpers of baby Ellen, obviously fighting against sleep with every ounce of energy she had left in her.

"So how did she leave it?" Kate asked. "Did she tell you to go to Hell?"

Andy looked up from where his face rested in his hands and he took a deep breath. He shook his head.

"No. I thought not. And another man?"

"No."

"So are you going to go and see her?" Kate asked.

Andy frantically searched the floor at his feet, his face twisted in torment. "How can I, Kate?"

"Sam's in there fighting for her life. You of all people should know how hard that is. You can't let her keep believing you don't care. Go to her, Andy. She needs you." She paused for a second and then added, "before it's too late."

Andy turned on her suddenly. "Don't you dare say that."

Kate matched his tempo. "Well I'm sorry, but it had to be said. I really hope it doesn't come to that – I love the girl, you know I do – but you haven't seen her, Andy." Kate's eyes began to glisten with fresh tears, but she bit them back and kept herself strong. Her voice softened. "You haven't seen her."

Spike walked back into the room and immediately asked Kate if she was all right. Kate sniffed and dabbed at her eyes. "Fine, love. Thanks," she said. "How's Ellen?"

Spike walked through to the kitchen and grabbed a beer from the fridge. "Sleeping."

Andy stood up. "I'd better go," he said. Spike walked back in and saw Andy to the door.

"She's on Sherborne Ward," Kate said as he turned to thank her. "Think about it, please, Andy. She needs you."

Andy looked at her and then at Spike.

Kate went to say something more, but Spike put a hand on her shoulder to stop her. "Let him go," he said. He nodded at Andy and then he closed the front door and pulled Kate against him and held her for the longest time.

By morning Andy was like a caged animal, restless and tortured. He paced the living room, trying to figure out what he should do. What could he do? He had slept little overnight and it showed. His eyes were haunted, shadowy creatures in a restless face. He was clean shaven and his clothing pressed and as smart as it had always been, but this thin veneer of daily routine in no way hid the turmoil that battled inside him.

By nine he had already been out for a run, showered and changed. He sat in his living room and stared into space, desperately seeking the right words to say when he met her again.

At ten o'clock he rang the hospital ward and asked for the visiting hours. The next one was two till three that afternoon. Four more hours to fill.

He began watching the clock like a man on death row and suddenly it hit him what he should do. He fetched over his laptop and looked up everything he could find out about lymphomas. By half past one he was armed with all the knowledge he could take in and had worn his carpet to threads. He checked his appearance in the long mirror by the door and walked out to unlock his bike then cycled off into town to the hospital and his only hope of redemption.

He arrived early and decided to prepare himself on a small area of garden with a couple of benches he found beside the car park. People with serious faces passed him by. He thought about how he was going to greet her; what he was going to say. Perhaps she would refuse to see him. He wouldn't blame her if she did. He took a few deep breaths and thought that if he had the choice of going back to the front line, or facing Sam right now, he would not have to think twice. The enemy, in whatever guise it could choose, had never been so terrifying as facing her right then. He stood tall, straightened his clothing and then strode off purposefully toward the entrance to the building.

At the door to the ward, Andy paused, and for a second he thought he was going to walk away. A patient walked past in her dressing gown, drip stand wheeling by her side. She smiled and Andy was stilled in his retreat. From beside him, a man appeared. "Going in?" he asked.

"Er, yes, sir." He looked down and realised the man was pushing a frail looking woman in a wheelchair.

"You need to press the button up there." He pointed to the intercom on the wall and Andy did as he was told. A lady's voice spoke out. Andy told her his name and that he was visiting Samantha Litton, and then the porter leaned over and spoke too. The door buzzed and they walked in. Andy walked up the ward looking, despite himself, at the faces of the patients on each side of him. Through every window a tale unfolded. The smell of the hospital, which had pervaded his senses up until this point, was heightened as he turned the corner.

He arrived at the nurses' station like a little boy lost and quietly asked for directions. The nurse asked him to wait where he was while she went to see if Sam was up to receiving visitors. Andy waited and watched the comings and goings of the ward as he held his breath in anticipation.

A few minutes later she returned and led him down the corridor to where a man was waiting. "This is Mr Litton, Sam's father. Can I leave you with him?" Andy nodded and thanked her and she swept away to see to her business. Andy turned to Mr Litton, who offered his hand and introduced himself.

"You've come to see Samantha?" Mr Litton asked.

"Yes, sir. If that's all right?"

"Can I ask how you know her?"

"I'm a friend, or at least I was." Andy searched hard for the right words to say. "We… I was in Afghanistan last summer and…"

"You're Andy?"

"Yes, sir."

"Walk with me, would you?" Mr Litton escorted Andy down the corridor to a quiet room with no one else around. "Would you like to sit?"

"No, thank you." Andy was too anxious to be still. "I didn't know whether to come, whether she would want to see me again."

"I only know a little about what happened between you two last summer. I realise that something went wrong and I have no idea who was to blame. But I know she cared about you, a lot I expect. What reason do you have to think she wouldn't want to see you now?"

Andy took a deep breath. "I let her down." Mr Litton said nothing, only waited to see what more Andy had to say. "It was all a complete mess. She tried to apologise, she did, but I wasn't in a good place after I got back. It's no excuse, I know, but that's just how it was. She wrote to me… for months."

"Well then?"

"But I never wrote back."

He seemed to consider this for a minute. "Why not?"

"At first I think it was self-preservation. I had to block her out to get through, but in the end? Stubbornness… and pride. You have to understand, it has been the thought of her that has kept me going for so long." He pointed to his head. "In here, she was… perfect. She could never do anything wrong."

"That's a hard mark for anyone to live up to."

"I know. And when she eventually did make a mistake… I couldn't deal with it. I couldn't forgive her." Andy hung his head.

"But you have now?"

Andy moistened his lips. He paused for a moment. "Last night a good friend forced me to read Sam's letters, and I did. All of them. Several times, in fact. They forced me to take a long hard look at myself and my own flaws." He shook his head. "I didn't like what I saw." Andy looked up, his eyes pleading for one last chance. "Sam may not be perfect, Mr Litton, but she's a Hell of a lot closer to it than I am. I…" His voice trailed off.

"Well, I'll certainly ask her for you. Let's just see what she says, eh? You do know how poorly she is, don't you?"

"I think so. Kate came to see me."

"Ah. She's a good girl, Kate. Well she's been off for radiotherapy this morning, so she's very tired now, but I'll see if she's up to seeing you." He put his hand on Andy's shoulder. "Come on."

Andy was left alone outside the room while Mr Litton went in to see Sam. He felt a little calmer. Her father had heard his confession and was still willing to let him in. There had to be some hope.

He watched through the glass as inside the room Mr Litton whispered to his wife and she turned around and mustered a smile. She leaned over and talked gently to the young woman lying in the bed in front of them, and Andy's heart rate quickened. Then Mrs Litton turned round and beckoned him in. Andy walked inside and Sam turned to look at him. He had tried to prepare himself for seeing her again, but the thin, pale face and enigmatic smile that greeted him was almost more than he could stand. He hid his pity as best he could and smiled back. She was still the most beautiful thing he had ever seen. "Hello, Sam."

Mr Litton offered the chair on the far side of the bed and Andy slowly walked around and sat down. The pale blue covers were undisturbed by her quiet form. He reached out to touch her delicate hand and noticed the bracelet dangling loosely around her wrist. Regret pierced his side and his heart squeezed harder. It was the gift he had given her the previous summer, when she meant everything to him and he to her. She was his songbird and he was her soldier. He looked up into her eyes and was immediately engulfed in the tide of love that swept through him. But did she feel it too? Andy could only hope.

Chapter 15

Sam was unsure why Andy had come to see her. She tried to smile, but her body trembled. She must look terrible, she thought. She had lost so much weight since he had last seen her. Her hair was lank and unkempt and she was wearing, of all things, her comfy old puppy pyjamas. Had one of the girls forced him to come? Did he resent being here? "You're here," she whispered, wishing more than anything that she had had time to prepare for his arrival. He had been through so much more than her and he still looked good.

Andy gently touched the thin strand of gold lying across her wrist. "I had to. I hope it's okay?"

Sam fought the urge to throw herself at his feet and beg for forgiveness. She didn't know what had prompted him to come. He had not yet said anything to give her hope, but he was there. "As long as you haven't come to tell me off. I'm not sure I'm up to that at the moment. I'm a bit under the weather."

Andy laughed and squeezed her hand. "If anyone deserves a telling off, it would be me."

Mr and Mrs Litton stood up. "We'll leave you two to it for a bit, okay?"

Sam nodded, grateful for the time alone. They looked back at each other and then Andy spoke. "I don't know where to begin. I've thought about what to say to you over and over again, but now I'm actually here and you're in front of me, I'm…"

"I'm sorry," Sam said.

"No, don't. I didn't deserve you. I behaved so badly toward you. How can you ever forgive me?"

Sam tried to sit herself up a little and Andy jumped up to try and help her. She rested back, exhausted. "You didn't do anything."

Andy shook his head. "I know. That's exactly it; I did nothing. All those letters you wrote to me… I never read them. Not one."

Sam was a little disappointed, but not surprised. "Yes. I guessed as much. Probably for the best. They were a load of rubbish anyway."

"No. You're wrong. I read them last night. All of them. I read them all twice over, some of them more. I was a fool, Sam. I realise that now."

"What made you read them after all this time?"

"Kate. She finally managed to knock some sense into me. I've been too wrapped up in my own problems to see clearly."

Sam smiled. "I know. The lengths a person has to go to to get any attention round here. It's ridiculous."

Andy shook his head in dismay. "I'm so sorry."

"You're here now." She squeezed his strong, warm hand. "A bit late, maybe, but…"

"Yeah, well you know how it is, I've been busy." His face fell serious again. "How did you do it, Sam? All that time with no reply. How did you find the strength to keep writing?"

Sam thought for a second. "I had to show you I wasn't going to give up on you again, even if I heard nothing. I had to prove it to myself, really. I just hoped that one day you would see that and understand." A tear welled up in her eye and trickled down her cheek to the pillow beneath.

"Shhh. Don't cry. I can't bear to see you cry." He wiped the tear away. "I've missed you so much, Sam. I can't think how I managed without you all this time."

"You did just fine. The returning hero, remember?"

Andy gave her a look. "No. Tina was right all along: I wasn't really living."

Sam smiled warmly at him. She understood what he meant. She had suffered along with him. "How have you been, really?"

Andy leaned down and knocked on his artificial leg. "Well I'm not up for any marathons yet, but I'm getting there."

"And everything else?" she asked, pointing to the scars on his face and arm.

"Well, yes, the modelling career does seem to have dried up, but I get by. I think my days as a gigolo are over, though." He winked.

"Oh, I don't know. I'm sure there are plenty of women-"

"I don't want any other women." Andy looked at her for a long moment and then leaned slowly down to her and kissed her. Tears began to well up and flow down Sam's face again, the relief she felt at the emotional reunion had a dramatic effect on her delicate state.

"Oh, God, I'm sorry. I shouldn't have…"

Sam smiled. "No. No. I'm glad you did. I'm just tired, I'm sorry. I get tearful very easily at the moment."

"Should I go? Would that be for the best?" Andy asked.

"Don't you dare." Sam held on to his hand with all of her strength.

"There's been so much wasted time, Sam. Tell me if it's too late, but I would really love to see you again. I promise I won't let you down." He pulled her picture out from his wallet. "Look. Kate gave me this."

Sam looked at the picture and smiled at baby Ellen. "I looked a bit better then. I'm not in such great shape now. Are you sure you wouldn't like to reconsider?"

Andy shook his head. "You look great to me. I… I love you, Sam. I always have. It's as simple as that. You came to me when I was going through Hell and I turned you away." Sam opened her mouth to object, but Andy stopped her. "Let me love you, please."

Sam was in heaven. She had no right to be there, but she was nonetheless. "I'm not in Hell," she said. "Not anymore."

Andy stroked her wrist. "I mean it, Sam. I want to be with you." Sam held out her arms for a hug and Andy went willingly. He sat back. "So, how's the food in here?" he asked.

Sam was relieved at the ease with which they had seemingly slipped back into each other's lives and it was still hard to believe after all they had been through. They talked a little about Andy's recovery and kept to the lighter side of their days spent alone, then before they knew it, Sam's parents were back and their time was over.

Andy looked as his watch and then at Sam's parents, not moving an inch from Sam's side. The two of them smiled back at him. Andy turned to look at Sam. "You never did tell me your middle name," she said, leaving him in no doubt that she was definitely expecting satisfaction.

He leant back down again. "Peter," he said.

Sam was confused. "Peter? Is that it? Really? But why all the mystery?"

Andy smiled. "It kept you writing."

Sam chuckled. God, she loved this man. She was very reluctant to let him go. She implored him to stay with her eyes, but Andy smiled down at her, kissed her on the forehead and withdrew his hand. "I'd better go, or they may not let me back in tomorrow."

These words were great comfort to Sam. He would be back tomorrow. He had to go, but he was coming back. She looked at his face for the reassurance she needed and Andy leant down to kiss her again. His lips hovered near her face. "I'll see you tomorrow, beautiful," he said.

Sam nodded and he walked around the bed, pausing briefly to say goodbye to Sam's parents by the door and then looking back at Sam, he winked and then walked away. Sam was exhausted, but happier than she had been in a long time. He had said that he loved her. After everything that had happened, he still loved her. And after saying goodbye to her parents until later that evening,

Sam slipped off into a peaceful sleep.

Andy stepped outside into blazing sunshine and walked for almost an hour, not caring where he went. He would not be caged in such an emotional state and the day was dry and warm and crammed full of promise. Only when he was at ease with himself did he find his way back to the hospital and his black and red bike and cycled home. There was much to do and Kate deserved to be told.

Kate was out when Andy arrived back home, so he got changed into his sports gear and went round to the gym to work out. He worked harder than usual in the hope that he could take his mind off Sam's plight for a short while, but all it achieved was exhaustion and further frustration.

Dean walked in and sat down at one of the benches. The two regarded each other with cool disdain. Dean began to pull on the weights as Andy sat there, a towel slung round his neck, drinking water from a bottle and catching his breath. Minutes passed before Dean finally showed his colours. "How's the love life then, Prof?"

Andy's body suddenly found sharp focus for his anger. He launched himself from where he was sitting, not giving a thought to his new leg, and pummelled the tormentor in front of him. Fists slammed into flesh and bone as splatters of blood flew out from the fray. It wasn't more than a couple of minutes before the fight was broken up by some other lads who wandered in and found the two trying to kill each other. Dean started to spit fire at Andy for being out of his mind, but Andy just wrenched himself free and stormed out to cool off.

The following evening Andy was back at Sam's side. The weather was warm and still, but high up in her room, the curtains found a delicate breeze and danced happily with it. Apologies were no longer wanted from either side. They talked about their friends, about Kate and Ellen and about how much Humphrey was enjoying being spoiled by Sam's mum's neighbour. They even discussed the poetry Sam had read and her favourite parts. Sam asked Andy what had happened to cause such a nasty bruise at the corner of his left eye, but he told her it was just a low signpost he had walked into. She did not know of the many sores and bruising that went unseen beneath the veil of his clothing, of the pain that ceased to bother him when he was with her.

Kate turned up, but not for long. She had cadged a lift in with a friend, who was kindly sitting in the car park watching Ellen while she popped up to see Sam. Kate was pleased to see Sam looking happier, even if she did still look incredibly frail. She winked at Andy on her way out. He opened the door for her and she mouthed a 'thank you' to him. Andy stopped her with his hand. "No. Thank you," he said and a look of understanding passed between them. Kate smiled and walked away.

The following day, Sam took a turn for the worse. Her breathing had been a problem all day and by mid-afternoon she was fitted with some nasal specs for oxygen. More drugs were added to her long list of medicines and her parents stayed close by her side.

Sam watched the clock. She knew Andy would be coming in at some point and as the afternoon visiting had already been and gone, it couldn't be that much longer before he would be with her.

She was frightened. She could take the pain and discomfort that she was having thrown at her on a daily basis, but her breathing was not good and she knew it. If only Andy would come, she thought, she could face anything. His strength buoyed her up. Her parents, she could see, were as scared as she was, but they were valiantly doing their best to hide it. She concentrated on the pattern on the curtain opposite. It was pale blue, like the bedding, with a pattern of leaves running through it. She tried to focus on calm, regular breaths, but it felt like she really needed to take a deep breath and she couldn't. Just a little more time, she thought. 'Come on, Andy, I need you.'

And then he came.

Mr Litton greeted Andy at the door and whispered to him.

Andy looked across and Sam tried her best to smile. He smiled back and she held out a hand and patted the bed. Andy nodded to Mr Litton and walked around the bed to sit down. He took her hand and held it in his. He kissed it and then looked into her eyes.

"Hello, Beautiful. Are you misbehaving again?" he said.

Sam wanted to cry out with joy. The fear that had built up inside her throughout the day brimmed over and the relief of seeing him again forced a solitary tear to trickle down her cheek.

"Shhh. I'm here now. I won't let anything happen to you." He smiled a gentle smile and wiped the tear from her face. Mr and Mrs Litton did not leave the room that day and so Andy just talked to Sam softly, as best he could, and helped her to drink her water little and often as the oxygen made her throat dry.

"What's it like out there?" she asked when they had come to a pause in the conversation.

Andy looked out of the window. "It's a warm summer's evening," he said. "Park weather. I think we're going to have a good summer this year. I'll take you outside when you're a bit better. They tell me there is a little garden here somewhere."

Sam was exhausted. The thought of a stroll through their park on a warm summer's evening was wonderful, but she was too tired to even imagine it now. The golden sunlight stretched across her pillow and warmed her weary face. She smiled up at Andy and closed her eyes. "Keep talking," she said. "I am listening."

Andy looked across at her parents and then back at Sam. He hesitated for a moment and then holding her hand in his, he began to stroke the delicate skin over her knuckles with his thumb and he began again.

"When you're better I'm going to pick you up around eleven and we can cycle to your old park on our bikes – Yes, I have one too now. You didn't know that, did you? It's good for me apparently. The sun is going to shine down on us as we park up our bikes and lift Humphrey out of your basket and plop him down on the ground. He'll bark at all the butterflies as usual, the silly old mutt, and run round and round while we set out a blanket on the ground for a picnic. We'll drink old fashioned lemonade and there'll be fresh strawberries and soft bread rolls with paté. The ducks will be basking on the banks of the pond, their heads folded under their wings and the warm air will be filled with the sound of the bees buzzing lazily around us. We will eat good food and drink until we're no longer thirsty and I will hold you in my arms and promise you that I'll never let you go again and you will look at me with your beautiful smiling eyes and promise me that you will always be mine."

Sam's hand fell heavy in his and Andy stopped talking. Sam did not move. He opened his hand and her hand did nothing to retain it. He looked across at Sam's mother, concern flooding his features. Mrs Litton stepped towards the bed and saw Sam was breathing steadily and her colour was good. She put a hand on his shoulder. "She's worn out, Andy. Let her sleep a while. It's been tough on her today." So he stayed with her as long as he could, holding her hand in his, but she did not wake up again and so with his spirit crushed, he left her in the care of her parents that night and walked out of the hospital and into the rain on that beautiful summer evening.

The next afternoon, Andy got a call from a tearful Kate. Sam's health had worsened. Kate had been at the hospital visiting when it happened. Her parents had asked her to call him.

Despite his leg, Andy fairly sprinted up to the ward, taking the stairs two at a time, only slowing as he neared the doors. Sam's parents were with her, one either side of her bed, their faces drawn and pale. Fear clutched at his heart. He knocked on the door, more gently than usual. Mr Litton looked up and beckoned him in.

Andy walked slowly inside and stood at the back of the room, afraid to move closer. Mrs Litton's eyes were red-rimmed and frightened. He pulled a chair to the bed and sat down. Mr Litton caught his eye for a moment, but obviously could not trust himself to speak. Andy turned to look at the woman he loved, lying unconscious in the bed, only her labouring chest showing any sign of life. He looked at the harrowed faces of those who loved her and it was more than he could bear.

"I'm sorry," he said, bolting for the door as panic gripped him.

Mr Litton looked across at his wife and got up to follow him out. He found Andy a short way along the corridor, his back pressed hard against a wall and his teeth clenched. His eyes glistened with unshed tears. Mr Litton put his hand on Andy's shoulder. "Follow me," he said.

Andy followed him into the day room where one of the nurses was tidying up. She smiled and then took one look at their faces and immediately excused herself.

"They've tried all they can," Mr Litton said, the effort clearly visible on his face. He took a deep breath. "It's not good, I'm afraid."

Andy was in Hell. He was finally with the love of his life and she was being ripped away from him before her time. This was not the way it was supposed to be. If anyone was meant to check out before their time it was him. He was the one putting his life on the line in dangerous places. It was meant to be her facing the possibility of life without him, not the other way around. Why hadn't he died in Afghanistan? She would have found someone new, someone who would have taken care of her and listened when she told him about her fears. She could have been saved and he…? He would not be facing the possibility of life without the woman who meant everything to him; the woman he loved. His eyes filled with tears, but he wiped them away as quickly as they appeared. He shook his head. "It's all so wrong. It's so bloody unfair."

"You were the last to speak to her," Mr Litton said and Andy looked up. "She never regained consciousness again after you made her smile, telling her about your picnic in the park." He patted Andy on the shoulder. "We'll be in there with her when you're ready."

Alone, Andy slumped down into a seat and held his head in his hands. He sat for a few minutes like that, until he found the strength to hold his head up and pull himself together. She was still there for now and if he had anything to do with it, she was going to stay there. She was going to fight for her life, for his sake, if not her own. He stood up and braced himself. "Right," he said and walked purposefully back around the corner and in to where Sam needed him.

For a long time he sat there saying nothing. No nurse came to hurry them along at the end of visiting time. Sam was in a room on her own and he supposed the nurses were allowed to bend the rules in cases such as this, and for that he was grateful. After a while, Sam's parents started to ask Andy about the time he had spent with Sam and he was pleased to be able to explain to them all that their daughter had meant to him. He asked them too about her childhood and learned a little more about the woman they all loved so much.

As the evening drew in, Andy asked Mrs Litton if she minded him staying with her. There was a grave anticipation among the staff and he couldn't bear to leave her in case that time left with her was all he got. Mr and Mrs Litton seemed to see the pain behind his eyes and agreed to his presence in their vigil overnight.

Andy made sure Sam's parents were as comfortable as they could be and made the best of what seating was left. He had managed to sleep in far worse conditions than this and he doubted very much if sleep was going to find him that night anyway. A nurse came in to check on Sam's condition every once in a while, but there was little change for the better, and so the night dragged on.

A second day passed in limbo, each of them reluctant to leave her side, just in case. But they needed to at times. Sometimes Mr and Mrs Litton would go for a little walk and leave Andy to be alone with Sam and then at other times, Andy would take a stroll up to the vending machines or the canteen in search of sustenance to keep them going. They took their turns to spend a few moments with Sam, saying all the things that should not be left unsaid, or just sitting in silence holding on to her hand and praying, making deals with God. Then finally as the sun rose on the third day, Sam's frail little hand began to move.

Her father was with her at the time. At first he didn't believe he'd felt it, but as he stared in shock he saw her hand move again. Then her lips twitched and parted. Mr Litton almost cried out in wonder. "Sam? Mary, she moved, look!"

In an instant, both Mrs Litton and Andy were by his side, watching Sam closely for any signs of movement. Mrs Litton started to talk to her and she stirred again.

Mr Litton turned to Andy. "Quick. Get a nurse."

Andy hurried out into the corridor of the ward, his shirt half out and his face creased from resting against a rolled-up blanket. He found the night nurse sitting at the desk in the centre of the ward. She looked at him and stood up immediately. "Can you come?" he said.

The nurse followed Andy down to Sam's room where Sam was just beginning to wake. She opened her eyes a little and groaned as she moved. The nurse was amazed. She walked up to Sam and began to check on her. "Her breathing is better," she said. She asked Sam how she felt and a hoarse whisper crept from the corner of Sam's lips. The nurse asked Mrs Litton to pass her some water from the cupboard on the other side of the bed and she put it to Sam's lips. Sam took a small tentative sip and opened her eyes a little more. She looked around and smiled weakly at her mum and dad, who gushed with tears at the relief of it all and then she noticed, behind everyone else, at the back of the room, Andy.

Andy was still too afraid to believe his eyes. His face echoed his pain and Sam shone her warm gaze on him. "Andy?"

Andy crept slowly forward and stood at the end of the bed, his gaze fixed on her face, unable to tear his eyes away, as the nurse wandered around checking on Sam's signs and writing everything down in her charts. Sam was alive. He had no idea if this was it, or whether she would relapse at any second.

For the next couple of days, Andy found it impossible to tear himself away. He was too afraid that he would wake up to find Sam had slipped away in the night, or while his head was turned. Eventually the staff managed to reassure him enough, and Mr and Mrs Litton promised to ring him if there was any change in her condition and only on that understanding did he agree to go home, spend some time away from Sam and let them all get some rest.

Against all the odds, Sam continued to improve and over the weeks that followed she battled on with her treatment and fought against all the difficulties that her illness threw at her. The hardest of all these was the news that as ill as she had been, the doctors had been forced to act quickly and due to the drugs they had used, she would no longer be able to have children. Sam was devastated. Apart from the personal tragedy of never holding her own baby in her arms, she knew this would mean the end for her and Andy. She was not prepared to lose him again so soon. So she kept it to herself for the time being and learned to hide the creeping pain it caused her.

Chapter 16

Andy knocked on the door of Lieutenant Durbin's office and was beckoned inside. He saluted. "At ease, Sergeant. Take a seat." Andy sat down opposite. "I won't beat about the bush, Sergeant; it's about your personal conduct."

Andy had been half expecting something like this. "Sir?"

"You're an outstanding soldier, Andy. Nobody is denying that. But some of us are having doubts about your suitability for the recruit training position you have applied for. It's a position of great responsibility and it requires a good instinct for searching out weakness and dealing with it in a positive way. The latter part we feel you may struggle with. You always have high standards, Andy; we all do. You have to, to be the best; but the ability to spot potential and nurture that potential are where we think you may not be suitable. Do you have anything to say to that?"

"Yes, Sir. I am aware that I tend to criticise others too harshly at times. It's one of many lessons in life that I have had to learn of late."

"Yes, I am aware you've been through the mill recently. But it's important we can rely on you to find the spark in every man that comes through the training system and make sure he reaches his potential."

"Yes, Sir."

"How is your woman doing, can I ask?"

"She's getting there, Sir, thank you."

"And you're happy with her?"

"Hopefully, Sir. Very soon."

"Good news. Right, well, I'll put this through to be considered. That will be all, Sergeant. Thank you."

Sam was resting quietly in her room when Andy's face appeared around the door and winked. "Your chariot awaits, my lady."

Sam smiled; pleased as always to see him, but a little uncertain of exactly what was going on. Everybody had been behaving oddly that day so far, from the daftly grinning nurses to her distracted parents.

"I've been given the okay to break you out of here for a couple of hours and it's a gorgeous day outside. What do you say?"

Sam looked out of the window and felt a mixture of anxiety and release. Her hair was all but gone, which she had dealt with in the controlled environment of the hospital, but outside? That was a whole different thing. She touched the scarf around her head, self-conscious about the way she looked.

"You look beautiful," he said.

Sam got up out of the chair where she was sitting and looked at the nurse for reassurance. The nurse nodded eagerly. Sam looked back at Andy and then down at her lightly crumpled clothes. She tried to smooth out the creases with her delicate hands until Andy came over and took her in his arms. "Stop fretting," he told her. "You look wonderful and besides, we're not going out among hordes of people. I want you all to myself." Sam hoped that was true.

Over the weeks since they had been back in each other's lives, Sam had found such devotion and peace in Andy's presence and she dreaded more than anything that the moment she was back on her feet, he would disappear again, or only stay with her through pity, or guilt.

"What do I need?" she asked.

"Nothing. Everything's taken care of." He held out a wide-brimmed sun hat that Sam's mother had brought in for him and Sam put it on delightedly. "I just need you."

Sam picked up her cardigan from the back of the chair and started to walk out but Andy was having none of it. "Get in the chair, you foolish woman. You're in a hospital for heaven's sake. Nobody takes a blind bit of notice of a person in a wheelchair."

Sam knew he was right, although her need to fly under the radar was strong. She sat down in the chair and rested her hat in her lap. Andy kissed the top of her head and turned the chair around and made his way back up the ward. As they passed, the nurses on the ward waved them off one by one and wished them both a lovely day.

Sam was wheeled out into the fresh air and sunlight and it dazzled her. She shut her eyes and turned her face to the sun, enjoying the warmth she found there. A taxi pulled up and Andy helped her in and then climbed in the other side.

"I'm afraid they wouldn't quite sanction a trip out on our bikes just yet," he joked, and Sam squeezed his hand and said "Thank you."

The taxi drove out of the town and into the countryside, finally pulling up by a gate to a field. He helped her out and swung a rucksack up onto his shoulder. Andy turned to Sam and held out his hand. "Ready?"

Sam nodded and took hold of his hand. Andy opened the gate and told Sam to rest her weight on him as they walked very slowly across the field, away from the trees and out into the sunshine. The field sloped away from them and after they had gone a little way, she could see a large oak tree in the middle of the field and Andy suggested they aim for there. Sam was weary with the effort of walking so far for the first time in months, but she was determined that she would get there under her own steam. Although he never complained, Sam was well aware that Andy's stump was causing him a fair amount of discomfort and she was not about to add to that.

When they reached the shade of the tree, Andy opened up his rucksack and settled down a blanket on the ground so that Sam could rest. He sat down next to her and they looked around. The forget-me-not sky sang to them as a dozen different birds went about their daily business. Lower down the hill, a second field ran gently down to the river beyond. The air was still and warm with only the occasional wisp of a breeze to stir the leaves from their sleep. "It's beautiful," Sam said as she wondered how she had ever been reconciled to leaving this heaven on earth.

"I hope you're hungry," Andy said after a minute or two of admiring the view. "I've got plenty."

Sam watched in amazement as Andy unpacked tub after tub of wonderfully prepared picnic food. He tried to tempt her to eat a lot, and although Sam was not up to big meals yet, she did try a little of most of the things he had brought.

It was an idyllic spot and for a while, Sam found it hard to believe the events of the last year had even happened. But then she looked across at Andy's scarred arm and the lines on his face and she knew they had. But they had made it, at least for now. She looked at her man, even more beautiful to her now than he ever was, and she was momentarily content with her lot. If all that she had been through was to bring her to this place and time, then it had to have been worth it.

With her mouth full of fresh strawberry, Andy turned to Sam at last and said, "Are you happy, Sam?"

Sam finished what she was eating and said, "Yes, very."

"Good." Then, from the side pocket of his trousers Andy pulled out a small red box. He hesitated for a second as if considering something and then held it out toward Sam. "I love you, Sam, I always have. I know I'm not the man you fell in love with anymore, but I've got the chance of a job training new recruits, so I wouldn't be round your feet all day. It's a good living and

I'm good at what I do, so I won't be a burden on you. What I'm trying to say is I can still provide for you, for us, so you wouldn't have to work, unless you want to. I mean, I wouldn't stop you, but... kids."

Sam tried to speak, but Andy stopped her. "No. Let me finish, please, or I'll never get this out. I know now that life is too short to throw away the things that really matter to you. And I'm a better man when I'm with you Sam. I can't promise I'll never be a stubborn bugger again, but I'll do everything in my power to make you happy."

Sam was getting more and more anxious by the second. There was nothing she had longed more to hear, but she had a huge flaw in her appeal now, and it could well mean the end for them. She struggled to fight the rising panic within, until trembling and pale. Andy suddenly stopped and looked at her. "What is it? You look dreadful, Sam. Are you all right?"

"I can't have children, Andy." Hearing the words for the first time spoken from her own lips, Sam began to weep. She had wanted children so much. They had always figured largely in her plans for the future. But there it was. There was nothing she, or anyone else could do about it. But if he was serious about her, Andy needed to know. She had done the right thing, but it hurt.

Andy paused, motionless for a minute and then he spoke. "I'm sorry," he said. "I know how hard it must have been for you to hear that. How long have you known?"

"A couple of weeks."

Andy said nothing.

Well at least she had saved him the embarrassment of having to take back a proposal.

"Marry me, Sam."

"Didn't you hear me? It's not a 'maybe'. I won't be able to have kids. You have to understand that."

"I know. I heard. I need to tell you something, Sam. I met a girl once, while I was on holiday in Tenerife. She was beautiful.

She was the kindest, most gentle girl I had ever known and it was love at first sight. I couldn't help myself falling for her. We spent hours just talking and when we parted on that first night I felt like a piece of me had been taken with her. And when she didn't show up the next day I was lost, Sam. I searched all over for her, but I never found her again.

"I got married and let that chance of happiness slide through my fingers because I was still in love with another woman. Can you imagine that, Sam? All those years of waiting and wanting.

"And then one day, just over a year ago, I walked into a bar and heard the most beautiful voice singing to me and I followed it and found… you. It was you."

Sam's stomach clenched as she suddenly realised how the story related to her. Her eyes opened wide with wonder.

"I have been waiting to find you again for so long, Sam. I should have told you straight away, I know. But I didn't want to scare you off, and then Dean and Afghanistan happened and it was all such a mess. But you're here, now, with me. I love you, Sam. Nothing can change that. If you can bear to live without having your own children then I'm sure I can manage it too. We can adopt if you like. Or not. I don't care. I want you. I'm no good without you, Sam. The rest is still to play for, but if I have you by my side I can take on anything. But the question I'm asking is: Do you still want me?"

Sam could see Andy's hands beginning to tremble as he opened the little box. He looked more afraid in that moment than Sam had ever seen him before. She looked down at the trio of diamonds nestled in a delicate gold ring and looked back up at Andy. Her heart was smashing holes in her chest as the rush of overwhelming love raced through her. A solitary tear sprung from one eye and wound its way down to her beaming smile. "Yes," she said softly and then again with more vigour. "Yes, of course I do. How could you ever think anything else? I love you, Andy Garrington. I've loved you from your very first letter. I was just afraid you wouldn't want me."

Andy shook his head in disbelief. He put the ring on Sam's ring finger and pulled her into his arms. "I could never love anyone more." And they kissed under the oak tree on a warm summer's afternoon, and Sam was content that Andy could not make her any happier if he tried. And then he did.

Not ten minutes after Sam had agreed to marry him, another car pulled up at the top of the field. Sam noticed its arrival, but thought little more about it until she heard a familiar yapping and down the hillside raced none other than Humphrey himself, fresh from her parent's house and following him over the horizon, they were there too.

Humphrey reached her and erupted in a frenzy of licks and wags as Sam did her best to contain him. She waved at her mum and dad as they wandered down the hill towards them and as soon as they arrived, Sam's mum looked from Andy to Sam and for the ring, and seeing it in its rightful place she beamed with delight. She looked expectantly at Sam and Sam held out her hand. Her mother cheered and hugged them both, congratulating them on the wonderful occasion. Humphrey leapt up and down and managed to get muddy paw prints all over Sam's clothes, but she didn't care. She was too happy for words, for on that glorious afternoon Sam knew that a long journey still lay ahead of her, but that with Andy by her side, whatever life chose to throw at her from then on, they would be able to handle it, together.

www.ingramcontent.com/pod-product-compliance
Lightning Source LLC
Chambersburg PA
CBHW010635100726
47900CB00011B/2843